HAVE YOU SEEN DAWN?

STEVEN SAYLOR

SIMON & SCHUSTER

New York   London   Toronto   Sydney   Singapore

SIMON & SCHUSTER

Rockefeller Center
1230 Avenue of the Americas
New York, NY 10020

SIMON & SCHUSTER and colophon are registered trademarks
of Simon & Schuster, Inc.

For information regarding special discounts for bulk purchases,
please contact Simon & Schuster Special Sales at
1-800-456-6798 or business@simonandschuster.com

Manufactured in the United States of America

10   9   8   7   6   5   4   3   2   1

Library of Congress Cataloging-in-Publication Data

Saylor, Steven, date.
    Have you seen Dawn? / Steven Saylor.
        p. cm.
    1. Missing persons—Fiction. 2. Teenage girls—Fiction.
3. Young women—Fiction. 4. Texas—Fiction. I. Title.
PS3569.A96 H38 2003
813' .54—dc21   2002070619

ISBN 0-7432-1366-1

Acknowledgments

No book is an easy birth, but some require more midwives than others. This book would never have been born were it not for the hindsight of my first two readers, Rick Solomon and Penni Kimmel; the foresight of my agent, Alan Nevins; and the insight of my patient editor, Chuck Adams. Thank you, all—or should I say "y'all"?

To the memory of
Juanita Reeves

$$1$$

Rue counted the landmarks as she drew closer—the dirt road that turned off the highway toward the old American Legion Hall, the ugly little power substation surrounded by a chain-link fence, the one-room farmhouse nestled in the crook of a limestone cliff. Nothing much had changed since she was a little girl, except that the Legion Hall was abandoned now, the power substation was painted silver instead of green, and the little farmhouse was almost completely obscured by a pair of oak trees. When had the trees grown so big? Rue had taken this drive hundreds of times through the years, but she had never noticed the trees before. Some changes happen so slowly they seem to occur all at once.

She passed the last landmark, a little historical marker by a dry, ruined windmill where the first settlers had found water in the 1850s. Then, as she approached the crest of the hill, she came to the city limits sign: AMETHYST, TEXAS, POP. 2,067. The town had shrunk a little since the last census, but it was still bigger now than when she was a child. The population then was 1,973—not hard to remember, since that was also the year she was born.

The little blue rental car shifted gears uneasily as it topped the hill. In a bowl of umber hills skirted by dark oaks and pecans and eroded limestone cliffs, Amethyst lay sleeping beneath a cold, gray sky.

The courthouse appeared first, a white-and-yellow wedding cake of Greek columns and plaster flourishes. The American flag atop the little dome hung lifeless as a shroud in the still December air. The big Texaco sign was next, a giant steel pole with branches at the top to hold up each giant red letter; the *X* was shattered and half blown away, and had been ever since Rue could remember. Some fool with a deer rifle, her mother had said, probably out drunk on a Saturday night.

She stepped lightly on the brake as the car descended the hill, eager to take in the view even though she had seen it so many times before. Each time coming home it was the same, as she passed each station on the journey: the long flight from San Francisco, the layover in Dallas, the short hop to Austin, the car rental at the airport, the steady hour-and-a-half drive across the rolling hill country through a string of small towns, each town smaller than the last, and then the final few minutes before she crested the hill, passed the familiar landmarks, and then saw the whole town spread out below her.

It was not a particularly pretty town, especially in winter, when the oaks and the junipers turned dark, the pecans lost their leaves, and the spotty patches of grass amid the cactus and limestone withered and turned gray. The town was naked in winter, and from the hill you could see all the houses jumbled together, the nice ones and the tacky ones, the brick ranchettes and the mock-Tara mansionettes, along with the clusters of ramshackle clapboard houses with rusted tin roofs, where the Mexican families lived. It was not even a particularly welcoming sight; there was a part of Rue that had always wanted to leave Amethyst behind, that had never felt at home there, just as there was a part of her that always brought her back no matter how far away she ventured. Still, each time she descended the hill for the first time on a visit home, she slowed down for the view, wanting to take it all in, wanting to somehow make some sense of the place before she stepped back into her past, their present.

Rue glanced at the clock on the dashboard. It was almost five thirty. If things were still the same, and of course they would be, on a Friday evening Schneider's Grocery would be closing at six. Gran would have supper waiting for her, but there were always little things Rue wouldn't find at the house—decaffeinated coffee, herbal tea, nonfat milk, magazines. She had just enough time to make a trip to the store.

The highway turned into Main Street and took her past the courthouse to the only stoplight in town. There were only a few cars and pickup trucks parked around the square; downtown Amethyst was never very busy even at midday, and after five just about everything in town except Schneider's shut down. The little community announcements board at the corner of the courthouse square read, BAPTIST LADIES BAKE SALE SAT. 12–4, and on the next line, BEAT THE GIANTS! GO TIGERS GO! The S in TIGERS was really an inverted Z—perhaps there weren't enough S's to go around. As Rue watched, an automatic timer switched on and the sign lit up, sending a sickly yellow light through the clear plastic panels, silhouetting the black letters.

Schneider's was only a block beyond the light. She pulled into the parking lot, taking a space with no cars on either side. That was one good thing about Amethyst, so different from San Francisco; there was always plenty of space to park. The only other vehicles in the lot were a rusty old Ford station wagon and a huge black pickup covered with dust from country roads, and inside the cab was a gun rack filled with rifles. Schneider's employees parked in back. It had always been that way, ever since Rue worked there summers and afternoons as a checker when she was in high school.

But there was something new: when Rue stepped onto the black pad in front of the entrance, the glass door automatically slid open for her. Milton Schneider had finally invested in electronic doors. She started to smile and then stopped, because something unexpected caught her eye.

Affixed with Scotch tape to the glass beside the door was a yellow placard. A small color photo was pasted to the heavy cardboard, a picture of a teenaged girl, and underneath, in big handwritten letters, the words HAVE YOU SEEN DAWN? The picture looked like a class photo. The girl was pretty, smiling in spite of her braces, with permed blond hair. LAST SEEN SATURDAY, NOV. 30TH, the sign said. Almost a week ago, Rue thought; two

3

days after Thanksgiving. There was more—the missing girl's full name, her age, a description, a number to call. She was only seventeen. It was the kind of thing Rue had gotten used to seeing in the city, but certainly not here. She suddenly felt the cold, shivered, and pulled her coat more tightly around her.

"Well, come on in, honey! It's too chilly to stand there with the door open!"

Rue stepped inside. The door hissed shut behind her. It was Maybelline Schneider, standing behind the nearest cash register, who had called to her. Maybelline's dyed red hair was done up in a bouffant and her large bosom strained against her store apron. "Why, if it's not Rue Dunwitty! You weren't here for Thanksgiving, were you? When did you get in?"

"Just now." Rue tried to think of something else to say, a little disoriented as she always was when she first arrived back in Amethyst and people started talking to her as if she were a girl again.

"Well, get your shopping done, hon. We close in twenty minutes." Maybelline turned back to the customer she was checking out.

Rue took a cart and walked up and down the aisles, thinking of things Gran wouldn't have in the house. From behind the butcher's counter, Milton Schneider smiled and said hello. He was a tall, heavyset man with a florid complexion. He had lost quite a bit of hair since Rue had last seen him. She smiled vaguely. Why was she suddenly in a bad mood? It was that placard in the window, the picture of that missing teenager . . .

When Rue checked out, she was the last customer in the store. Milton was striding up and down the aisles with a broad-headed broom. Maybelline checked as slowly as she talked.

"How's your grandma, hon?"

"I'm sure she's fine. Actually, I haven't been to the house yet. I only just got in."

"Milton! Do me a price check on this yogurt—the low-fat vanilla. And how's life treating you out there in California, hon?"

"Fine. No complaints."

Maybelline smiled sweetly. "Except you better watch out for those earthquakes! And your older brother's still in Austin?"

"Yes."

"I'll bet his kids keep him busy." Maybelline raised an eyebrow. "You got yourself a boyfriend out there in San Francisco?"

"Well . . . not exactly."

"You sure about that?" Maybelline flashed a smug-looking smile, as if she had heard some gossip and knew something she wasn't supposed to. But how could Maybelline Schneider know anything about Rue's private life in San Francisco? "Well, don't you worry, hon, I'll bet some handsome fellow's likely to pop the question when you least expect it, and then the two of you'll have your own house full of brats before you know it."

Rue hummed and nodded.

"Milton! Well, did he hear me, or not? Dwayne, you go check on that yogurt for me." She turned to the sack boy, a tall, sullen-faced teenager with dark blond hair. Over his store apron he was wearing an orange-and-black football letterman's jacket. Rue looked at him closely for the first time and was startled to see a zigzag cut into his hair and a small gold ring in one earlobe. He could have been a San Francisco teenager. How did kids in Amethyst keep up with trends and fashions? From television, probably, even though the local cable company had always refused to carry MTV, saying it was too controversial. Rue also noticed he wore a more conventional silver signet ring with the initial D in onyx.

"Actually, I'm pretty sure the yogurt is eighty-nine cents," Rue said.

"Good enough for me. Never mind, Dwayne, just keep sacking. So, is that everything, hon?"

"I think so."

While Maybelline totaled the bill, Rue took another look at the boy sacking her groceries. She sensed that she had seen his face before, but where? That happened all the time in Amethyst, seeing faces she couldn't quite place. Maybe he was some classmate's baby brother all grown up. He was wearing a little name tag, which seemed silly, since everyone in Amethyst would know him. The name meant nothing to Rue: *Dwayne Frady.*

Maybelline announced the total with a sigh that said she was finished for the day. Rue reached into her shoulder bag. Then she remembered what had been bothering her. "The sign on the door," she said. "The missing girl . . ."

"Oh . . . yeah. Since last week. The Saturday after Thanksgiving." Maybelline wrinkled her brow and turned toward the boy, not quite looking him in the eye. "You can go ahead and take that bag out to the lady's car, Dwayne."

"Oh, that's all right," Rue said. "It's not very heavy. And it's awfully cold out there."

"Well then, Dwayne, why don't you go help Milton close up the produce department?" Maybelline kept her eyes averted from the boy. He turned and walked slowly away, glancing furtively over his shoulder at Rue. Maybelline lowered her voice. "If you want to know about Dawn, you should buy a *Bulletin*," Maybelline said, pointing to a stack of thin newspapers by the checkout. "It's all in this week's edition. All that anybody knows, anyway, which isn't much."

"Oh, that's all right. I'm sure Gran will have a copy at the house." Rue gathered up her groceries.

"Well, you and your granny stay warm tonight. S'posed to be a mean cold front coming our way. Weatherman predicts record lows."

"We'll bundle up." Rue smiled.

The door hissed open to let her out. A gust of frigid wind blew against her face. The cold front had arrived. Across the parking lot she saw naked treetops thrashing in the sudden wind.

The parking lot was empty now except for her little blue rental car. Rue fumbled for her keys, balancing the groceries on her hip. She slipped inside and slammed the door shut against the howling wind.

Rue searched for the headlight switch and clicked it on. In the store window, beyond the glare of the reflected headlights, the boy named Dwayne was standing and staring at her. When she caught him looking, he gave a start, or perhaps it was Maybelline's voice from inside that made him jump. He flashed a nervous, crooked smile, then turned away. His braces glinted in the headlights.

It was the braces that made her realize who he was; the braces, and the fact that he had been standing practically side by side with the picture in the window. He and that girl had the same smile, the same braces, and the same last name. From this distance Rue could barely read the name on the placard—*Dawn Frady.*

The boy was the missing girl's brother.

2

Rue took Main Street back to the stoplight by the courthouse square, then turned left. Under the lowering clouds the streetlights came on. Past the very last one, just beyond the city limit, where the street officially turned into a state highway, she turned off onto the road that led to Gran's house.

After about fifty yards, the road turned from pavement to graded dirt. Beyond a thicket of mesquites and cactus the little asbestos-shingled, tin-roofed house, barely visible from the highway, sat on a lot strewn with weeds. They had all lived there together when Rue was a little girl—her mother and brother and Gran. Now Rue lived in California, Reg was in Austin with his wife and kids, and her mother was dead. Gran lived in the house alone. The porch light was on.

Rue gathered up the groceries and, shivering from the cold, hurried to the porch. She opened the screen door, then reached into her coat pocket and pulled out the rental car key chain, to which she had added her old house key. She pressed it into the lock and twisted it, but met no resistance. As usual, Gran had left the door unlocked, despite all the times Rue had tried to nudge her into the habit of locking it. When Rue was a little girl, they had never bothered to lock the front door, or even the doors to the car parked outside. Eventually her mother had started locking everything, but her mother was gone now, and Gran never seemed to do it herself unless Rue was there to remind her.

She opened the door, then called out as she shut it behind her. "Gran, I'm here!"

From deeper in the house came Gran's voice, calling, "Come on in, hon," and the unmistakable smell of Gran's winter stew.

The living room was dark, or at least it seemed that way after the glaring porch light. Rue threaded her way past the television and the chairs by memory, giving a final shiver as she pushed against the swinging door and stepped into the warm, brightly lit kitchen. She set the groceries on the table and let out an exclamation against the cold as she reached up to undo the scarf around her neck.

Gran looked up from her wheelchair and smiled her shy smile. She had been in a wheelchair since before Rue was born. Polio had crippled her long ago, but she had always managed to do things for herself. Today she was busy stirring the stew atop the oven. "Cold, honey?"

"It is *freezing* out there!" Rue stamped her feet and hugged herself. "It was cold when I landed in Austin this afternoon, but nothing like it is now. It seemed to come in all of a sudden, just a few minutes ago."

Gran nodded. "They say there's supposed to be record lows tonight."

Rue moved toward her, and when she was close enough Gran reached up her spindly arms to give Rue a weak hug. Rue hugged her back, careful as always not to squeeze too hard. Gran seemed so delicate. When Rue pulled back, Gran was smiling up at her, looking straight into her eyes with that quizzical, loving look that more than anything else always made Rue feel at home.

"Well, go ahead, hon, sit down at the table. Are you hungry? I made you some stew and I think it's pretty good."

Gran had already set the table. She spooned the stew into bowls and handed them to Rue, reached for the crackers on the low shelves beside the oven, then wheeled her chair around and drew up to the table.

Like everything Gran cooked, the stew was simple—lean meat, onions, potatoes, carrots, canned tomatoes. But everything Gran made

9

was always delicious. After the long drive and the cold air, the stew was perfect, especially since the only food Rue had eaten all day had been in airplanes and airports. She slowly relaxed, letting the stew warm her inside, as she took stock of the kitchen—the familiar knickknacks that had been there since she was a child, the crowded shelves built low so that Gran could reach them, the decorative plates painted with scenes of bluebonnets.

Gran asked her about the flight, the drive, the weather in San Francisco. She ate slowly from the half-filled bowl she had served herself and pushed it away before it was empty. Gran seemed to eat very little these days. Perhaps she was just getting old—she was almost eighty, after all—but it seemed to Rue that the real change had come all at once, two years ago, when Rue's mother had died of cancer. Since then, no one in the family had been quite the same.

Rue asked about Thanksgiving. "So how were the holidays? Reg and Cathy drove up from Austin with the kids, like they planned?"

Gran crossed her hands in her lap, done with eating, and made a face. "I swear, those are the most rambunctious children I have ever seen."

Rue laughed and shook her head. Gran laughed too.

"Well, it's the truth, Rue. The way they run and scream! Of course, it's not their fault, it's the way they've been raised. Reg lets those children run wild, and that Cathy doesn't lift one finger to control them."

Rue leaned back from the table, full of stew. "Yes, Reg's kids are pretty rowdy."

"I guess it's all right you didn't come this year," Gran said, looking away. "I had my hands full. But I'm glad you could come now." She reached across the table and squeezed Rue's hand.

Rue shrugged, her face suddenly warm. "Sorry I'm a week late. I just couldn't get away until now. Last week we were running a big simulation—" She stopped herself. It was no use trying to explain what she did for a living. Rue worked for a dot-com survivor in San Francisco's Silicon Gulch, and Gran's grasp of modern technology barely extended to the television remote control. Once, on a previous visit home, when Rue had connected her laptop to the phone line to receive a fax from the San Francisco office, Gran had asked what she was doing. Rue's explanation of how a newspaper clipping in San Francisco traveled over the phone line and arrived on her computer screen had met with a look of blank incomprehension from Gran. Rue's mother had never fully understood what Rue did for a living, either, but she had been able to comprehend modems and e-mail. Gran couldn't begin to grasp such things, and Rue felt sad at the gulf between them. It made her miss her mother. It wasn't right that she and Gran should be there at the table without her mother . . .

On this trip, Rue had intentionally left her laptop behind. She hadn't even brought her cell phone. The only gadget in her carry-on bag was a CD player. While she was in Amethyst, she was going to give Gran all her attention and keep her mind completely off her work.

"Anyway, there was a big simulation scheduled—" She pressed on, but stopped herself. Why was she dissembling? Could Gran sense it? Why couldn't Rue simply tell her the truth—that Thanksgiving in Amethyst the year before, for the first time without her mother, had been too hard to bear. Christmas had been even worse. The fact was, Rue had volunteered to work over the Thanksgiving holidays, in exchange for extra time off a week later.

"Anyway, I'm here now. It's just the two of us, and we can have a nice, long visit."

Gran said nothing. Were the holidays as hard for her? Of course, they had to be. Rue should have been here when the rest of the family gathered, for Gran's sake. It had been selfish of her not to come. But it was hard enough simply to be in Amethyst now, in the house, with her mother gone.

"I'll take care of the dishes," she said, standing up.

"Oh, you just sit down and rest."

"Don't be silly. I've been sitting all day."

"Well, so have I," said Gran dryly.

Rue prevailed; there was room enough for only one person at the sink. Gran insisted on putting the stew away, ladling it into a plastic tub and putting it in the refrigerator. "So they're working you pretty hard at that place, are they?"

Rue smiled. "Pretty hard. But I like it. And the benefits are good." Rue had once tried to explain to Gran about stock options, which had proven as incomprehensible to her as the fax transmission. How remote it all seemed from Amethyst!

Gran abruptly made a face and pursed her lips—the exaggerated expression that meant she had just remembered something important. "Oh, Ada, I clean forgot! You had a phone call."

Ada. Rue cringed a little. That happened sometimes—Gran would call her by her mother's name and not even realize it. "Who from?"

"Oh, that McCasland girl—what *is* her name?"

"Ginger."

"That's right. She called not ten minutes before you got here. Said she'd seen you driving through town and wanted you to call her right away when you got in. I'm sorry, I just clean forgot."

"That's okay. I wouldn't have called her back until after we finished eating, anyway." Rue dried the spoons and walked into the living room, turned on the lamp beside the overstuffed chair, and picked up the phone. She reached for the slender phone book on the shelf underneath, in which Amethyst was listed along with a dozen other towns in the adjoining three counties. She paused for a moment, trying to recall Ginger's married name—Sutherland, she remembered. *If* she was still married to Marty Sutherland. Rue hadn't spoken to Ginger in almost two years, not since her mother's funeral, and the last she'd heard, the Sutherlands were not a happy couple.

The phone rang six times, then there was a noise as if it had been lifted off the hook and dropped. After some muffled clattering, a tiny voice said, "Hello?"

Rue started to speak, then heard a loud male voice in the background. "For Pete's sake, sweetheart, why the hell do you let her answer the phone?" Even muffled by the distance, Rue could recognize Marty Sutherland's nasal twang. As always, it sounded as if he had a mouth full of chewing tobacco.

"Well, what the fuck am I supposed to do about it?" That was Ginger speaking. She became shrill when she was angry; her voice carried as if she were speaking right into the receiver. "I'm busy doing the dishes and you're in here sitting on your fat ass not ten feet from the phone." There was a pause, and then Ginger's voice, impossibly loud: "Hello!"

"Ginger? It's Rue."

The voice on the line changed immediately to a sweet singsong. "Well, Rue honey, how are you? I *thought* that was you I saw going by on Main Street this afternoon. I was in the drugstore and I turned to Jackie Odom and I said, 'Wasn't that Rue Dunwitty in that little blue car?' I was sure that was you, even with your hair so short. You been in town all this time since Thanksgiving?"

"No. I just got in today."

"Well, then, I'm glad I caught you. I'm always hearing from somebody down at Schneider's or the post office that you've just been in town, but then I call up your granny and you've already left. How long are you here for?"

"A few days. I've got a whole week off. I'll probably spend some of the time down in Austin with Reg and his family, but for now I'm here with Gran."

"Well, good. You know, I called because I thought you might want to go to the game with me tonight."

"Game?" Rue smiled, remembering long evenings around the kitchen table in Ginger's parents' house. "I suppose I could go for a few rounds of Yahtzee."

"Yahtzee? I mean the *football* game, girl."

Rue rose from the chair, stepped to the window, and parted the drapes. The slender peach tree, the one her mother had planted but had never seen bloom, stood naked against the blue-black sky, trembling in the wind, its shivering outline faintly illuminated by the light of the distant streetlight that leaked through the mesquite thicket. It was dry outside, and the wind seemed to have died down, but it looked very cold to her.

"Football? In this weather?"

Ginger laughed. "Oh hon, I know you've been living out in California for a long time, but this is still Texas. Yes, football in this weather. You think a little cold front is gonna stop a high school football game in Amethyst?"

13

"I guess not. But it'll be freezing in the bleachers."

"Hon, I'm up for anything that'll get me out of this house and away from these kids for a couple of hours. Marty can stay and look after 'em. He'd come, except his foot's bothering him. Crazy fool stepped in a hunting trap and hurt himself. Just you and me, girl, like old times, huh? Everybody in town will be there. You can say hello to people you haven't seen in years."

"Well, Gran does go to bed early . . ."

"Okay, then! I'll pick you up in ten minutes."

3

Girl, you are looking *great!*"

"Well . . ." Rue smiled.

"No, really. Your clothes—what kind of designer jeans are those, any-way? And that leather coat is beautiful. I wish I could afford stuff like that, but I wouldn't even know where to shop for it. And is that how they're wearing their hair out in California these days?"

"Ginger, I always kept my hair short, even back in high school."

"Yeah, but not that short. It's a great cut. Really suits your face."

They were standing in the living room. Rue was bundled up and ready to go, but it would have been rude to leave the house without exchanging a few pleasantries in front of Gran.

"Well, really, girl, I mean it," Ginger said. "You look terrific!"

"Thanks." Rue wasn't sure what else to say. It would have taken a certain amount of pretense to say the same thing back to Ginger. She had gained at least twenty pounds since high school, but in spite of her plumpness she had a haggard look. Her straw-colored hair was medium length and must have been permed at some point in the distant past; now it hung in unruly clumps. While they stood and talked, Ginger produced a brush and started brushing her hair, wincing now and then through her smile. She was wearing faded jeans and an olive green ski jacket with a dark stain on the front.

"I swear, Rue, nobody would ever believe you're a day over twenty-two. Would they, Mrs. Lee? You look like a college girl. Shoot, you haven't got a ounce of fat on you."

Rue shrugged. "I guess I do try to stay in shape." It was true. When she wasn't in front of a computer screen, she was usually at the gym or out running along the Embarcadero. It sometimes seemed that she never slowed down for a minute, except when she came to Amethyst.

Ginger was still fawning over her. "You're so skinny, you ought to be a model."

"Actually . . . I *have* done a little modeling."

"No kidding!"

"It was nothing, really. Just a picture of me in my office with the skyline behind me, for an in-house brochure. But they did make me sign a release, and they took me to dinner at Farallon."

"Well, hell, Rue, you're just turning into a star out there in California. Listen, we better get going or the good seats'll all be gone. You ready? It was nice seeing you, Mrs. Lee." Ginger gave a little wave to Gran. "You stay warm tonight."

"I will. You girls have a good time at the game. Rue, I'll probably be asleep by the time you're home. I'll leave the porch light on for you, hon."

"Okay, Gran. And keep the door locked."

Ginger lit a cigarette as soon as they were outside the house. When they got into her car she snubbed it out in the already full ashtray. The old Pontiac reeked of cigarette smoke. She had left the engine running and the heater was on full-blast. The radio was turned up loud, set to a country station from Waco. Ginger executed a three-point turnaround and headed out on the highway, spinning her wheels and throwing pebbles in her wake.

"So it's still Rue Dunwitty?" Ginger asked, checking over her shoulder for traffic.

Rue had been waiting for the question. "Yes, I'm afraid so, Ginger."

"Those fellows in California must be blind. Or hell, in San Francisco they're all gay, from what you hear. Or are you just picky?"

Rue smiled. "I suspect it may be a combination of all those factors."

"No steady boyfriend?"

Rue sighed. "Well . . ." Her last boyfriend had moved out in August, taking a cat Rue was allergic to, a guitar he couldn't play, and a shoe box full of heavy metal CDs. The relationship had lasted for almost a year. He had been considerably younger than Rue; she would never have started up with him if she'd known from the beginning that he was only twenty-three, but the scruffy goatee had made him look older. He had been phenomenal in bed. He had also been unable to keep a job, which didn't matter all that much, since Rue was making plenty of money. What did matter was his inability to keep his hands off other women. When Rue came home unexpectedly from work one afternoon and caught him in bed with a UC-Berkeley student—so Rue had assumed anyway, from the girl's T-shirt, which was the only thing the girl was wearing—that had been the last straw. Rue briefly considered telling Ginger all about it, but if she did, the next day half the people in Amethyst would know the details. Ginger had never been good at keeping secrets.

"But I'll bet you've got your eye on some fellow," Ginger said, raising an eyebrow.

"Well . . . maybe." Rue couldn't suppress a faint smile. There was, in fact, a man she had her eye on. Dylan Jeffries, from work. Nothing had really happened yet. They'd been to lunch a few times, then started jogging together along the Embarcadero after work. Lately they'd gone to see a few movies together. But she hadn't yet slept with him. She had told him from the first that she was in between and not ready for a new boyfriend yet, and Dylan hadn't pressured her. That was what Rue wanted, not to rush things as she usually did, and she was enjoying their slow, gradual courtship—if that was what it was. Dylan was the exact opposite of her last boyfriend. He liked dogs, not cats; classical music, not heavy metal; and he was so clean-cut it was almost comical. Her last boyfriend had pouted and brooded; Dylan was always in a good mood, always joking. He wasn't model handsome, but he had unruly chestnut hair, hazel eyes, and a cute grin. If anything, Rue worried that Dylan was *too* steady and predictable for her. But maybe that was what she needed. She was tired of the bad-boy types. In the end, they never turned out to be really bad, just boys.

"Well," said Ginger, "it'll be ten years for me and Marty next month. Marty Junior started third grade this year, and April's in the first grade. Being a mother is a hard life, let me tell you. But no more kids for me—I made Marty get the operation last year. He kicked and squealed, but I told him it was either snip those tubes or else wear double rubbers every time, 'cause I can't tolerate the pill. Actually, our sex life improved afterwards, for a while, anyway. Now if I could just get him to stop going out hunting every chance he gets—and stepping in other people's traps. Oh listen, I forgot to mention it! You and me are practically neighbors now."

"You're not still renting that house on Kline Street from Marty's dad?"

"Not since the spring. Moved into that new little development up north of town, on the far side from your Gran's house. Just north of the old Dunwitty place, where your other grandparents used to live. Not more than a mile away from your grandmother as the crow flies, except there's no road that goes straight through. To get from our place to yours, you have to drive all the way through town."

"North of the Dunwitty place? But there's nothing up there but pastureland for miles."

"Not anymore. Developers put in six houses this year, and hookups for six more. We almost had a lawn started when this cold weather kicked in. This norther'll probably kill every blade of grass."

Up ahead Rue saw the glare of the football field lights. Through the car windows, above the radio, she heard drumbeats. Ginger sped by the yellow brick high school building with its dirt parking lots and turned onto the little road that led to the bleachers. She clicked off the radio.

"You remember the old fight song, Rue. 'Fight, fight for Amethyst'—come on, sing along! I know you remember the words, you were a cheerleader your last two years in high school. 'Fight, fight for Amethyst . . .'"

Rue hummed along, feeling silly but not unhappy. She was a long way from San Francisco.

The turnout for the game from the other team's town was dismal, just a few carloads of people huddled together in the visitors' bleachers along with their school band. But as Ginger had predicted, the home bleachers were packed. People Rue hadn't seen in years waved and said hello as they walked past—old teachers, friends of her mother, distant kinfolk whose relation to her she had never quite worked out, and a few old classmates, some of them changed almost beyond recognition. They found a place to sit high up, just under the announcer's booth with its sheet-metal walls. Rue wore a wool cap, her scarf, and gloves; Ginger brought blankets for them to snuggle in. Between bundling up and sipping some of the worst coffee she had ever tasted (fresh from what Ginger called "the concession stand from hell"), Rue managed to keep tolerably warm.

The game was no contest. Perhaps it was partly the home team advantage for the Amethyst boys, but by halftime the score was 24–0. Even the Giants' band made a poor showing, straggling out onto the field and executing some of the sloppiest pinwheels Rue had ever seen, while playing a march version of the theme song from *Titanic*. As they marched off, a whole column turned the wrong way, then broke apart as the kids turned and ran to get back into formation. Some of the people in the stands laughed out loud. Rue felt sorry for the kids, imagining what a miserable night they must be having.

The Amethyst band wasn't much better, but at least the director kept the show simple. They marched onto the field, filed into concert formation, and stayed that way while a drill team strutted onto the field and did a high-step routine. The drill team was something new since Rue had been a student. The girls wore orange stockings and skimpy tiger-stripe outfits with fake fur at the collars and wrists.

"The Tigerettes," Ginger explained, blowing out a mouthful of cigarette smoke. "You're supposed to roll the *r* like you was a Mexican—Tigerrrrrettes. Or like you was freezing your ass off, which ain't hard to imagine—Tigerrrrrettes. They're pretty good, don't you think? Most people seem to like 'em. I liked it when we had twirlers, though—remember, like back when we were in school? I tried out and didn't make it."

The drill team wasn't half bad, Rue thought, especially considering that they must have been freezing in those outfits. While the band played a halting version of "Who Let the Dogs Out?" the girls strutted and kicked. The movements reminded her of the latest aerobics routine at her gym.

She leaned toward Ginger. "Who choreographs the drill team?"

"Liz Frady. I'm sure they don't pay her much, but somehow she talked the school board into letting her teach the drill team for an hour a day, and then I think she also teaches some sort of kiddie aerobics over at the grade school. Then in the afternoons she does bookkeeping at the bank."

"Liz Frady? I don't think I know her."

"No, you wouldn't, she just moved here a couple of years ago. From San Angelo, I think. A widow with a couple of teenage kids. Twins, a boy and a girl. Juniors this year. Except . . ." Ginger raised an eyebrow. "But then you wouldn't have heard about that. Not if you just got in today."

"Oh—yes." Rue nodded slowly, connecting the names. "The missing girl. Dawn Frady."

"Uh-huh. Missing for almost a week now. People in town are pretty upset about it."

"A runaway?"

Ginger shook her head sagely. "No way. Not that that kind of stuff doesn't happen around here these days. There was a couple of teenage girls up and disappeared last summer, but they were from those white trash Sumpter and Keegan families. Those girls were always in trouble. Everybody just figured they hit the road together. But that's not Dawn Frady; she'd never run off, especially not in the middle of the fall semester. See the girl in the middle of the drill team, the head girl with the whistle in her mouth? She's filling in for Dawn. Dawn's really talented. When her momma made her head of the drill team, nobody complained about it being unfair, because Dawn really is good. I've seen her do a backwards somersault from a standing position. She's pretty, too. And a straight-A student. Athletic *and* smart, sort of like you were."

Rue suddenly felt incredibly cold. She shivered inside the blanket.

Ginger shook her head. "I hear her mother is a real mess. In fact, I don't think she even showed up tonight." Ginger craned her neck to look up at the announcer's booth behind them. "Nope, or else she'd be up there now with the band director, helping him to announce the halftime show."

Rue pictured the placard in the window at Schneider's and saw Dawn's face clearly in her memory—the blond hair, the smile, the braces. "Who saw Dawn last?"

"The way I heard it, the Saturday after Thanksgiving, Liz sent Dawn down to Schneider's to buy some laundry soap. She could've sent Dawn's brother, Dwayne, but he works at Schneider's and he had the day off, so she didn't want him to have to go down there. The Fradys live just a few blocks from the store, on the other side of the railroad tracks, so Dawn walked. But she never showed up at Schneider's. Nobody knows what happened. The sheriff and the deputy questioned everybody along the route, and not a soul saw her coming or going. I guess that's not too surprising. You know how it is around here over the holidays, there's not a body stirring. People just shut themselves up in their houses and watch football on TV. Dawn left her house on foot—and then she just up and vanished."

"How awful," Rue said.

The band reached the finale of "Who Let the Dogs Out?" with a barrage of squealing trumpets. The drill team bowed in a ripple. After polite applause from the stands, the band marched forward to the beat of clicking drumsticks, merged into single file along the sideline, and marched toward the end zone. They halted at the sound of a shrill whistle, faced right, took up their instruments, and played the Amethyst fight song while the team charged out of the field house.

Everybody in the stands stood up and sang along. Rue joined in, amazed that she could remember the words:

Fight, fight for Amethyst,
Fight till they desist!
We're bound to beat the Giants,
Victory, and then—
On to district championship,
The Tigers must win!

She laughed out loud, it was all so silly and sweet.

The third quarter was slow going. Amethyst scored twice; the Giants stayed at zero and made some humiliating fumbles. People started leaving the stands, satisfied the Tigers had won and tired of the cold. By the start of the fourth quarter the visitors' stands were deserted except for a few diehards under piles of blankets and the band, which kept playing, with less and less enthusiasm, the only tune they seemed to know, the theme song from *Titanic*. Their band director had no sense of irony, Rue thought.

Bored with the game, Ginger gossiped about who was divorcing whom in Amethyst, who was pregnant, and where all their old classmates were living. Most of them were still in Texas, in small cities like Abilene and Lubbock. A few of the more ambitious ones had settled in Dallas or Houston.

The few times Rue mentioned San Francisco, Ginger showed no interest. She seemed to have no curiosity about life in California, and no conception of San Francisco beyond the old clichés about "fruits and nuts" and leftover hippies from the sixties. She seemed to be interested only in the life and the people she knew in Amethyst, and about them she could talk endlessly.

Rue's mind wandered until she found herself thinking about the cold more than anything else. She should have brought a down ski jacket with her, but she had forgotten how cold it could get in Texas at the beginning of December. Ginger suddenly nudged her with her elbow. "Now, *there* goes a fine hunk of a man."

"Where?"

"Are you blind? Right down there, walking in front of the bleachers. Feast your eyes, girl!"

Rue looked down at the tall, broad-shouldered man who had just paused at the silver-painted rail to watch the play. He was wearing boots, tight black jeans, a red down jacket, and a black felt cowboy hat. When the man looked over his shoulder and spoke to someone behind him, Rue caught a glimpse of a blue-stubbled jaw and a flashing white smile.

Ginger sighed. "I swear, if God didn't make that man, the devil did!"

"Who is he?"

"That heavenly creature's name—and I kid you not—is Justice Goodbody."

"You have *got* to be joking."

"Justice Goodbody is no joke, I assure you. He's the new deputy sheriff. Well, not all that new, he's been here for over a year, but that still makes him a newcomer in Amethyst. Probably just got off patrol duty and decided to drop by the game. Just about the finest specimen of manhood you're likely to see in Amethyst County. Not married, either, which makes him *the* most eligible bachelor." Ginger made a low, amorous growl.

The man turned and looked up briefly toward the announcer's booth. Rue saw his eyes, deep blue beneath fine black brows. For a moment their eyes met and Rue felt a slight jolt. Goodbody smiled and tipped his hat before turning back to watch the game.

Ginger let out a little shriek. "Did you see that? He practically made a pass at you!"

Rue's cheeks were suddenly warm despite the cold. "Hardly! He was tipping his hat to both of us, I imagine."

"I don't think so, Rue. Juss Goodbody has never once looked at me, at least not that way. He was looking straight at *you!* And look—that's Hank Fender he's talking to down at the rail . . . and now Hank's looking up here—smile, Rue!—and now Hank's whispering into Goodbody's ear. Rue! Juss Goodbody must have been asking Hank to have a look and tell him who you are!"

"You have a very active imagination, Ginger," said Rue. But even as she spoke, the deputy turned his head again and glanced up at her. When he looked away, the lingering eye contact left her with a residual tingle of excitement.

Ginger stirred and sat up straight, suddenly interested in the game again. "Well, would you look at that, they're finally letting the Frady boy play."

"Dwayne Frady?"

"Yep. Dawn's twin brother."

Rue nodded. "I saw him this afternoon at Schneider's."

"Yeah, he's worked there ever since the family moved here. Even working on a Friday afternoon, with a game tonight! Well, I imagine they need the money. Normally he's the starting quarterback, but I guess what with Dawn and all, and the Giants being such wimps, the coach started the Nelson boy instead. Well, I'm glad to see Dwayne finally out there on the field. Whoa! Go, Dwayne!" Ginger started yelling and cheering. So did a lot of the people around them. It was sentimental cheering, the kind they might have given for a player injured on the field or a retired coach taking a bow. The boy's sister was missing, and so everyone wanted to cheer for him.

The first play was a short pass, good for a first down. The Frady boy's timing was perfect. There was a shift in the mood in the bleachers, as if the crowd had warmed up. There was more yelling and cheering. The band struck up the fight song.

The next two plays were a muddle. The Tigers were held in check, then were pushed back five yards. The coach called Dwayne to the bench. The boy twisted and turned with his hands on his hips, looking angry. The coach jabbed the air with his forefinger. They seemed to be yelling at each other, then Dwayne suddenly turned and ran back to the huddle. The coach paced back and forth.

On the next play Dwayne attempted a handoff and fumbled. One of the Giants' linemen scooped up on the ball before it touched the ground and started running with it.

Dwayne was after him like a shot. Authentically tigerlike, Rue thought, incredibly fast, a blur of long, sprinting legs. He made a leap and came down on the lineman's shoulders, knocking him to the ground. The ball flew off toward the sidelines, but Dwayne ignored it. Instead he grabbed the tackled boy's face guard and yanked him halfway to standing, threw him down again, then jumped on him, flailing with his fists and knees.

It was all so strange that Rue simply stared. It was only when people started standing up around her that she realized the controlled violence of the game had turned into something out of control. Officials ran onto the field. Spectators started shouting, then booing. Rue stood to peer over the heads in front of her and saw the referees pulling Dwayne Frady away from a knot of Giants players. He broke free and started shoving them, then throwing punches.

"Disgraceful," Ginger said. "I mean, there's just no excuse . . ."

Rue saw a black cowboy hat among the football helmets and referee caps on the field and realized it was Justice Goodbody. Even without his hat he would have stood out, thanks to his height and his broad shoulders. He grabbed Dwayne Frady's arm and pulled him away from the tangle, then held up his hand and told the others to back off. The boys seemed to defer to Goodbody naturally, as if they recognized his authority instinctively. He was only doing his job, keeping the peace, but Rue felt a stirring of admiration for him.

People stayed on their feet, stamping and shaking and rubbing their hands to keep warm. It had been a long, cold night and a boring game, but finally they had something to talk about. They laughed, joked, shook their heads, cupped their hands, and shouted down at the field. Rue pulled the blanket around her and shivered.

"Do you think you could take me home now, Ginger? All of a sudden I'm very cold."

4

The porch light was on when she got home, but Gran had forgotten to lock the door again. Rue shook her head, exasperated, as she stepped into the house, making sure she pushed the lock button on the knob as she quietly closed the door. Maybe she was just being silly to carry her San Francisco habits home with her. Then she remembered the missing girl. Bad things *could* happen in Amethyst.

Gran already had gone to bed. On the kitchen table she had left a note:

> Rue, I left all the faucets running at a trickle, otherwise we'd have
> busted pipes in the morning for sure. Just in case they freeze up,
> I already filled the teakettle and the coffeemaker with water so
> we'll have it in the morning. Hope you and Ginger had fun at the
> game.

Rue had to puzzle over several of the words before she could make them out. When had Gran's handwriting become so shaky?

She found a blanket and snuggled up in the easy chair in the living room, then reached for the television remote control, smiling to remember how Gran, even in her wheelchair, had resisted the remote at first, suspicious of any new gadget that appeared in the house.

The standard cable service in Amethyst provided only twelve channels. One of them was a regional weather channel from Dallas. The report confirmed what Gran and everyone else had been saying. Temperatures were continuing to drop all over Texas, record lows had already been set in Fort Worth and Dallas, and a second front was expected to move into the state in the early morning, bringing even colder temperatures.

Harsh weather, thought Rue. Poor Gran, having to fret about the water pipes. It was a good thing Rue was home to look after her. What if the pipes did freeze, or the power went off, or the phone went dead? How would Gran cope? Perhaps Gran should no longer be living alone. Surely she would be safer in a nursing home or some kind of managed care facility. But Gran would hate that. She had always put so much stock in doing things for herself and in having her own place. If only Rue's mother hadn't died. Her mother had always taken care of everybody . . .

Rue awoke to the sound of someone talking about Jesus.

It was a white-haired man on the television with prim, pursed lips and a silky-smooth Southern accent, standing with upraised arms on a platform surrounded by rose-covered lattices. The roses looked fake and the minister looked too young to have solid white hair. Apparently, at some point in the night, the regional weather station changed over to a TV ministry. There were so many religious programs on Texas TV—not like San Francisco, where psychics and weight-loss hucksters dominated the late-night channels.

"Let me read you a letter, now, brothers and sisters," the minister said, staring into the camera and wrinkling his brow. "It comes from a viewer who has written to us before, who always signs his letters 'Outcast from the Body of Christ.' The Outcast writes, 'Brother Zack: I continue to be filled with unclean longings and foul desires. I struggle against them every hour of the day and every night, and I do not find an instant of respite. My flesh burns and I can hear the devil laughing in my ears. I pray to Jesus, Brother Zack, but I cannot hear his answer. I only know that I am consumed by urges so unspeakable that I dare not name them, even to a man of God like yourself. I am ashamed, Brother Zack, and yet I cannot help myself. These are sexual cravings that consume me, Brother Zack, lustful appetites that rise up from the foul bodily regions and pollute my mind. Everywhere I turn—"

Rue turned off the television. She switched off the lamp and made her way across the dark room to the door that opened into her bedroom. She stepped inside and started to reach for the overhead light switch, then realized she didn't need it. If there was one room in the world she could negotiate in the dark, it was this one. She had slept in this little room virtually every night of her life until she left for college, and each piece of furniture remained exactly where it had always been—the narrow bed, the bedside table, the old-fashioned dresser, and the stool . . .

It was chilly in the room, shut off from the gas heaters that warmed the living room and kitchen. She switched on the electric blanket and turned back the sheets. She undressed in the middle of the room, letting her clothing drop to the floor. There was a nightgown somewhere in her luggage, but she was too tired to look for it. She climbed into bed. As so often happened when she was back in Amethyst, she dozed off almost at once.

Later—how much later, she had no idea—something woke her. Her mind was so heavy with sleep that it seemed she might only be dreaming as she rolled onto her stomach and rose onto her hands and knees. Why was she suddenly awake? What was it she needed to do? It was cold air that had awakened her, coming from somewhere above her head. She had forgotten to pull down the shade and close the curtains of the window above the headboard, and the cold from outside was penetrating the windowpane. Groggy, her eyes barely open, she reached up to pull down the shade. Then she felt a shiver that came from something other than the frosty air on her naked skin.

Somewhere, out in the empty fields to the east of the house, there was a light.

It was small and distant, and while she watched, it flickered and disappeared, then appeared again. The light seemed to swing up and down, this way and that, like a flashlight carried in someone's hand. It seemed to be very far away and was slowly moving from right to left, south to north. She watched the slow progress of the flickering light until it suddenly disappeared altogether.

She pulled down the shade, blocking the cold air, then abruptly raised it again. The fields were dark. There was no sign of the light she had seen before. Or *had* she really seen it? Could she only have imagined it? Why would anyone be out on a night like this, carrying a flashlight? She looked at the bedside clock, with its old-fashioned glow-in-the-dark hands, and saw that it was after three o'clock.

She pulled down the shade again, closed the curtains, and snuggled under the electric blanket. She lay unmoving, her eyes open. Finally she sprang out of bed and began putting on the warm clothes she had shed earlier, until she was fully dressed again.

She stepped out of her bedroom and crossed the living room. The little button lock sprang out as she turned the doorknob on the front door, making a noise that seemed loud in the utter stillness. Rue stepped onto the front porch and closed the door behind her.

The night was moonless, but a feeble illumination from the distant streetlamp seeped through the mesquites, casting a faint, dappled light across the front yard. Rue stepped off the porch onto the walk, took a deep breath of cold air, and looked up at the stars, glinting bright and frosty in the black sky. She never saw the stars in San Francisco, where they were always hidden by fog or by the glow of big-city lights. In Amethyst, on a cold, clear winter night, the sky was pure black and spangled with endless stars.

It was quiet, too, so quiet that it seemed as if the air itself had frozen solid. She listened harder and realized there were sounds to be heard—a faint rustling of grass, even though she felt no wind on her face; the sound of her own breath; and from somewhere on the highway, outside of town, miles and miles to the north, the low, faint rumble of a big-rig truck shifting gears. Lonely sounds, the sounds of isolation and darkness.

Rue walked to the side of the house that faced east and stood beneath her bedroom window. She looked out at the fields where she thought she had seen the light. Surely there was no one out there at this time of night.

No one had any business being there, at any time of day. Those fields were Dunwitty property.

Far away, as small as a doll's house in the distance and almost hidden by pecan trees, was the old Dunwitty place, the two-story house where her father's parents had lived and died and where her father had grown up, hiking across the fields to come court her mother.

The house was abandoned now, and had been ever since Grandmother Dunwitty died, ten years ago. That was about the time that Rue and her father had stopped speaking to each other. There had been no dramatic falling-out, no sudden rupture, just a gradual but steady drifting apart. They had never been close, not since her parents divorced, when Rue was a first-grader. Neither of her parents ever remarried. Her mother stayed in Amethyst, living with Gran, and Emmett Dunwitty moved down to Corpus Christi, on the Gulf coast. After that, Rue saw him only on holidays, when he would drive up to visit his parents and stay at their place. After they died, he inherited the property and for a while continued to drive up to Amethyst from Corpus Christi occasionally to check on the place, but as far as Rue knew he hadn't come back in years. He had never rented out his parents' house or sold it. Instead he'd left the place just as it had been when Grandmother Dunwitty died, allowing it gradually to fall into neglect and disrepair.

At some point during her visit home, perhaps Rue would hike across the fields and have a look at the place. She knew where the key was kept and how to get in. It was always depressing, seeing how much more dust had accumulated inside and how much wilder the yard had grown. But it was one of the special things about coming to Amethyst, getting back in touch with her childhood and the places that would always be important to her.

But not tonight. It was much too late and much too cold. The frigid air was already penetrating her clothes, chilling her flesh. The only reason she had left the warmth of her bed to step outside was to take a better look at the dark, scrubby fields where she thought she had seen the light. But now she was even more uncertain than before that she had actually seen anything. Could it have been a glimmer of headlights somehow reflected from the highway? No, that was impossible; Gran's house stood between the highway and the fields. It seemed even less possible that anyone was actually out in those fields at this time of night, in such cold weather. Rue had heard rumors that hunters occasionally trespassed on the Dunwitty land, but surely not at three in the morning on the coldest night of the year.

And yet . . . she thought she had seen a light moving slowly from right to left, in a general direction away from the old Dunwitty house, across the fields dotted with barns and sheds, toward the hills to the north. Could someone have been leaving the Dunwitty house? Surely not. Even her father, on the very slight chance that he was in town, wouldn't be staying there—the gas and electricity had been shut off years ago. Rue shivered to think how cold it would be inside that dark house. There was not much left inside now that any burglar would want, not even much for any vandals to destroy.

Nevertheless, Rue stood and stared at the fields, half expecting the moving light to reappear. She stayed there until her nose burned from the cold and her fingers began to grow numb inside her gloves. It took only a few minutes; this night was colder than any she could remember. She shivered and hugged herself and hurried back into the house.

She hurried out of her clothes and into bed. The electric blanket felt toasty as she wriggled her toes against the tucked sheets at the foot of the bed and pulled the covers snugly about her neck.

As she fell asleep, a disturbing thought flitted across her consciousness: had she remembered to lock the front door? After all her admonitions to Gran, what an irony that would be if she had forgotten. She told herself she should get out of bed again and go check the door, but not yet. In a minute . . . after she had warmed up a bit more . . .

Rue fell into a deep sleep.

5

Rue! Rue, honey, you need to get up now!"

It was Gran, calling her from just outside the bedroom door. Rue smelled bacon. She rolled onto her side and glanced at the alarm clock. It was almost ten. No wonder Gran was impatient for her to get up.

She rolled over, slipping from under the warm electric blanket and reaching over the headboard to roll up the shade. The sky was overcast, pearl gray, but the light from outside was still bright enough to hurt her eyes.

"Rue, honey, can you hear me?"

"Yes, Gran," she called out huskily, clearing her throat. "I'll be out in a minute."

"Okay, hon." Rue heard the heavy roll of Gran's wheelchair withdrawing toward the kitchen.

She put on her nightgown and robe and a pair of thick woolen socks. As she brushed her hair, she leaned over the bed and peered out the window toward the Dunwitty house and the fields where she had seen—or imagined—the light. There was nothing to see except the decaying view so familiar from childhood: the scattered barns and sheds with rusting tin roofs, standing amid overgrown fields and uncared-for pecan orchards.

Everything was gray and umber, bleached and lifeless beneath the mantle of cold, gray clouds blown in on the fresh norther.

The whole house was chilly, despite the fact that Gran had turned up all the gas heaters. According to the weather station, temperatures were below zero all over central Texas. There had been heavy sleet in Dallas and two fatal car accidents. A fire in Waco had spread to several houses and killed ten people. Drivers had been stranded on icy highways all over the state. The unusually cold weather was expected to continue for at least another day.

Breakfast was bacon, scrambled eggs, toast, and homemade jelly made from the tart wild plums Gran had always called hog plums. Gran ate a single slice of bacon and half a piece of toast, then sat back to sip her coffee and ask Rue about the ball game. Rue laughed, remembering how awful the Giants' band had been. She also remembered, with a slight tingle, her lingering eye contact with the new deputy sheriff, and the way he had stood out in the crowd when he broke up the fistfight on the field. That led to less pleasant thoughts about poor Dwayne Frady and his missing sister. Did Gran know about Dawn Frady? She must; Maybelline Schneider had said there was a story about the disappearance in the weekly *Bulletin,* which Gran read religiously.

Rue avoided the subject and instead told Gran the local gossip she had picked up from Ginger, about who had married or divorced or had a baby. It was Gran who brought up the missing girl.

"Oh, and isn't it terrible about that Frady girl, gone missing?" Gran shook her head. "I remember them coming up here last Christmas, I guess it must have been before you and Reg and the kids got here for the holidays. That Liz Frady runs the Methodist youth group, and she took them out caroling in the church van. There must have been about a dozen kids, and most of them I didn't know who they were or even who their folks were, but Liz comes up here every now and then with your great-aunt Claudia—they've got this program at the Methodist church where some of the younger women drive older people around town to visit and shop. So I knew Liz Frady, and she introduced me to her boy and girl. Good-looking kids. Identical twins."

Rue shook her head. "I believe twins have to be the same sex to be identical."

Gran nodded. "Well, of course you're right. I knew that! Even so, those two kids look an awful lot alike. You and Reg looked almost that much alike when you were teenagers." Gran nodded toward some family photos on the wall, which included matching portraits taken when Reg was a senior and Rue was a sophomore. Rue had cut her hair very short that year; she had read a magazine article that said a brunette with her features—dark eyes, a long nose, full lips, and high cheekbones—looked better with short hair, and the result had worked so well that she never changed back to longer hair. Gran was right; in the photos, with her boyish hairstyle, she and Reg looked very much alike. Since then, Rue had changed less than Reg, who had gained thirty pounds and grown a beard. It was no longer so obvious that they were siblings.

Gran sighed. "That Dawn Frady is such a pretty child. It's a terrible thing, what this world's coming to. A girl like that can up and vanish and nobody seems to know a thing about it."

"Somebody must know something," Rue said.

"I guess that's the truth. Of course, if she didn't just up and run off on her own, then when they do find her, I imagine she'll be dead."

"Gran!" Rue got up from the table and started gathering up the dishes. Gran sometimes said the most appalling things, coming right out with the worst possible conclusion. Her mother had been the same way.

"It's only the truth. Course, she could be like these two girls that up and disappeared last summer. Everybody says they just ran off. What could you expect from those white trash Sumpters? And the Keegans aren't much better, from what I hear."

"Gran, you really ought not to talk about people that way."

Gran sat back in her chair, crossed her hands in her lap, and drew up her thin shoulders. "Well, maybe you haven't known the Sumpters as long as I have. They were just the same when your mother was a girl. That Elizabeth Sumpter would drive all over the county, and try to get your mother to go with her. She took up with a wetback cook out at the

Davis turkey farm and had three little half-breed babies before she even got married."

Rue started to say something but kept her mouth shut and stacked the dishes by the sink. How many hours had she and Reg wasted as kids arguing with her mom about things that didn't matter in the end, anyway? Generations were different. So were small towns and big cities. Gran might sometimes sound harsh and judgmental, but Rue had never known anyone with a better heart. There was a smug, unforgiving intolerance that characterized so many people in Amethyst, so many people all over Texas; Rue had inherited some of that judgmental nature herself, but she tried to direct it toward better targets than poor Hispanics and the kind of people Gran called white trash.

Rue put Gran's words out of her mind but couldn't shake a sudden bad mood. It was always like this when she came back to Amethyst, even when she was alone in the house with Gran—something would happen to remind her that no matter how nostalgic she might feel about the place, she no longer belonged in Amethyst. She could come home to visit, but never to stay. And since her mother had died, what did home mean, anyway? Gran was old; sooner or later she would be gone, too, and then—but Rue wasn't ready to think about that.

She started to do the dishes, but when she turned the handles, nothing came out of the faucet. Something was wrong. Gran had left the faucets dribbling overnight, but now there wasn't even a trickle. The pipes under the floorboards must have frozen solid, just as Gran had feared.

Rue bit her lip. What would her mother have done? Go under the house and have a look, Rue told herself, and wondered again how Gran would have coped alone, without her.

Rue found a flashlight. She dressed as warm as she could, putting on gloves and a muffler, but even so, her fingers and nose began to hurt almost from the moment she stepped outside. She couldn't remember it ever having been so cold before. This was a harsh, stabbing cold that seemed to penetrate straight to the bone.

At the side of the house there was a little door with a latch that opened into the crawl space under the house. It actually was a tall space, high enough for a child to stand upright without grazing the floorboards. Rue remembered being under the house only once before, years ago when she was a girl. The experience had left her with very unpleasant memories. Reg had dared her to do it, knowing how much she hated dark places and insects. She had been ten, and Reg twelve. As soon as she was through the little door, Reg had slammed it shut behind her and latched it. Rue had screamed and wailed, imagining every sort of creepy monster converging on her in the musty darkness—scorpions and tarantulas and giant flying cockroaches. Reg had laughed and laughed, and kept her locked under the house until her mother and Gran arrived home from visiting relatives in Halleyville. Rue had taken little satisfaction in the whipping Reg received. For months afterward she had nightmares about the crawl space, and she had never ventured back under the house—until now.

She started to reach for the latch, then turned and looked over her shoulder, toward the Dunwitty house across the fields. She was remembering another time Reg had locked her in a confined space. The memory was hazy at first, but gradually came back to her . . .

She and Reg had been upstairs in her grandparents' house. Rue had been no more than six or seven; it must have been shortly after her parents' divorce. Part of the house's attic was a pine-paneled room, her father's bedroom when he was a boy but by that time a playroom for Reg and Rue. A little door in one wall opened into the rest of the upstairs, which was unfinished attic space. For some reason, Rue had ventured into the attic space on her own—or more likely, Reg tricked her into doing so—and then Reg had closed the door on her. Rue had a vague memory of a dimly lit space with exposed beams and rafters, and something flitting through the air—something that buzzed and could sting her, a red wasp or a yellow jacket. She must have screamed, because their grandmother came upstairs to investigate. Grandmother Dunwitty didn't believe in corporal punishment, and Reg had escaped with only a scolding—but afterward, Rue seemed to recall, the door into the attic space somehow disappeared. How was that possible? Was her memory playing a trick on her? At any rate, Rue had never gone into the attic again, and had forgotten it even existed until this moment . . .

Amazing, how a trip home to Amethyst could stir up so many buried memories. Rue shook her head and told herself she was stalling. She had to take a look at the pipes under the house, and already she was numb from the cold. She switched on the flashlight, unlatched the door, and pulled it open. A musty, earthy smell wafted into her nostrils. The crawl space was not as dark as she remembered. Dim light seeped in through ventilation grates in the foundation walls. She stepped through the doorway, ducking to avoid a tangle of spiderwebs.

She walked stooped over among the wooden pillars until she found the cluster of pipes directly below the kitchen sink. With her flashlight, she found the other pipes and traced their courses. She saw no visible leaks or damage. That was a good sign. Still, a crack in one of the pipes might not show until the ice thawed and water began to flow again.

Suddenly, with a bang, the door into the crawl space slammed shut. Rue gave a start, and a terrifying claustrophobia jolted through her, more stabbing than the cold. Just as suddenly, the door flew open again. It was only a gust of wind, moving the door back and forth.

She hurried back toward the little door, eager to leave the crawl space. But passing by one of the supporting pillars, she almost tripped over something. Startled, she jumped back and lowered her flashlight. It was an old cardboard box.

Curious, she tried to pull the box out of the shadows, but the cardboard was so old and moldering that the flap in her hand pulled free. She carefully opened the other flaps and shone the flashlight onto a stack of water-stained magazines, their pages stuck together—copies of *Playboy*, *Penthouse*, and *Hustler*. As she leafed through the pages, her fingers awkward inside her gloves, the brittle paper cracked and crumbled. The photos of naked women were no longer erotic but crumpled and stained and spotted with black fungus. Their mother would never have allowed Reg to keep magazines like these in the house. He must have kept them hidden here when he was in high school, and then forgot about them when he went to college. Rue had discovered his secret teenage stash of sex magazines.

Another memory flashed through her mind. Once at Reg's house in Austin, rummaging through a trunk of old family photos, Rue had come upon some porno videos. The photos on the boxes showed men in leather with riding crops and women in chains, trussed and gagged. Was that what Reg and Cathy were into? she had wondered. Or did the videos reflect only Reg's private fantasies? Rue had considered saying something—if she had found the videos, then so could Reg's children—but she had kept her mouth shut. Who was she to tell her brother how to run his household?

The stale air and the cold and the dark, confined space were suddenly too much for her. Rue hurried out from under the house, pulling spiderwebs from her hair. She drew in a gasping breath so cold it seemed to cut her lungs. She hurried to the front porch and back inside the house.

The front passed through, followed by warming temperatures. The sun came out. At three that afternoon, the water started to flow again. Rue forced herself to take another look under the house. The beam of her flashlight showed nothing amiss. The pipes were dry and intact.

Rue washed the dishes, then took a long, hot shower. The day passed before she knew it. Darkness came early, and with it memories of the light she had seen, or imagined, in the field the previous night.

They were sitting at the kitchen table. Gran was doing the crossword in the San Angelo newspaper. Rue put down the *Vanity Fair* she was reading. "Gran, you can see the old Dunwitty place from your bedroom window, can't you?"

"What, hon?" Gran looked up from her crossword.

"The Dunwitty house. You can see it across the field from your bedroom window."

"Yes. Why do you ask?" Gran put down her pencil and flexed her narrow shoulders.

"Oh, it's nothing. Would you like some mint tea?" Rue sipped from her cup. "I could make some for you."

"No, that's all right, hon. I'm not thirsty."

They sat for a long moment, neither of them speaking. In Amethyst, there was never a hurry. "Do you ever see or hear anything over at the Dunwitty place?"

Gran shrugged. "There's not a soul over there, and not anybody else for a mile on either side, except for me."

"I wonder if Dad ever drives up from Corpus Christi anymore."

"If he does, he never comes to see me. I don't reckon I could see if there was a car parked over there or not. There's a high hedge all along that driveway."

"But have you ever noticed any . . . any lights at night?"

"Lights? I don't reckon there's been any power to that place for years now."

"No, I don't mean in the house. Out in the fields."

Gran shook her head. "Why? Did you see something over there?"

"I don't know. Last night, looking out my bedroom window . . ." Rue shook her head. "I guess I just imagined it."

Gran drew herself up and looked shrewdly into the distance. "Well, now, Rue, there have been people who broke into the Dunwitty house."

"Really? When was this?"

"Back in the summer. I don't reckon it was anybody trying to steal anything, probably just some kids up to no good. It was July—I remember I had all the windows open and I couldn't get to sleep, on account of the heat. It was after ten o'clock when I heard the strangest noise, like a phone left off the hook too long. You know how sound can travel across these fields on a still night. I kept trying to imagine what on earth it was until I realized it had to be coming from the Dunwitty place. Then I remembered you and Reg saying your father has some kind of alarm installed on the door over there."

Rue nodded. The alarm was a cheap battery-operated little box that fit onto the top of the door with a pin on a spring that would go off if the door was opened. There was a switch right on the alarm to turn it off; Rue did it every time she went into the Dunwitty house. Of course, the door had a lock, but the key wouldn't be hard for anyone to find; it was hung on a nail behind a hat on the screened porch.

"So what happened?"

"Well, it just went on and on and I finally figured there was probably nobody who could hear it except me!" Gran shook her head and laughed. "Your father always was a strange bird. I don't know what good he thought an alarm like that could do, except I guess it did scare off whoever was over there. Anyway, I called Sheriff Boatwright, and he said he'd check on it. Sure enough, it wasn't but a few minutes before I saw headlights over there and that alarm stopped."

"And?"

"In the morning he and that new deputy came by."

"The new deputy?" Rue flashed on the memory of two blue eyes connecting with hers.

"Good-looking young fellow with a funny name. Now, what is it?"

"Justice Goodbody," said Rue.

Gran smiled. "Now, how did you know that?"

Rue smiled in return. "Ginger pointed him out to me at the football game last night. But go on. The next morning he and the sheriff came by?"

"They did, and they told me they found the front door of the Dunwitty house standing wide open with the key in the lock. Course, they couldn't tell if anything was missing, that place is such a mess, I imagine, but they didn't find any windows broken, or anything like that. Sheriff Boatwright asked me for your daddy's number down in Corpus and said he'd call him about it, and that's the last I heard. Oh, and they brought me the key that was in the door and asked me what to do with it. Well, Reg and his kids came up a couple of weekends later, and I gave Reg the key and he went over and put it back wherever it belongs. Reg said he couldn't see that anything had been stolen or damaged. I imagine the real worry is that somebody might start a fire over there. Lord, wouldn't that be awful? But from what you kids say and what the sheriff told me, that place is just a shambles, anyway. Why on earth your father just lets it sit there empty I can't imagine."

Rue nodded in agreement.

"And then, of course, every now and again I can hear shots from over that way."

"Shots?"

Gran shrugged. "Sounds like a rifle. Somebody hunting, I imagine."

"Day or night?"

"Both. I can't imagine there's much worth shooting this close in to town, besides squirrels and birds. Maybe a fox or a deer. And people hunt coons at night. I told Sheriff Boatwright about hearing shots, and he figured the alarm might have been set off by some hunter trespassing over there at night who decided to go nosing around the house. He claimed whoever it was must've been on foot."

"Why?"

"Because that night, when the sheriff radioed him to check on that alarm, the deputy happened to be parked at the Dairy Queen, which is right where the road to the Dunwitty place comes out into the highway. The deputy didn't pass anybody heading out, and that's the only road to the Dunwitty place, so whoever was over there and set off that alarm must have got there on foot."

"So it was the deputy who checked on the alarm?"

"I think they both went over there, but I guess it was the deputy who got there first. Justice Goodbody—with a name like that, he should run for office!"

Rue smiled and nodded. Where else but Texas had people ever elected a state treasurer named Jesse James? "I believe they call him Juss for short. That's what Ginger called him."

Conversation ended, and in the silence that followed, Rue put down the *Vanity Fair,* bored with it. She leafed through a stack of newspapers until she came to the latest edition of the *Amethyst Bulletin.* Dawn Frady's photo was printed four columns wide across the front page. The headline read: LOCAL GIRL MISSING.

Rue skimmed the story, but it seemed she knew all the details already—the lack of any witnesses, the absence of any leads, the consensus that it wasn't likely that Dawn had simply run off. The story included a plea from Liz Frady, but no statement from the girl's brother. Rue remembered his initial surliness at the grocery store and the fight he'd started at the ball game. She also remembered the sudden, nervous smile he had given her as she pulled out of Schneider's parking lot, his braces glinting in the headlights, just as in the school photograph Dawn's braces caught the light from the flashbulb.

6

On Sunday morning the sky remained clear. The weather was still chilly but there was a definite warming trend. Rue put on the designer dress she had brought, and went to morning services at the Methodist church. Gran declined to go with her; she said it was still too cold for her to venture out. Rue saw lots of people she knew, most of them her mother's age or older. After the service, people lingered in the foyer for a while, talking about Friday's football game and the cold snap.

Driving home, Rue noticed that the community announcements board had been changed. The bake sale was over and there was no football game the next Friday. Instead, there was only one message—HAVE YOU SEEN DAWN?—followed by a phone number.

Back at Gran's house, after a lunch of pot roast and potatoes, Rue hardly stirred for most of the afternoon, as a quiet lethargy crept over her. San Francisco and the hectic pace she maintained there seemed more and more remote. What was there to do except lie on the sofa and read an old book, or sit at the kitchen table leafing through magazines and old newspapers while Gran dozed or worked her crosswords, or look through boxes of her old things or her mother's old things, or browse through scrapbooks and photo albums? She moved from room to room, absorbing the memories that lingered in framed photos on the walls and in drawers that no one had opened since the last time Rue was home.

Eventually she grew restless. She needed to move, to breathe, to feel her blood pumping. Rue decided to go for a run. She put on her sweats and running shoes and set out into the cold.

The route she followed was one she had been running since she was a track star in high school: up the highway for a short distance, then a right turn onto the paved road that cut east past the farms and ranches spread out in the rolling hills north of town, then another right turn onto the road back into Amethyst that would eventually take her past the Dairy Queen. From there she could head up the road to the old Dunwitty house and cut across open fields to get back home. The entire route was about ten miles.

Despite the bright sun, the day remained almost too cold for this kind of exertion, but once Rue got away from the highway and onto the farm-to-market road, the countryside was so beautiful and the air so crisp that she managed to ignore the occasional stab in her chest and the rings of cold moisture around her nostrils. On such a clear day she could see for miles across the gray hills, all the way to a smudged purple horizon. Fence posts strung with rusted barbed wire lined the road. The grasses and weeds along the shoulder were gray and brittle. The mesquite trees stood naked and gnarled against the sky. The junipers were wrapped in shaggy, dark green mantles, dotted with pale, blue berries and hung with mistletoe. Farther from the road, deep in the fields, she saw stands of cactus and what the ranchers called tanks, seasonal watering holes for the livestock. The highest objects were windmills, with gray metal blades that stood idle in the cold, still air.

The road seemed to be abandoned. The fields were empty; all the livestock had been herded into barns to protect them from the cold. The widely scattered houses along the way were tightly shut up; the driveways and open garages were mostly empty. Where was everyone? At the crest of a hill Rue turned to take in the view behind her, jogging in place. All was quiet and still in every direction. The only movement was a big-rig truck heading north up the highway, as tiny as a thumbtack in the distance.

She turned and plummeted down the short hill, feeling the air burning cold on her cheeks and in her lungs, exhilarated by the absolute simplicity of everything around her. This sense of freedom was what she could never find in San Francisco, or even in Austin. In those places she was a woman with ambitions and desires, preferences and opinions and projects, obliged to plan ahead and fill up every moment with either work or pleasure. Here, running alone on a quiet road outside Amethyst, she had no identity, she was nobody. Nothing existed here except the endless blue sky above and the slumbering earth below, the gray metal windmills that dotted the hills like frozen sentinels, the road beneath her feet, the air in her lungs, the blood pounding in her ears. She was anonymous and alive and alone, and that was enough. She had been born in Amethyst; twenty-nine years later, running on this road, it was as if nothing had happened in the time between. The changeless things remained unchanged: sky, earth, windmills, road, breath, blood. She belonged to this place, and the place belonged to her. The moment was perfect and hard, like crystal.

Suddenly her foot landed on a jagged rock that had been thrown onto the graded shoulder. The rock upset her balance and pitched her forward. To compensate she skittered sideways across the loose gravel. She almost fell, but caught herself and stamped forward taking big, awkward steps. Finally she came to a halt. Breathless, cursing softly, she reached down to squeeze her left ankle.

The pain was sharp. She winced and took a few steps and knew that further running was out of the question. Walking was possible, but still painful. She looked around, feeling suddenly very isolated and very far from the comfort of Gran's house. She was probably three quarters of the way through her run; it would be better to go forward than back, though it might be easier to hitch a ride on the highway, if it came to that. She stood for a while, catching her breath, loosening her shoulders, scowling at herself and testing her ankle against the road. It was only a very mild sprain, the kind of injury that meant she wasn't a girl any longer, endlessly resilient. She was a grown woman, and whenever she used her body she had to take more care.

Walking actually seemed to relieve the pain. She remembered the quote that Reg's high school football coach was famous for: "You've got to learn the difference between pain and injury!"

She reached the turnoff that would take her back toward Amethyst. The road was a little busier than the farm-to-market, but not much. Rue thought about hitching a ride, but decided firmly not to. Even in Amethyst, it probably wasn't a good idea; there were so many townspeople she didn't know now. Whenever a car passed, she tried to hide her limp and kept her eyes straight ahead.

She passed what once had been a garbage dump. It was covered over now, made redundant by a landfill south of town, and looked almost parklike, a smooth expanse of high gray grass without trees or cactus. Across from the old dump, on her right, there was something else that was new—a broad paved road with a street sign. It was the new housing tract, she realized, the little development where Ginger lived, north of the old Dunwitty property.

There were only six houses, three on each side of the road, sprawling one-story ranch houses with two-car garages and huge air-conditioning units outside. They looked out of place amid the rocky land that surrounded the tract. Someone had bulldozed through the jumbled limestone and dirt, laid down black asphalt for the street and dirt for yards, and put up houses, but it didn't really seem like a neighborhood. It would look more settled, Rue thought, once the landscaping matured. In Amethyst that would mean Bermuda grass lawns with lantana bushes and crepe myrtle trees for color.

Rue didn't see Ginger's Pontiac in any of the driveways, but there was a mailbox on a post in front of each house. The last mailbox on the left had pink butterflies and yellow daisy decals on the side. That looked like Ginger's idea of decoration, she thought. When she got closer, Rue saw *The Sutherlands* hand-painted in dainty, uneven pink-and-yellow strokes across the front of the box.

There was a gigantic black pickup truck covered with road dust in the driveway, with a gun rack filled with rifles in the cab. It seemed oddly familiar, and then Rue remembered having seen it in the parking lot at

Schneider's when she first arrived in town. At one corner of the rear cab window was an NRA decal and at the other a Christian fish. A Mexican Day of the Dead skeleton dangled from the rearview mirror. The rear bumper was crowded with stickers: FLAG BURNERS SHOULD FRY; BAN MY GUN & YOU BETTER RUN; and a much-weathered, barely decipherable red-white-and-blue BUSH FOR GOVERNOR.

Rue stepped onto the front porch and pressed the bell. There was a mumbled shout from inside. A few moments later the door opened.

It took her a moment to recognize Marty Sutherland. Ginger had not aged particularly well, but Marty was hardly recognizable. He had been kind of sexy in high school, or at least had seemed that way to Rue within the narrow confines of Amethyst. Rue remembered him coming to school in skintight Lee jeans and cowboy boots, wearing V-neck T-shirts with the sleeves rolled up and an old green-and-yellow John Deere cap. He had been strong and barrel-chested, with big hands and feet and the kind of face Rue's mother called cute-ugly—big cheeks and squinty eyes and tousled blond hair.

Marty looked at her oddly, then grinned. He suddenly looked like himself, and Rue realized it was the glasses that were different, above and beyond the extra weight he had put on. Marty had never worn glasses in high school, and he'd had just one chin back then, but his grin hadn't changed. He still wore the same type of V-neck T-shirt, which now showed a big bulge around his middle, but he had switched from tight jeans to baggy khakis.

"Rue, is that you? Damn! Ginger said you was in town. I'd've gone out to the ball game with you the other night if my damn foot wasn't aching me. Come on in."

Rue stepped inside and returned Marty's smile, then winced at the smell of whiskey mixed with cigarettes on his breath. His body had a strong odor as well, like worn clothes from a hamper. Or perhaps that was the house itself, the smell of a house with two children and a mother who didn't have much time for cleaning. The living room carpet was cluttered with toys and games. The sofa was strewn with newspapers and discarded clothes. There were dirty dishes on the coffee table.

Marty didn't seem embarrassed about the state of the house. "Have a seat, anywhere you can find a place that's clear. You want a beer or something?"

Rue stepped toward the big easy chair nearby, then saw the butt-filled ashtray on one arm and the cocktail glass on the other, and the well-worn indentation on the macramé pillow in the seat. She glanced at the television, which was turned to a raucous talk show. The participants, a group of heavy black women, were yelling and pulling one another's hair. Marty followed her gaze and chuckled. "Crazy niggers," he said. "Always trying to steal each other's boyfriends."

Rue sighed. Very likely the only people of color Marty ever saw were on TV, on shows like this one. "Where's Ginger?"

"Drove to Mayhew with the kids to visit her sister. Left me to fend for myself. Are you limping, Rue?"

"A little. I was out running and hurt my ankle. Nothing serious. But I was going to ask Ginger for a ride home."

"Shit, I'll give you a ride."

"Would you? Thanks."

Marty looked at her and grinned, but it was a different grin from the one he had given her at the door. Rue didn't like it. She stepped toward the sliding glass doors that opened onto the backyard. The hill fell away steeply beyond the stillborn lawn, giving a view of the town below. She could see the top of the Texaco sign and the courthouse, and farther to the south the high school and the football stadium. Closer landmarks were blocked by the trees and scrubby growth of the hillside; she couldn't see anything at all of Gran's house, though she could guess its location off to the right. Nor could she see any of the Dunwitty property, which was directly below the hill.

"I hadn't realized these new houses were so close to the old Dunwitty land," she said. "Practically up against the property line."

"Not practically," Marty said. He walked to the easy chair, picked up the glass, and took a swig. "Your daddy's land starts about forty feet past my back patio. There's an old barbed-wire fence that marks the line, same fence that's been there for about a hundred years."

"The fence my grandfather built."

"I reckon so."

"All this used to be just fields. Thicket and cactus."

"Progress," said Marty. "I wanted a house out in the country where I could go shooting when I wanted, and Ginger wanted to stay in town. So we sort of compromised."

"Where do you go shooting around here?"

Marty shrugged but didn't answer. He took another drink. "You sure you don't want something? A little whiskey to kill the pain?"

"It's not that painful."

"Well, mine is. My damn right foot."

Rue nodded. "Ginger said something about a hunting accident."

"Yeah. I stepped in a goddamned trap. Hurts like a son of a bitch when I'm on it too much. So we're both invalids, huh? A couple of crips."

"Looks like it." Rue took a deep breath and restlessly flexed her shoulders. "Why don't we limp together out to your pickup?"

"What's your hurry?" Marty stepped toward her. She hadn't noticed it before, but now she saw that he did have a slight limp. When he got close enough for her to smell his breath again, she took a step back.

"I need to get home, Marty."

"Your grandma expecting you?"

"Yes."

"I'm sure she could wait a while longer. Old lady in a wheelchair most all her life, I bet she's learned a lot of patience."

Rue looked Marty in the eye. He stared back at her and didn't blink. She looked away, through the sliding glass doors, at the rooftops of Amethyst in the valley. Marty had always been big, and he was even bigger now, even if a lot of him was fat; big enough to block her way if she tried to step past him toward the door.

"Forget the ride, Marty. I'll walk home."

"Aw, don't get mad. Damn, you are a good-looking woman, Rue Dunwitty. Always were." He stepped closer. Rue was suddenly backed against the Formica bar that separated the kitchen from the living room. "You're not married, are you? That's what Ginger said. You must get up to some pretty wild stuff living by yourself out in San Francisco."

"That's really none of your business, Marty. Now why don't you back off and give me room to breathe?"

"Is it too hot in here for you?" He sucked in his breath and grinned down at her. "Damn, I'm hot, that's for sure. Feel of it, Rue."

"Marty—"

"Feel of it, damn it!" He grabbed her wrist and pressed her hand against his crotch. The ridge down his pants leg was stiff as a pipe. Ginger had always claimed it was big; it was a boast when she and Marty first started screwing in high school, and a complaint after they married. For just an instant, Rue was fascinated in spite of herself.

"Oh yeah, baby." Marty let go of her wrist and braced his hands against the countertop, trapping her. He lowered his face, crooning and parting his lips for a kiss.

Rue turned her face away and pushed at him with both hands. His stomach and chest were soft and fleshy, not at all like the bodies of the men she was used to touching. "Marty, I said to stop it, right now."

Marty narrowed his eyes and started baby-talking. "But Daddy don't wanna stop, baby Rue. Be a good baby and touch it for Daddy again, squeeze it real sweet."

Rue laughed, in spite of herself. Was this how he and Ginger did it? Marty started nuzzling her forehead. The smell of stale cigarettes and whiskey was overpowering.

"Look, Marty." She tried to keep her voice even. "I'm not enjoying this, okay? I really want you to back off, right now."

"Touch it for me, baby. Wrap your little hand around it. Daddy's good little girl." He moved one hand onto her shoulder and slid his palm onto her breast.

She gathered her strength and pushed at him as hard as she could. When that didn't work, she punched him in the gut. He staggered back, looking hurt. Then he suddenly grinned. "You are so goddamned pretty!" he whispered. The grin turned into a smirk as he lumbered toward her.

Rue stepped to one side and reached behind her, searching for the latch to the sliding glass door. She snapped it upward, pushed the door open, and felt a rush of cold air on the back of her neck. She stepped back, still looking at Marty, and unexpectedly felt something soft but restraining against her back. It was the screen door. She hadn't accounted for that. Nobody had screen doors in San Francisco. She turned and fumbled with the second latch and heard Marty chuckling behind her. As she slid the screen door open she felt Marty's hands gripping her shoulders tightly.

She ducked, slipping out of his hold, and turned to face him again; he hadn't counted on her agility. She looked once again at his smirking face before she brought her knee up hard against his crotch.

Marty gasped and hopped backward, leaving her free to slip out the door. Rue ran to the front yard and onto the street. Surely he wouldn't follow her into the open. She slowed her pace to a fast walk, glancing over her shoulder. It wasn't until she reached the highway that her adrenaline began to ebb and her ankle began to throb again. She winced and cursed under her breath. She started limping down the hill, so rattled that she didn't even hear the car approaching until it was almost on her.

7

Rue heard the crunch of tires on gravel and spun around. The movement twisted her ankle and she cursed at the pain.

Her heart sped up. She expected to see the huge black pickup truck looming behind her, with Marty grinning behind the wheel. But it wasn't a pickup. It was a banged-up little two-door Toyota with a long crack running down the front windshield. The paint job, or what was left of it, was metallic green.

Rue caught her breath and tried to swallow the anxious swelling in her throat. A red glare from the lowering sun reflected off the windshield so that she couldn't make out the driver. If only it was someone she knew! She squinted and stepped haltingly forward.

The driver's door opened and a shock of dark blond hair emerged. A kid, she told herself, but big for his age, wearing an orange-and-black football letterman's jacket. She tensed and felt her hands draw involuntarily into fists. Then he smiled shyly, just enough to show a glimpse of braces, and she recognized him. It was the boy from the grocery store, the missing girl's brother. The quarterback who had lost control at the football game. Dwayne Frady.

His smile wavered, then vanished as he drew his eyebrows together. "Are you okay? I thought I saw you limping."

Rue took a deep breath, still keeping her distance from the car. "Actually . . ."

"Are you lost?"

She had to laugh. "You could set me down blindfolded on any road within a fifteen-mile radius of Amethyst and I would *not* be lost."

He looked at her oddly. "It seems awful cold to be out jogging. Are you sure your leg's okay?"

"Actually, I did sprain my ankle. Just a little."

"Can I give you a ride?"

"Well . . ." She hesitated for a moment, then heard the noise of an engine and saw another vehicle farther up the hill, turning onto the highway from the road to Ginger's house. It was Marty's black pickup.

"Yes," she said. "If you could give me a ride, I'd appreciate it." Dwayne nodded and ducked back into the car. He reached across the passenger seat to unlatch the door for her. As Rue pulled the door open and bent down to slip into the low bucket seat, she looked over the roof of the Toyota. The pickup approached and passed by, going recklessly fast, but not so fast that she didn't catch a glimpse of Marty behind the steering wheel. He turned his head as he passed and for an instant made eye contact with her. He looked furious. As she slammed the flimsy door beside her, Rue shivered, only partly from the cold.

"Asshole!" the boy murmured, shifting the car into gear. "Driving like a bat out of hell."

"The pickup?"

"Marty Sutherland. Notorious blowhard and blue-ribbon asshole. Pardon my French." He grinned and looked at her sheepishly. "You're not related to him, are you?"

"To Marty? Hardly. But I know him."

"Oh yeah?"

"We went to school together, a long time ago."

"You're kidding. You're the same age as Marty Sutherland?"

"Same class at good old AHS. Do the kids still call it Ass Holes Supreme?"

He laughed, then squelched it as his voice broke high enough to embarrass him. "Actually, it's Ah, Holy Shit! So you don't live here anymore?"

"Not since high school. I went to college in Austin, then moved out to California."

"Oh, yeah?"

"San Francisco."

"Really? San Francisco." He seemed impressed. "What is that, four hours on a plane?"

"Either that or three full days of driving."

"That's a long way. Wow, San Francisco. You like it?"

"Yes, very much."

"But you *still* come back to Amethyst?" He said it like someone who couldn't imagine coming back if he ever had the chance to leave.

"Sure. To see family."

"Oh. We're kind of new in town. I still don't know who-all's related to who."

"Actually, I don't have much family here anymore. Not close family. Just my grandmother." They had reached the bottom of the hill and the beginnings of town, an area where several Mexican families lived in simple frame houses with peeling white paint. The packed-dirt front yards were strewn with rocks. Goats and chickens lived in little lean-to sheds built against the houses. Barking dogs ran along the chain-link fences as the Toyota passed by.

"My name's Dwayne, by the way."

Rue nodded. "Dwayne Frady."

He frowned. "How'd you know that?"

"Well, it's printed on that name tag you wear at Schneider's, for one thing."

"You've seen me in Schneider's?"

"Friday afternoon, just before they closed."

He looked ahead at the road and shrugged.

"You don't remember me?"

"I guess we were kind of busy. That's when the cold front came in, wasn't it? Plus we had the game that night."

"But you looked straight at me when I was pulling out. You smiled."

"Did I? I guess I was off on some other planet." He shrugged again.

"Anyway, my name's Rue. Rue Dunwitty. My grandmother's name is Lee."

"Oh, yeah, I know her. Old lady in a wheelchair, lives alone."

"How—"

"My mom took a bunch of us caroling last Christmas. Plus I've been by your grandma's house a few other times. My mom does stuff like drive old ladies around town to visit each other."

Rue nodded. "I remember Gran mentioning that."

"So is that where I should drop you off, at your grandmother's house?"

"Yes, please."

When the road intersected with the main highway from Austin, Dwayne turned right. As they passed the Dairy Queen, Rue saw the black pickup pulled up at the drive-through window. She said nothing and looked in the opposite direction, at the turnoff onto the dirt road that eventually became the private drive that led to the Dunwitty house.

Dwayne bit his lower lip and kept his eyes on the road ahead. "You know, you really shouldn't be out hitchhiking."

"I wasn't hitchhiking. I was running."

"Even so, you shouldn't be out like that. Alone, I mean."

"I know."

"I mean, really."

"I hear you." Rue looked out the window, at the storefronts that lined the highway as it turned into Main Street—the hardware store, the drug store, the *Bulletin* office, all closed on a Sunday. "Listen, Dwayne, I heard about your sister. I'm very sorry. I really hope it turns out all right."

He turned and looked her in the eye. He was so young, Rue thought, to be having to face something so awful. Nothing like that had ever happened in her family. It had been sad when Grandfather and Grandmother

Dunwitty died within months of each other, and terrible when her mother's lung cancer was diagnosed, but those things were different. Besides, Rue was a woman now, as able to face life's tragedies as she ever would be. Dwayne Frady looked like a child to her, hardly old enough to be driving a car, though he was at least seventeen and bigger than most of the men she knew. When he blinked and looked back at the road, she saw the sparkle of tears in his eyes.

They came to the stoplight. Rue felt a twinge of uneasiness, then realized the reason when she glanced at the community announcements sign. HAVE YOU SEEN DAWN? the sign said. Rue noticed that the W was actually an upside-down M.

Dwayne was staring at the sign when the light changed. The car behind them honked. Dwayne gave a start, and when he tried to shift gears the engine died. He restarted it and the Toyota lurched forward.

"Sorry," he muttered.

"That's okay."

"We talked to the milk people. The man told us it would take six weeks."

"I beg your pardon?" said Rue.

"Milton Schneider got my mom in touch with the people who make the milk cartons. You know, with pictures of missing kids. We gave them a photo and everything. But they said it would take six weeks before they could get Dawn onto any milk cartons."

"Oh."

"You really shouldn't be out walking on the highway alone like that. Especially with a twisted ankle."

"I know. I guess I just wasn't thinking."

"Every chance I get, I've been going out and driving up and down the highways around town. Driving all over. Just looking, you know. You're the only woman I've seen out alone like that. Another half hour and it'll be dark."

"Looking for what?" The answer seemed obvious and she instantly regretted asking.

"I'm not looking for Dawn, if that's what you think. The sheriff's already had people doing that, walking on foot. Because they say a lot of times that's where they find somebody, just . . . dumped along the highway." He shook his head. "I've just been driving and looking. Keeping an eye out. Seeing who's out on the roads. Somebody's out there who shouldn't be. It's not just Dawn, you know. Last August it was Brittany Sumpter and Kandy Keegan."

Rue frowned. "I thought they were runaways."

"Yeah, that's what a lot of people think. Just 'cause they were wild. But the kids at school know different. Dawn knew they weren't runaways."

They reached the Amethyst city limits and passed the final streetlight, glowing dull yellow against the steel gray sky. Dwayne slowed and turned onto the dirt drive. He pulled up behind Rue's rental car. The front porch light was on. That meant Gran was waiting for her and wondering where she was.

"Hey, thanks for the ride," said Rue. "You're my Good Samaritan."

"Yeah, sure. I don't suppose—I mean, I guess you already have plans for dinner?"

"Just leftovers with Gran. But if you'd like to come in . . ."

"No, my mom's expecting me, too. I'd better get home."

As Rue reached for the door handle, Dwayne cleared his throat. "So— you live in San Francisco . . ."

"Yes. Dwayne, my ankle's starting to bother me."

"Oh, yeah, look, I'm sorry. Glad I could give you the ride."

Rue smiled and started to pull up on the door handle.

"So—is it really like that out in San Francisco?"

"Like what?"

"You know . . . like they say on TV."

"That depends on which TV shows you watch."

He smiled. "Yeah, I guess. I mean, is it really like that, with the, you know . . . all the gays and lesbians and everything?"

Rue smiled. It was such a typical question. "Everything you've ever heard about San Francisco is absolutely true. It's usually just the way they tell it that makes it a lie. Why do you ask?"

"I just . . . never met anybody from San Francisco. It must be really different from here."

She let go of the door handle and looked at him, but he wouldn't look her in the eye. His skin was so fair that even in the dim light she could see him blush. Rue felt a twinge of conscience. He seemed to need someone to talk to, at his own pace. On the other hand, her ankle was beginning to throb, and Gran would be worried about her, and she was suddenly very tired.

"Dwayne, I really have to go now. But we should talk sometime. You know my grandmother's name, right? She's in the phone book. Call me. I'll be here at least a few more days."

"Okay." He stared at the steering wheel.

"Or I'll call you. Would that be all right—with your mother, I mean? I don't want to embarrass you or anything."

"No, that would be fine . . . I guess."

Rue took a deep breath and laid her hand on his. "Thanks for the ride, Dwayne." She opened the door, but when she stood up she put too much weight on her injured ankle and staggered a bit. She let out a hiss of pain.

He was out of the car and beside her in seconds, offering his arm for support. It wasn't really necessary, she told herself, but it helped as she limped up the walk.

At the door he wouldn't come in, but waved and said hello to Gran, who was anxiously waiting in front of the television. Gran excused herself, turned around, and rolled into the kitchen to get dinner ready.

"Well, I'm finally home." Rue shivered, anxious to close the door. "Thanks again, Dwayne."

"Yeah."

"And do call me, okay?"

"Sure."

"And—and I really hope everything turns out all right. With Dawn, I mean."

His jaw stiffened. "It won't."

"Why do you say that?"

"Because Dawn's dead."

Rue shivered. "You shouldn't say that."

"It's the truth."

"But you don't know, not for sure."

"Yeah, I do. Don't ask how. I just know. Maybe because we're twins. I knew that first day, when she didn't come home from the store, I knew that she was never going to come home. And not because she ran away. She'd never up and run off, not without me. But it wasn't until this cold front hit that I knew for sure that it wasn't any good looking for her anymore. I woke up Saturday morning and it was so cold in the house. I don't mean just the temperature. I mean . . . cold as death. Friday night, that's when the cold front hit. And that's when Dawn died. In the middle of the night. Late Friday or early Saturday. Don't ask me how I know, I just do." He stared off into the darkening fields, his eyes hard and glinting.

He walked away without another word, got into his Toyota, and backed out of the drive.

Gran made a fuss over Rue's injury and insisted on fixing dinner while Rue elevated her leg and put an ice pack on her ankle. After they ate, Gran stayed up to watch the weather report. The forecast was for decreasing cold, with clear skies and highs in the low fifties.

Gran went to bed. Rue turned off the television, made herself a cup of cocoa, and propped her foot on the ottoman in front of the easy chair. She was almost asleep when the phone rang.

The ringing sounded unnaturally loud in the quiet room. Rue realized that Gran's bedside extension would also be ringing, and quickly reached for the phone. She cleared her throat and managed a husky hello.

The voice on the phone was a man's, speaking softly. "Rue, is that you? Did I wake you?"

"Who is this?"

"It's me, Rue. I wanted to apologize."

It was Marty Sutherland. "Yeah, well . . . ," said Rue, her voice flat.

"Really, Rue, I'm sorry about the whole thing. I guess I was drunker than I realized. Took a nap and woke up with a hangover."

"Good."

"Oh, Rue! Don't be that way. You're not mad at me, are you?"

Rue sighed. "Look, Marty, I accept your apology, for what it's worth. Why are you really calling, to ask me not to tell Ginger?"

"Rue, I know you better than that. You were never the type to kiss and tell."

"Good-bye, Marty."

"I saw you getting into that car with the Frady boy." The edge in his voice stopped Rue from hanging up.

"So?"

"You shouldn't have done that."

"Why not?"

"There's something wrong with that boy, Rue."

"You're one to talk, Marty Sutherland."

"No, I mean it, seriously. People say it's not natural."

"What?"

"How close he is to his sister. Or was. I know they're twins and all, but still, brothers and sisters aren't supposed to be that close. They did everything together, even dressed alike sometimes—matching jeans and T-shirts, shit like that. He may seem like a normal kid, playing football and all, but there's something funny about him."

"Funny?"

"Just ask anybody in town. Dwayne Frady's got a screw loose. Now they say he spends all his spare time driving up and down the highway, staring at people. Something queer about him. Not somebody you ought to get in a car with. You should've let me take you home instead."

"Is that all you have to say, Marty?"

"Yeah, I guess so. Except . . ." His voice grew huskier. "When are we going to finish what we started this afternoon, huh? I saw the look on your face when you touched it. You want to touch it again, don't you? Baby wants to make Daddy feel real good—"

Rue hung up the phone. Her hand was trembling.

She went to bed but tossed and turned for what seemed like hours, until finally she drifted off to sleep.

8

Rue woke Monday morning with the sun streaming through the window onto her face. Gran had let her sleep late again.

She stepped out of bed cautiously, remembering her injury. If she bent her left ankle a certain way she could produce a twinge of pain, but otherwise she was fine. She had always been a quick healer. *That's how I was, too,* she could hear her mother say, *until I turned thirty.* Rue looked at herself in the mirror, spied a gray hair, and plucked it.

Gran had already eaten, but insisted on fixing Rue toast and bacon. Rue let herself be fussed over and sat quietly at the kitchen table. In the cheerful morning light it was easy to forget about Marty Sutherland, and even about Dawn Frady.

The sunshine was so brilliant that she couldn't stay indoors. She tried to talk Gran into going for a ride in the car, but Gran insisted it was still too cold. Rue dressed in some knockabout clothes she kept in her old bedroom closet, jeans and a flannel shirt and sweater. She searched in her dresser drawer, found an old elastic band left over from her high school track days, and wrapped her left ankle, just to be safe, then slipped on some old wool socks and sneakers she hadn't worn in years.

She paused on Gran's porch and looked out across the fields. She had intended to walk straight to the old Dunwitty house and take a senti-mental journey through the rooms of her grandparents' home, as she often did on visits to Amethyst. But something about the quality of the day—the bright sunshine, the crisp, cold air—filled her with a nostalgia for when she and Reg had wandered the fields as children. The extent of her grandparents' land had seemed endless then, vaster than she and Reg could ever hope to explore: the pecan orchard, the giant oak tree ringed by a stone wall, the barns filled with derelict machinery, the wooden bee-hives, the chicken coop, the windmills, and up on the hill, the big cistern covered by a cement dome thirty feet across.

Her grandfather had built every bit of it himself. By the time Rue was born, Grandfather Dunwitty was already in his seventies. Rue had seen the property in the very last years of its flourishing, when the hives still had bees, chickens laid eggs in the coop, and the windmills pumped water up to the cistern on the hill, where it was stored to irrigate the pecan orchards. She could remember her grandfather dressing up in his bee-keeper's outfit and bringing back great dripping wedges of honeycomb as a treat for Reg and her. She remembered going with Grandmother Dunwitty to gather fresh eggs from the chicken coop. She remembered gathering pecans off the ground, and how for days afterward her hands would be stained a rusty brown.

Now the Dunwitty property was run-down and neglected. High grass had overgrown everything. The windmills were frozen with rust. The barns were falling down. The pecan trees had withered. The hives and the coops were empty.

Her father hadn't lived in Amethyst for many years, not since the divorce, which happened when Rue was a first-grader. After that he drove up from Corpus Christi a few times a year for holidays; Reg and Rue would go over for dinner at the Dunwitty house and sit around the fire-place afterward, or in summer eat watermelon and chase fireflies on the lawn. Grandfather Dunwitty died the year Rue was a high school senior; only a few months later her grandmother followed. Her father held on to the property after that, never renting it out, refusing to sell it, and staying too busy with the hardware store he owned down in Corpus Christi to keep the place up himself. Unpainted wood moldered and rotted, trees died without tending, stone and cement cracked under the blistering sun and the hard Texas winters.

It was a sad place to her now, but achingly special. For years after her grandparents' deaths, she had been able to go into their house and find everything exactly as it had been when they were alive. But as the years passed, the slow process of decay took its toll, and various objects—pieces of furniture, vases, paintings—had been removed by her father or by Reg or sometimes by Rue herself, so that the house became more and more derelict. In the earlier years, Rue had often seen evidence that her father had been to the house, sometimes for an extended stay in his old bedroom upstairs; but as the years passed, he came less and less often. Eventually he had the utilities turned off and he stopped coming altogether, or so Rue assumed. She hadn't spoken to him in years.

Rue had never stopped visiting the house, but she hadn't gone walking through the fields in a very long time. Following a whim, she left Gran's front porch, crossed the yard, stepped carefully over a low wire fence, and walked past a faded yellow-and-black No Trespassing sign into the high grass of the Dunwitty fields. She had the sensation of stepping back in time. This was where she had wandered as a girl; this was where her mother had walked as a teenager, crossing the fields to meet with Emmett Dunwitty during their courtship.

Rue spent the morning revisiting the secret places of her childhood— the hole in one of the barns that was just big enough for a little girl to crawl through, the ruins of the tree house Reg had built in the towering oak tree, the stone wall bordering the pecan orchard that Reg had said was as long as the Great Wall of China.

She finally turned south, intending to head toward her grandparents' house, but then, on another whim, she changed her mind. She was remembering a part of the property she hadn't stepped onto since her grandparents died. She turned around and headed uphill toward the far north end of the property, beyond the orchards and barns, into the tract her grandfather had left mostly undeveloped. Even as a child she had seldom gone there; there were more grass burrs, more ant beds, more prickly pears than elsewhere on the property. Grandfather Dunwitty had warned her about snakes up on the hill, and even now Rue couldn't step through the high, rustling grass without keeping her ears peeled for the sudden shiver of a rattle. She told herself not to be silly—it was the middle of winter, a time when no cold-blooded snake would be stirring.

She crossed an open field and entered a wild thicket of junipers and elms hung with desiccated grapevines. The ground underfoot was littered with fallen leaves. Every step she took made a loud crunching noise in the still, cold air.

And she was not alone.

From nearby, she heard the same crunching noise, as if someone else were walking slowly though the copse, unseen. Rue felt a little thrill of fear and stood absolutely still. The noises continued and seemed to be coming from more than one direction—a crunching sound here, another there, scattered and occurring seemingly at random.

Rue stood still for a long time, her heart beating fast. The footstep noises were all around her, some close, some distant. It made no sense—until she heard a trilling and chirping in the high branches above and saw a bird swoop down and rummage among the blanket of leaves.

Having finally seen one, she now saw the little birds everywhere around her. There must have been dozens, maybe hundreds of them in the little copse, chirping, diving, shrieking warnings to one another about her presence, desperately hunting for something to eat. They must have arrived overnight, stopping here on their way south. How had they survived the killing cold of the weekend? What could they possibly find to eat amid the dry leaves and twigs? Juniper berries, beetles, mistletoe? When she got home, Rue would set out bread crumbs and a shallow pan of water for them.

She stepped out of the copse, suddenly exhilarated. The somber colors all around her were ravishing in their quiet way: the gray-green of the cactus, the bone white of the limestone, the desiccated yellow grass, the dark junipers, the frigid blue of the cloudless sky. She walked up the hillside, trudging as it grew steeper, hardly remembering what was there until she came upon it.

It had amazed her as a child. How vividly she remembered the first time she had seen it; her grandmother had taken her and Reg to have a picnic on its gently curving concrete surface while they gazed down on the rooftops of the barns and the orchards below. The cistern had been one of the first things her grandfather built. The windmills pumped water up the hill to be stored in its cool, deep vault; the cistern provided water for the house and the fields through the hot, dry summer. It had seemed immense to her then, the largest dome on earth, its sloping surface falling away from the central apex with such a gradual curvature that, standing there, she could imagine she was standing on the face of the moon.

At first, all Rue could see of it was the circular wall that supported the dome, rising a few feet above the soil. The circumference was not as wide as she remembered, but it was still impressive. The cistern was built into a shelf scooped out of the hillside, a natural little amphitheater ringed by eroded limestone cliffs that ascended up to the property line. Somewhere higher up, obscured by thickets and junipers, was the fence that separated Dunwitty land from the new development where Ginger and Marty lived.

Rue turned around and paused to take a deep breath of cold air. The day seemed captured in crystal, a day made of perfect, frozen light, the kind of day that made her want to shout out loud, to wave her arms, to sigh, to dance. She looked out over the withered trees and the ramshackle barns. She looked farther, catching glimpses of rooftops here and there. Beyond Amethyst, beneath the pale blue sky, lay the bruised purple smudge of the horizon.

She turned back toward the cistern. As she stepped nearer she saw immediately and with a shock that the dome had caved in. The damage didn't look new; it could have happened years ago. The ruin saddened her. Everything her grandfather had built was falling into decay, even this. She stepped closer to have a look over the knee-high circular wall into the dry cistern below. Her eyes ran down the far side of the wall as she approached—down, down, deeper than she had expected. The cistern was at least twelve feet deep.

Her foot bumped against something and she noticed a long wooden ladder lying flat on the ground. It had been out in the open for a long time; exposure had turned the wood as gray as the scrubby grass around it, camouflaging it. She stepped over the ladder, reached the wall, and stopped, peering downward.

Open to the sky, the cistern was filled with midday sunshine, glaring and white. The bottom was a flat cement circle piled with huge blocks of concrete, the remains of the fallen dome. Lying atop the jumble, her limbs unnaturally splayed, her neck bent at an impossible angle, her mouth open in a frozen scream that showed braces glinting in the sunlight, was the naked body of a girl.

9

Gran sat quietly in the living room, shaking her head and fretting with her hands. Rue glanced at her and tried her best to smile reassuringly even as she spoke into the phone through gritted teeth. "I just don't understand why someone's not here yet."

The woman at the sheriff's office answered in a nasal drawl. "I told you already, hon, I have radioed the deputy and he radioed back. Unfortunately, he was all the way across the county, so it'll take him a while to get there. When you called back the second time, I went ahead and contacted the sheriff, too, even though he's off duty for lunch. I can radio 'em both again if you want me to, but I'm sure they're getting there as fast as they can, Rue."

The woman on the phone seemed to know her, but Rue couldn't conjure up an image of the woman's face. Her name was vaguely familiar—a Monahan or a Miller, one of the Baptist women older than her mother but younger than Gran. Whoever she was, she seemed to take the matter about as seriously as a beauty shop receptionist trying to straighten out an appointment for a manicure.

"Would you do that for me? Would you radio them both again, Bertha?" The name suddenly came back to her—Bertha Miller. Her husband

Steven Saylor

owned the welding shop on the highway. "If you could just radio and make sure they've got the right address—"

"Address? Hell, honey, old Horace knows where your house is as well as I do."

"But the deputy's new, isn't he? Maybe he doesn't know."

"All right, hon, I'll radio again. Now, why don't you hang up and I'll call you back."

"No, that's all right. I'll hold."

"Whatever you say." There was a click. The line went dead, and then Rue heard a dial tone.

"She's cut me off!" Rue shook her head and stared at the ceiling. "The idiot cut me off!" She reached for the slender phone book but knocked it off the table. It fluttered to the floor, then snapped shut when she reached down and grabbed the spine. She thumbed frantically through the pages, suddenly forgetting what she was looking for as the pages dissolved and she saw *it* again—the girl's naked body lying twisted against the cold concrete, her face obscured by a tangle of blond hair, her flesh waxen and pale, her open mouth showing braces. Her legs were spread-eagled, her arms akimbo—whoever had left her there had shown no respect for her body. Her legs had been covered with scratches. There was a ring of bruised, abraded flesh around her neck, like a rope burn, and similar discolorations around her wrists . . .

There was a sound from outside. Rue was abruptly alert, as if she had been pulled from a dream. The sound was the low concussion of a heavy car door slamming shut. She hadn't even heard the car pull up outside.

"I'll bet that's them now," said Gran anxiously.

Rue sprang up and looked out the little diamond-shaped pane of glass in the front door. A porch pillar blocked her view of most of the car, but she could see the black-and-white hood, and then the heavy form of Horace Boatwright lumbering around the front of the patrol car and stepping onto the walk. He was wearing a Stetson, tan polyester slacks, cowboy boots, and a shiny green jacket that looked at least a size too small on his corpulent frame.

Rue unlocked the door and opened it, then unlatched the screen door.

68

Horace saw her and smiled vaguely, taking off his Stetson. "I hear you had a little shock," he said.

"Thank God you're finally here! Come inside."

Horace nodded to Gran as he entered. "Howdy, Mrs. Lee."

"Hello, Horace." Gran had never liked the sheriff, not in all the thirty years he had held the office. His sons had been school yard bullies; they had tormented Reg when he was little. Even after all this time, Gran had no use for the Boatwrights.

"So, what's this I hear about you finding a body?"

"On my grandparents' land," said Rue. "Or my dad's land, I mean. In the old cistern up on the hill. I can show you right now."

"Well now, whoa, slow down just a minute. Where's Juss? I figured he'd be here by now. Bertha said she radioed him a good half hour 'fore she called me."

Rue shook her head, exasperated. Didn't anybody understand? She had found a body. *The* body. "He's not here yet. Does it matter? Dawn Frady is out there, just a few hundred yards from here." Rue realized how loudly she was talking and looked anxiously at Gran. She should have driven somewhere else to phone the sheriff's office, and left Gran out of it. But her first impulse after seeing the body was to run straight home.

"Just calm down, young lady. If that body's as dead as you think it is, it ain't goin' anywhere. No point in rushin'." The sheriff looked over Rue's shoulder at Gran and gave her a nod, as if it might require someone older than Rue to understand his point.

Gran would have none of it. "Horace Boatwright, are you going to do your job and go see what Rue found, or not?"

Horace's smile faded, as if what he took to be a grass snake turned out to have rattles. "Relax, Mrs. Lee. I've been in this line of work too long to go traipsing through prickly pears and climbing over fences and poking around empty cisterns. That's what the county hired a young new deputy for."

Gran drew herself up and made a face as if her dentures pained her. "You always were a lazy dog, Horace Boatwright!"

"Now, Mrs. Lee—"

"This is ridiculous!" Rue had had enough. She put on her sweater. "Sheriff, I'm going back up there right now. By myself, if I have to. You're right, if she's dead, she's dead, but what if—what if she's still alive?" Even as she spoke, Rue knew there was no possible way that the body she had seen had any life in it.

She walked to Gran and bent down to hug her. "I'm sorry about all this, Gran. I'll be back as soon as I can."

"That's all right, hon."

"Young lady!" Horace called after her as she slipped past him and out the front door. He fingered the brim of his Stetson and looked disgruntled, then caught the baleful look in Gran's eyes and retreated out the front door, hurrying to catch up with Rue.

The sheriff was right; he was in no shape to go climbing over fences and traipsing through overgrown fields. Rue kept having to slow down and wait for him to catch up. She tried to imagine him chasing a criminal on foot and shook her head.

As they got closer to the caved-in cistern, Rue felt her heart pounding in her chest. Her breath grew short. Her palms were sweaty. When she was close enough to see the rim of the cistern she slowed down, letting Horace catch up with her.

"This the place?" he said. Between huffing and puffing, there was a note of trepidation in his voice. Horace Boatwright suddenly seemed as anxious as she was. Surely he'd seen some awful things in his career—the aftermath of car wrecks on the highway, if not the kind of gory crime scenes that occurred in bigger places.

They walked slowly up to the rim. Rue lifted a hand to her mouth, steeling herself. Horace cocked his head and grimaced, as if anticipating a flinch and trying to suppress it. Together they looked over the edge.

Rue sucked in her breath.

After a moment, Horace cleared his throat. "Well, where is she, then?"

Except for the concrete rubble of the caved-in dome, the cistern was empty.

"She was"—Rue shook her head and pointed—"right there. She was right down there."

"Well, she ain't there now!" Horace lengthened his face and worked his tongue inside his cheek.

"Oh my God, somebody must have moved her," Rue whispered. She scanned the hillside above them, then looked into the stands of live oaks and underbrush on either side. "Someone must have been watching when I found her, and then moved her after I left!"

"Now, Rue . . ."

"Sheriff, I saw her. She was right down there."

"And how the hell did anybody get down in there and out again? I don't see any way in or out. It must be twenty feet deep. The walls go straight down, and there's no kind of rungs anywhere."

"It's not twenty feet deep! Twelve, maybe. And I saw a ladder somewhere around here." Rue peered at the ground. She clearly remembered bumping her foot against the ladder and stepping over it, but where was it? "There!" she said, spotting the gray wood against the gray grass. She walked over to it and Horace followed. "You see?"

Horace gave the ladder a kick. The wood was weathered but still sturdy and the ladder looked long enough to reach the bottom of the cistern. But something was different. Rue wrinkled her forehead. "It's been moved," she said. "This isn't where it was before."

"You sure of that?"

The problem was, she wasn't sure, not really. It was all a blur in her memory—realizing that the cistern had caved in, noticing the ladder, peering over the edge, seeing the body, staring down at it for a long, horrified moment, then running blindly through the fields back to the house.

"Grass doesn't look like it's been disturbed," said Horace.

Rue had to agree, but what did that prove? If it were summer and the grass were high and moist and easily bruised, the surroundings might have shown if the ladder had been dragged, might even have registered footsteps, but who could tell if anyone had been there when the dry, cold earth was so hard and the vegetation so low?

"Sheriff, we've got to search around here. Look among those trees, and the fields—"

"Now, Rue." Horace Boatwright rubbed his chest, as if the mere thought of exertion threatened him with a heart attack. "Look here, what *exactly* did you think you saw?"

"I didn't *think* I saw something. I *did* see it. A body. That girl, that blond girl who's missing—"

"So you already knew about Dawn Frady being missing?"

"Of course I did! It's on that sign down by the courthouse, for God's sake. And that placard in the window at Schneider's. And I talked to her brother, yesterday."

"Did you now? So Dawn Frady's been on your mind?"

"Yes."

"And you're out here poking around in these fields, all alone, maybe getting yourself a little spooked—am I right so far?"

She shook her head, but then remembered how the footsteplike noises made by the birds in the dry leaves had startled and frightened her a little, sparking her imagination. "What are you implying?"

"Well, this kind of thing happens, young lady. Believe me, I've seen it before. A woman's thinking about something awful like Dawn Frady disappearing, and she's alone, and she gets herself all spooked, and maybe it's a certain time of the month, and then her imagination sort of—"

"No! You are *way* off the mark. I did not *imagine* seeing Dawn's body."

Horace thrust his hands deep into his pockets. "Hell, Rue, you can't imagine how many false alarms I've been called out on over the years, for one thing or another. And with this Dawn Frady thing, people have been calling me all week, thinkin' they heard noises in the middle of the night, or they saw a strange car pass through town—"

"Did anybody besides me actually see her body?"

"No. I'm just sayin' that everybody in town is on edge, and it's under-standable." He gave her a sympathetic look.

"You honestly don't believe me, do you?"

"It's not what I believe, Rue. It's what's there or not there. And this body you thought you saw is not there, is it?"

"Because somebody moved it."

"Who? When? How'd they have time?" He swept his eyes over the landscape. "There's not a soul in sight. Nobody lives anywhere close. Your grandmother's house is the only place around."

"That's not true. There are houses right up there, just past the top of the hill. That new subdivision where Ginger and Marty Sutherland live."

"Yeah, but they can't see down here and we can't see 'em up there, can we?"

"No."

"But you still figure somebody just happened to see you find this body, and then they ran down here, and put the ladder down in there, and heaved the body out, and then ran off with it? Think about it, Rue. It just don't make sense."

Rue felt like screaming. She started to pace, every now and then glancing down into the cistern. She shook her head in disgust, then gave a start as a voice called up from behind them: "Hey, Sheriff! What's up?"

Rue and the sheriff turned to see the tall figure of Justice Goodbody come scrambling up the hill.

10

"Where the hell have you been?" snapped Boatwright.

Goodbody was dressed, like his boss, in a tan uniform and green coat, but on him the outfit looked as if it had been tailored to fit his broad shoulders and narrow hips. Seen close up, his chiseled features were even more handsome than Rue remembered.

"Sorry, Sheriff. I was practically over in Mayhew when I got the call. When I arrived at Mrs. Lee's house, she wasn't able to give me very specific directions about where you'd gone. Took me a while to find you." He turned his attention from the sheriff to Rue, tipped his Stetson, and thrust a big, square hand toward her. "I'm Sheriff's Deputy Goodbody, ma'am."

"I'm Rue Dunwitty," she said, shaking his hand. "Mrs. Lee's granddaughter."

He nodded. "I believe I saw you at the ball game Friday night."

"Yes, you did," said Rue, missing the firm, warm grip of his hand as it slid from hers. The deep blue color of his eyes was distracting.

His smile faded. "I understand you've had an awful shock, Miss Dunwitty."

"Yes, well . . ."

He stepped to the edge of the cistern and peered down. He looked back at her, his fine black eyebrows drawn together. "I thought your grandmother said . . ."

"She's not there anymore," said Rue.

Goodbody turned and looked at the sheriff. "The body's plumb disappeared," said Horace Boatwright matter-of-factly. "Now, I don't know about you young folks, but I'm gettin' a little cold standing here. I suggest we go back to your grandmother's house."

"No!" said Rue. "We've got to search for the body."

"Search where, Rue? It didn't just up and leave by itself. If somebody came and got it, then they must have carried it off. I figure me and Juss'd do better to get in our cars and patrol the surrounding roads. See who's coming and going, or if somebody's parked where they shouldn't be."

Rue shook her head. "Someone should at least go down in there and see if there's any sign of her. There might be some—I don't know, something left behind, or maybe some . . . blood or something. We have the ladder right here."

"I'll do it," said Goodbody.

As he bent over to pick up the ladder, Rue touched his arm. The muscles beneath her fingers, flexed for lifting, were hard and sculpted. How different he felt from Marty Sutherland! "But if they used the ladder to bring her out, maybe we shouldn't move it," she said. "It's evidence."

Horace chuckled. "I think somebody's been watching too many reruns of *Law and Order*. Rue, hon, there's no way we could lift any fingerprints off that old gray wood. The grain's too raised and rough. Go ahead, Juss."

The deputy heaved the long, heavy ladder up and swung it down into the cistern. He jimmied it until the bottom was secure against a block of rubble, then stepped over the cistern wall onto the ladder. "Thing's a little rickety," he said, testing his weight on each rung as he descended. He reached the bottom, stepped off, and peered at the broken pieces of the fallen dome. "Where'd you think you saw her?" he said, his voice echoing slightly off the cistern walls.

Rue pointed. "There, on that big slab."

While the sheriff and Rue watched, Goodbody nosed about the broken pieces of concrete. Rue thought she saw something shiny. "What's that, Deputy? About six inches from your left foot. Like a piece of jewelry . . ."

Goodbody squatted, picked up the tiny object, and peered at it. "Jewelry? Well, kind of." He held it in the air so that it caught a flash of sunlight. Rue leaned over and squinted. Goodbody smiled up at her. "It's just one of those aluminum pull rings off a cola can." He held it to his ear like an earring. "The girls used 'em for play jewelry when I was a kid."

Horace snorted. "Probably been down there for years."

The deputy nodded. "Still, it proves that somebody must've come down here sometime, even if it was just kids playing." He pulled a small evidence bag from a pocket on his belt and put the ring inside, then continued nosing about the rubble until he had covered the entire bottom of the cistern. He looked up at Rue and raised his open palms. "I sure don't see anything, Miss Dunwitty."

"I want to look." Uncrossing her arms, Rue realized how tightly she had been hugging herself. Descending the ladder, her left foot slipped on the last rung and a sharp pain shot through her ankle.

Goodbody's hands were suddenly gripping her waist from behind, supporting her. "Are you okay?"

She turned her head. His face was very close. For the first time she noticed that he wore some sort of cologne. The musky scent was very distinctive. Like his touch, the smell sent a tremor of pleasure through her.

"I'm all right," she said, stepping off the ladder and pulling away from him, conscious of Horace Boatwright watching them. She retraced the same path Goodbody had taken around the rubble-strewn bottom of the cistern, stooping and peering. She found nothing. The deputy held the ladder for her, then climbed out after her.

"Are you satisfied, Rue?" said Horace.

She sighed and looked down the hillside. "There's something else I need to tell you. The other night, from my grandmother's house, I saw some sort of light in these fields."

"Saw—or *thought* you saw?" Boatwright raised an eyebrow.

Rue gritted her teeth. "It was late Friday night, after the ball game."

"How late?"

"I remember, the clock said three A.M. I looked out the window above my bed."

The sheriff cocked his head. "You were in bed, asleep?"

"Yes. I mean, I *was* asleep. But something woke me." It had been cold air from the windowpane that woke her; she rose up on her knees to pull down the shade. "I happened to look out the window. I thought I saw a light, like a flashlight . . ."

"You don't sound too sure."

Because I'm not, she thought. Rue saw the way the sheriff was looking at her and realized that mentioning the light had been a mistake. He was even more skeptical than before.

"Look, Sheriff," said Goodbody, "if you want to get back to your vehicle and patrol the area, I'll stay here for a bit and have a look around."

Horace nodded. "Good idea. You comin' back with me, Rue?"

"No, I'll help look."

"Suit yourself." He lumbered down the hillside.

Rue and Goodbody looked at each other. She had never seen eyes quite that color, almost a sapphire blue. "I'll start over here," he finally said, waving toward a stand of gnarly oak trees. "There's quite a bit of cactus, and I'm wearing thick boots. You'd be likely to stick yourself in those sneakers. Why don't you walk up and down across that open area?"

Rue nodded.

For twenty minutes they searched the hillside all around the cistern. Rue had to admit that she could find no indication that anyone had been there. At least the deputy seemed to be taking her more seriously than the sheriff—or was he merely being a good assistant to his boss, humoring her so that Boatwright could be on his way?

She *had* seen the body. Surely there was more they could do about it than this. By the time Goodbody shrugged to her from the far side of the field and came sauntering over, she was on the verge of tears from frustration, but determined not to show it.

"I'm sorry, Miss Dunwitty, but I just don't see a thing. I think the sheriff's right. I'd do better to take a drive hereabouts and look for anything suspicious."

"I think you should question everybody who lives in those new houses, up past the top of the hill," said Rue. "Maybe somebody up there saw something."

Goodbody nodded. "I was planning on doing exactly that."

As they walked silently back to the house, Rue studied him in sidelong glances and noticed that he seemed to be doing the same to her. She realized she had never seen him without a hat, and wondered what he would look like without it. From what she could see of his hair, it appeared to be thick and wavy and very black, as black as the eyebrows that gave his face such an expressive quality.

As they neared the house, she saw his black-and-white patrol vehicle parked alongside her blue rental car. He helped her step over the low fence, then walked to his car. He reached inside, pulled out a clipboard and a pen, and handed them to Rue. "I'll take a statement from you, if you don't mind. Write out exactly where you were and what you saw. Just make it as matter-of-fact as you can."

Putting the experience into words conjured up vivid images in her mind—the twisted body, the bruises around the throat and wrists, the braces glinting in the sunlight. When she was finished, Goodbody read the statement and nodded.

"In the morning, I'll round up some men and conduct a more thorough search. We'll scour that hillside. I promise you, if there's anything up there, we'll find it. I take it that land belongs to your father."

"Yes. Everything from the cistern down to the old Dunwitty house is his property. His name's Emmett Dunwitty and he lives down in Corpus Christi."

"You have his phone number handy?"

Rue lowered her eyes. "Actually, no. We don't have much contact."

"Well, whether we find anything on that hillside or not, I'll want to search the rest of the property as well—all those outbuildings, and of course the house. I'll try to get hold of your dad, but failing that, I'm asking you for permission."

"Certainly. I could go with you—"

He shook his head. "I'd rather you didn't go over there at all, not until I've had a chance to conduct a search. And I especially don't want you to go over there alone, not until this matter's resolved. I can't stress that strongly enough."

He suddenly sounded very official. Rue nodded. "I understand, Deputy. As far as I know, none of the outbuildings is locked, and the key to the house is pretty easy to find. It's hung on a nail behind a hat on the screened porch."

He smiled faintly. "You know, I've been in that house once before."

"Right. I'd forgotten. Gran said you answered her call last summer, when she heard the alarm go off over there."

"As far as we could tell, it was probably just a hunter, snooping. That battery alarm on the door doesn't amount to much security, especially with that key right there on the porch. Anybody could pretty much come and go in that house as they please." He frowned. "Look, Miss Dunwitty, I know you're not satisfied with the sheriff's response."

Rue pursed her lips. "He thinks I'm a hysterical female with a vivid imagination. It probably doesn't help that I come from San Francisco, the land of fruits and nuts and bad drug trips. What do you think?"

He looked away, toward the fields. "I'm not sure what to think. But it seems to me that if you did see Dawn, and somebody saw you find her, then you may not be safe here in your grandmother's house. Is there somewhere else you can stay while you're here, maybe a house with more people in it, where you wouldn't be so alone at night?"

Rue shook her head. "Not in Amethyst. I have a brother in Austin. I was planning to drive down there in a few days."

The deputy nodded thoughtfully. "Maybe you ought to go now."

"And leave Gran alone?"

"Your grandmother's not involved in this. And neither are you, now that we have your statement." He handed the form back to her. "Here, add your brother's phone number in Austin, alongside your permanent address in San Francisco. That way, if we need you, we can find you. But right now I figure the best thing might be for you to get on down to Austin."

"Maybe. I'll think about it."

He walked her to the front door. "Listen, if something else comes up, don't bother calling Bertha at the office." He pulled an official-looking card from his wallet, slid a ballpoint pen from his pocket protector, and wrote some numbers on the back. "Call me at this number. It's my private cell phone. You carry one?"

"Always, back in San Francisco. But this trip I didn't bring it with me, on purpose. Trying to escape from the world for a while." She smiled at the irony.

"Well, this way you can reach me direct and not have to go through Bertha or the sheriff. Okay?"

Rue took the card and nodded.

"If you see anything suspicious, or if you get scared, or if you need anything—anything at all—call me anytime, day or night. I'll come runnin'."

"Thank you, Deputy. I appreciate that. I really do." Rue resisted a sudden urge to touch his hand. Instead she ran her fingers over the card. "I only wish Horace Boatwright would show half as much concern as you have."

"Well . . ." He seemed to hesitate. "Listen, I really shouldn't tell you this. But things aren't quite the way you think."

"What do you mean?"

"I know it must look like the sheriff was hanging back, the way he waited for me to show up and then handed things over to me once I got there."

"If he's too old for the job—"

"It's not that. He and I discussed all this ahead of time."

"Discussed what?"

Goodbody bit his lower lip. He dropped his eyes and turned his head, looking in the direction of the ruined cistern and the gray hills. "I don't have the years of experience the sheriff has, but when it comes to looking for missing girls—well, I've had previous experience with this sort of thing. The sheriff knows that, and he's let me take the lead on finding Dawn." He let out a sigh and narrowed his eyes. "It's not easy to talk about this. It's not something I like to remember. Before I came to Amethyst, I was down in Corpus Christi. Out there in San Francisco, did you ever hear of the McCutcheon murders?"

Rue shook her head. "I don't think so."

"Maybe you heard it called 'the case of the Corpus corpses.' That's what the newspapers called it. Some guy wrote a book with that title."

Rue winced at the glib catchphrase. It sounded vaguely familiar.

"It was big news here in Texas," said Goodbody. "Very big. Some high school girls in Corpus went missing. Then a jogger along the waterfront found the first body, under a pier. That was just the beginning. More girls went missing. More bodies were found. The details—well, I won't go into it, but the investigation went on for months. Just about everybody in the department got called in to help. I was new on the force, just starting out, pretty much still a kid. Certainly not a detective or a forensic expert. But there was a lot of door-to-door on that case. They needed all the manpower they could get. I did my share of foot soldiering. I saw . . . I saw some things I wish I'd never seen, down in Corpus . . ."

His voice trailed off. His gaze, leveled at the hills, was so intense that Rue could almost imagine he saw something up there. But whatever Justice Goodbody was seeing was only in his memory. "Anyway, I learned a few things about that sort of crime, whether I wanted to or not. And when it was all over—well, that was the main reason I left Corpus and moved up here. I thought about leaving law enforcement altogether, but instead of doing that, I thought maybe if I just moved to a nice, quiet little town, a place like Amethyst, I wouldn't have to ever see that kind of thing again. Of course, I was wrong. You can't just leave that kind of thing behind, can you? There's nowhere you can go. It's anywhere and everywhere. No place is safe. And sure enough, here it is, happening in Amethyst."

He finally turned his gaze back to her. For an instant she glimpsed something fierce in his blue eyes, a kind of cold fury, then his expression softened. She again felt the urge to touch his hand, but hesitated a little too long. The moment passed.

"Did they catch whoever did it," she said, "down in Corpus Christi?"

"Oh, yeah. Fellow named Charlie McCutcheon. Sick bastard—excuse my French. Sitting on death row in Huntsville right now, probably working on his next appeal. Never would confess. But he's the one who killed all those poor girls." He shook his head. "Listen, Miss Dunwitty, I've got to go now. But you think about what I said—about heading down to Austin. If we need you, we'll reach you. Meanwhile, don't wear out that card, okay?"

Rue abruptly stopped her nervous fingering of the card and managed a chagrined smile. Goodbody smiled back at her faintly, and with a tip of his Stetson turned and walked to his patrol car, leaving behind the faint, musky smell of his cologne.

11

As darkness fell, Rue tried not to communicate her anxiety to Gran, who kept shaking her head and muttering about what a fool Horace Boatwright was. Rue fixed a simple supper, but neither of them ate much. Finally Gran said that she was going to bed. As she was rolling her wheelchair down the hall toward her room, she stopped and called back to Rue. "Honey, you be sure to lock the front door tonight."

Rue waited until she was certain that Gran was asleep, then picked up the phone and reached for the phone book. Inside the front cover there was a place to write personal numbers. Under her own phone number, written in Gran's shaky hand, she found Reg's home number in Austin.

She counted seven rings before someone picked up the phone. In the background she heard a blaring television and screaming children, and then an exasperated voice that announced, "Dunwitty residence."

"Cathy?"

"Rue? Are you in Austin already?" Cathy's voice went down, not up, as she asked the question.

"No, I'm still up in Amethyst. Is Reg there?"

"No, he's still not back yet."

"Back?"

"He had to go to a meeting today down in San Antonio, for this new job."

"New job?"

"What planet are you on, Rue? Didn't you know he just got a new job with this company that makes silicon chips?"

"No, I didn't know."

"Well, you would if you'd ever call him. Or if you had come to Thanksgiving at your grandma's."

Reg could call me when he has news, Rue almost said, but bit her tongue. She had been through this argument before. Where did Reg's and Cathy's tacit assumption come from, that the married sibling with kids was no longer responsible for keeping up communication? That obligation fell on the sibling who was still single. The fact was, she and Reg had communicated less and less over the years. With their mother gone, it seemed the family bonds only grew weaker.

Rue tried to focus her thoughts. "So Reg has to travel for this job?" she said.

"Yeah, the company's got offices in Austin and a factory down in San Antonio, and they're always sending people back and forth. He's down there a couple of times a week, at least. Mondays are always travel days."

"That must be an hour-and-a-half drive each way."

"Longer if you hit traffic. About the same as driving to Amethyst and back. He's never home in time for supper with the kids on his travel days, but he's usually back by now. If he doesn't buy a new car to replace that old junker of his, he's gonna have a breakdown on the freeway one of these days. I won't let him take my station wagon. I've got to have that for the kids."

"I really need to talk to him. Does he carry a cell phone?"

Cathy laughed. "Sorry, Rue, we can't all be hotshot dot-commers driving around in SUVs with a cell phone stuck to one ear."

I don't drive an SUV, Rue wanted to say, but kept her mouth shut. She and Cathy had never gotten along. *That girl's not the brightest bulb in the marquee,* Rue's mother had once said. *I can't imagine what your brother ever saw in her.* Rue suspected it had something to do with Cathy's D-cup breasts. Or maybe it was because Cathy liked the kind of kinky sex Rue had seen pictured on the video boxes in Reg's house . . .

"Oh, listen," said Cathy, "before I forget, somebody in San Francisco phoned here tonight, looking for you."

"From San Francisco?"

"Some guy who works with you. Said it wasn't important, just a friendly call."

"What was his name?"

"I didn't write it down, because it was such an oddball name I figured I wouldn't forget. Shoot! Now, what was it? Oh, yeah, Dylan. Like the old folk singer."

"Dylan Jeffries?"

"I guess. Didn't tell me his last name."

"What did he want?"

"Wanted to talk to you. I told him you weren't in Austin yet. So he asked for your grandma's number in Amethyst."

Rue cocked her head. "Is that how he asked for it? Did he actually say 'Amethyst'?"

"He said, 'Could I have the number of her grandmother in Amethyst, please?'"

Before she left for Texas, she had told Dylan that she would be spending some of her time in Austin and some at her grandmother's house, and she remembered telling him a few things about Amethyst, back when they had been at the stage of telling each other where they came from. Probably, on those long jogs along the Embarcadero, she had told him more than she realized—about her mother's death, about her grandmother being in a wheelchair, about the abandoned Dunwitty property. But she was surprised that he had actually remembered the name of the town itself. Where had Dylan told her he was from? A suburb of Minneapolis, she thought, but she couldn't remember the name of the place. And how had he found her brother's phone number? She couldn't remember giving it to him . . .

"So this Dylan guy hasn't called you yet?" said Cathy.

"No. If it wasn't about work, he probably just wanted to say hello. I'll call him tomorrow." She pressed a hand to her forehead, fighting off a headache. Why wasn't Reg at home? That was who she needed to talk to.

"Hold on a minute," said Cathy. "I believe I hear your darling brother's rattletrap pulling into the driveway now. Hang on." There was a loud bang as the telephone was dropped onto a hard surface. Rue again heard the blaring TV and the sound of children yelling, followed by a door opening and shutting, and then a muffled conversation that ended with Reg raising his voice. "Shoot, Cathy, why'd you tell her I was here? I'm beat from driving and I need to eat."

Then Cathy's voice: "No, talk to her now and get it over with. She sounds like she's got a stick up her ass."

Finally Reg came on the line. "What's up, Rue? Is Gran okay?"

"She's fine. That's not why I called. Listen—do you know about this girl here who disappeared?"

There was a long pause. The television blared in the background; it sounded like a pro wrestling show. She had never known the television to be turned off in Reg's house.

"I'm sorry, Rue. What did you say?"

"The girl who disappeared. Dawn Frady."

"I don't know what you're talking about. In Amethyst?"

"Yes. There was a high school girl named Dawn Frady who went missing Thanksgiving weekend."

There was another long pause. She heard a clinking noise like flatware dropped onto a plate. She pictured Reg sitting at the dining room table between the kitchen and the living room, one eye on the television and one eye watching Cathy fetch his supper.

"Reg, are you listening?"

"I heard you. Some girl went missing in Amethyst."

"The Saturday after Thanksgiving."

"That's funny. We were up there that weekend. Stayed from Thursday till Sunday and took Gran to church with the kids. I don't remember anybody talking about a missing girl."

"Reg, I called because . . . I found her body."

"What?"

"Today, over on the Dunwitty property. I was taking a walk . . ." Rue was suddenly close to tears. She had been working so hard to keep control of herself all day, first with the sheriff and the deputy, then for Gran's sake. Now a tide of emotion ripped through her. She fought against it and suppressed the quaver in her voice. "I was out walking and I found her."

"Where?"

"Up on the hill. You know the old cistern?"

"Of course."

"The top's caved in."

"I know. Happened years ago."

"Well, nobody ever told me. Anyway, down inside—I saw her body."

"Dead?"

"Of course, dead."

"Rue, that's terrible. What did you do?"

"I ran back to Gran's house and called the sheriff."

"And?"

"It took him forever to get here, and when he finally did, we went back to the cistern, but . . ."

"For God's sake, Rue, what happened?"

"The body was gone."

"What do you mean?"

"Her body just wasn't there anymore."

"Maybe she wasn't dead after all."

"No, don't you see? Whoever put her there must have seen me when I found her, and they knew I was going for help, and they came and took her away. Reg—"

"Just a minute." He muffled the receiver somehow, but Rue could still hear every word. "Cathy, this bowl of mashed potatoes is cold. Would you put it in the microwave for a minute?" His voice returned. "What are you trying to say, Rue?"

"I just told you. I found the girl's body, and then it was gone."

"How did you know it was this missing girl?"

"Her picture is up at Schneider's."

"You saw her that close, to recognize her face?"

87

"No. I didn't have to see her face. Who else could it be?" Rue thought for a moment. "I saw her braces."

"Her what?"

"Dawn had braces. I saw them . . . the metal . . . in the sunlight."

She heard a clinking of flatware on porcelain. When Reg spoke again, his mouth was full. "So what did the sheriff say?"

"The sheriff was useless. It's still Horace Boatwright."

"You're kidding! That old fart? They should have retired him years ago."

"Maybe they should have, but he's still sheriff. He seemed to think I was making the whole thing up. He was ready to just ignore me and walk away. At least the new deputy seemed to take it a little more seriously . . . I think. Only—"

"Goddamnit, Cathy, can't you shut those kids up! I'm on the phone! Sorry, Rue. What were you saying?"

"I . . . I don't remember."

"Rue, I'm sorry. Really. It must have been awful for you, seeing something like that. But if you called the sheriff, then you did all you could. Now it's his job."

"It's just so creepy, Reg. Her body was on our land. On Dad's land, I mean."

"I hear you. Up in the old cistern—that's really weird. What do you think happened? Did she fall in? God, I wonder—what's the liability if somebody trespasses on your land and breaks her neck? Dad probably doesn't have a scrap of liability insurance."

"No, Reg! Haven't you been listening to me? She was naked. She was dead. Somebody killed her and put her there!" Rue checked herself and lowered her voice, fearful of waking Gran. "And then the same person must have come and taken her."

"Jesus. I'm sorry, I didn't understand." There was another long pause. Was he fazed by the enormity of it? Or had Cathy put the mashed potatoes in front of him? "Have you told Dad about all this?"

Rue sighed. "Reg, you know that he and I haven't spoken in years. If he had bothered to come to Mom's funeral—"

"Christ, Rue, not that again, okay?"

"If he doesn't care enough to—"

"Rue, this is different. If you found a body on his land, then you ought to let him know."

"Maybe. I suppose so. It *is* his property, even if he hasn't been to Amethyst in years."

"Well, actually, he was just there."

"Dad? In Amethyst? When?"

"Over Thanksgiving weekend. Cathy and I ran into him shopping at Schneider's. Must have been the Friday or Saturday after Thanksgiving."

"What on earth was he doing in Amethyst?"

"I don't know."

"Where was he staying? Surely not at the old Dunwitty house."

"Of course not. I imagine he stayed at that ratty motel across from the park. Probably didn't even step foot on the old property. He told me once that he can hardly stand to go there anymore. Too many ghosts, he said. I'm starting to feel the same way."

"Then why would he come back to Amethyst? And why doesn't he sell the land, or pass it on to us?"

"I don't know, Rue. We hardly said more than hello at the grocery store. I'm not on much better terms with him these days than you are, but at least I *will* say hello when I see him. You really ought to call and tell him about all this, Rue."

"Why don't you call him?"

"And tell him the whole story secondhand? You're the one who saw it. You tell him. Maybe he can prod old Horace Boatwright into getting off his ass. Boatwright's more likely to pay attention to somebody who pays property taxes in Amethyst than to some kid who just comes home once a year to visit."

"I'm not a kid."

"You are to Horace Boatwright. He thinks Gran's a senile old woman, and you're a hysterical little girl. You know that's *exactly* what he thinks."

Rue sighed. "You're probably right."

"So you can forget about him providing you any protection. Listen, Rue, if you saw what you think you saw, then you should get in your car right now and drive to Austin. I'll wait up. We'll move Shawna into Tyson's room, and you can sleep in her bed."

"No. No, I need to stay here."

"With nobody but Horace Boatwright between you and . . ." He left the thought unspoken.

"It's not quite that bad," said Rue, glancing at Goodbody's card on the table beside the phone.

"You ought to come to Austin."

"No, I can't leave Gran alone right now."

"Well, it's up to you. In case you change your mind, I'll leave the house key in the mailbox and some blankets on the sofa. Just let yourself in and crash and we'll see you in the morning."

"Thanks, Reg. I appreciate that. But I don't suppose . . ."

"What?"

"I don't suppose you could come to Amethyst?"

"When?"

"Tomorrow?"

"Oh, Rue . . . I just started this job. I can't ask to take a day off."

"Sick leave? Family emergency?"

There was another long pause. Was he squirming, or just shoveling more potatoes into his mouth? "I'm sorry, Rue. I can't."

Rue felt a sudden chill between them, the kind that usually preceded an argument. Their last big falling-out had been after their mother's funeral. Rue had been angry that their father hadn't shown up. Reg had said she was being ridiculous, seeing that the two hadn't been married or even spoken to each other for years. Rue had said it would have been a chance for their father to put things right. Reg had said that a funeral wasn't an occasion to test people, and the argument had deteriorated from there.

She took a deep breath. "Okay, Reg. Maybe I'll come to Austin tomorrow. I'll call and let you know."

"Good. Listen, I'm really sorry you had such a shock. Call Dad, okay?"

"All right. Maybe. Well. . . . I love you, Reg."

"I love you too, Rue." It was Reg who hung up first.

They had never said, "I love you," to each other before their mother got cancer. Since she died, they always made a point of ending their talks on the phone that way. It had become a sort of ritual, almost superstitious, like knocking on wood. She listened to the line click and switch to a dial tone, then hung up.

Rue made a pot of chamomile tea. She turned on the TV, flipped aimlessly through the channels, then turned it off. She checked the doors and made sure all the windows were bolted. She turned on the TV again, then turned it off because she heard something outside the house. But the noise was only a tree branch scraping the roof in the rising wind. Finally she picked up the phone book and looked at the inside cover. Underneath her own number was her father's phone number down in Corpus Christi, not in Gran's handwriting but in Reg's.

She sat down, picked up the phone, and took a deep breath. She made a mistake the first time and reached a wrong number. She set the phone aside, stared into space for a long moment, then picked up the phone and dialed again.

She heard the ring at the other end. A second ring, a third, a fourth. She glanced at the clock. It was almost ten, too late to be calling anyway. The phone rang again. She was on the verge of hanging up when she heard a click. There was a pause, then a voice that she hadn't heard in years, older and gruffer than she remembered.

"Hello? This is Emmett Dunwitty . . ."

Rue took a deep breath. She opened her mouth to speak, but the voice at the other end kept talking.

"I can't come to the phone right now, but if you'll leave your name and number after the tone, I'll get back to you as soon as I can. And if this is a sales call, do us both a favor and don't waste my time."

The answering machine beeped. Rue sat frozen for a long moment, then gently placed the phone back on the hook.

12

After checking the locks again, and peering for a long time out her bedroom window in the direction of the Dunwitty fields and seeing nothing but darkness, Rue turned on the television again. The classic film channel was playing a Humphrey Bogart movie she had never seen before, and she willed herself to pay close attention to the plot, letting herself think of nothing else. When the movie was over, she switched to the weather channel. High winds and a drop in temperatures were expected due to the arrival of another, weaker cold front, but after that another warming trend was expected. Rue sighed and yawned . . .

Once again, as on her first night home, she awoke to the voice of the television minister, Brother Zack. She blinked, her eyes gummy with sleep. Amid white lattices and artificial roses, the minister with the young face and solid white hair smiled into the camera, then adopted a more serious expression.

"And now another letter, brothers and sisters, from a soul in torment who has written to us before, the lost soul who signs his letters 'Outcast from the Body of Christ.' He says, 'Dear Brother Zack: I write to you today not asking you to pray for me, for I am so foul that I am surely beyond the help of anyone's prayers. Instead, I ask you and all your television flock to pray for the souls of the young women who have tempted me into doing evil. It may be that a demon dwells inside me, driving me to do these terrible things, but surely there were demons dwelling inside those young women as well. Why else did they put on such lascivious and shameful displays of their womanhood, flaunting their legs and breasts and the unspeakable regions of their bodies, tempting me to do the things I know that no man ought ever to do?'"

Rue fumbled for the remote control, picked it up, and pointed at the set, but the batteries had gone dead. No matter how many times she pressed the Off button, Brother Zack, clutching the letter in his hand, ranted on.

"'Every one of those girls was born an innocent baby. Every one of them grew into a lovely girl, as sweet and fresh as rose petals. But inside each of them dwelled a Jezebel just waiting to cross over to the devil. In the morally debased world we live in today, what can any man do, short of the most drastic steps, to stop a young woman bent on pursuing whorish ways? How can a man of flesh and blood possibly resist such an onslaught of temptations . . .'"

Rue at last got out of the chair, stumbled sleepily across the room, and turned off the television.

The telephone rang.

Who would be calling at this hour, after midnight? She walked toward the phone. Her heart was suddenly racing, even though she was still groggy with sleep. Her hand hovered over the phone, reluctant to pick it up.

The ringing stopped. Just one of those mysterious wrong numbers, she thought, the kind you never even have a chance to answer. The caller realized the mistake and hung up without making contact. She turned away.

Then the phone rang again, making her jump. Before it could ring a second time, she picked it up.

"Hello?" Her voice was thick with sleep. She cleared her throat. "Hello?"

There was no response from the other end, no echo, no sound at all, only silence. She might have been speaking into a dead phone line.

"Hello? Who is this?"

She pressed the phone hard against her ear and listened so intently that for a moment she thought she heard something, a faint, distant pulse, but it was only the rush of blood in her ear. Outside, the wind howled. The tree branch scraped the roof.

Rue hung up. She was wide awake now. She stared at the phone, steeling herself for it to ring again, but it remained silent.

Just a wrong number, she told herself. Or maybe . . .

It must have been her father, she thought. He had been out when she called. He had arrived back home—after midnight?—and played his messages. Except that Rue hadn't left a message; she had simply hung up. But what if he had caller ID? Yes, probably he did, he was the type to screen his calls, wary of salesmen and fund-raisers, and when he checked his incoming calls he would have seen her number listed as a hang-up. It was unlikely that he would recognize Gran's number, but he would have recognized the area code, and must have wondered who was calling him from Amethyst. He had merely to press a button to call the number back, but he had fumbled it somehow (or thought he had fumbled it), as older people often did when using unfamiliar technology, however simple, and that was why he had hung up and tried again, ringing her twice. When he heard her voice, he froze up, just as she had done when she heard his voice, and then he hung up—just as she had hung up, without saying a word.

Yes, Rue thought, that must be it. Her father had unwittingly called her back. After years of silence, each had phoned the other and neither had the courage to utter a single word.

But what if it hadn't been her father? What if someone else was calling her and deliberately hanging up?

The phone abruptly rang again.

Rue swallowed hard. She told herself the hang-up had been her father, after all, and this was probably her father again. She reached for the phone, resolved not to be such a coward this time. She cleared her throat before answering. "Hello. Who is this?"

"Gosh, Rue, is that how people answer the phone in Texas?"

She frowned, feeling muddled and confused. "Who—Dylan? Is that you?"

"Yes. But . . . you don't exactly sound thrilled to hear from me."

"No, of course I am, it's just that . . ." Why was Dylan calling her from San Francisco, and after midnight?

"Hey, don't overdo the enthusiasm on my account. You'll give me a swelled head."

"I'm sorry. Only, I was . . . asleep. Sort of."

"Asleep? Oh, Jeez, I'm sorry! I forgot the time difference. I'm always doing that. It's only nine thirty here."

"Nine thirty? In San Francisco?" She looked at the clock, which showed half past midnight. "It's only two hours' difference, Dylan, not three. It must be ten thirty there."

"You're right. Ten thirty! I don't even know the correct time in my own time zone! Sorry, I'm still at the office. Working late. I meant to call you earlier, but I got busy—you know how it is."

"Did you . . . call my brother's house in Austin?"

"That's right. Hours ago. How'd you know?"

"I called him. My sister-in-law said you called there, asking for this number."

"So I guess you shouldn't be all that surprised to hear from me."

"I guess not." She shook her head, as if that might help to clear it. "But how did you get my brother's number?"

"Ah, now you're asking me for a trade secret. To reveal my methods would be a breach of the stalker's code of honor." He laughed. "Just kidding! It wasn't hard to track you down. There aren't many Dunwittys listed in Austin. But I guess you're still hanging out at your grandmother's house, in Amethyst?"

Rue smiled in spite of her muddle. "So you actually remembered the name of my hometown?"

"Why not? Amethyst is my birthstone. I told you that, didn't I?"

"Maybe. Yes, I guess you did." She remembered now. When she had told him the name of her hometown, Dylan had said, "Amethyst—my birthstone." That meant his birthday was in February . . .

"So—when will you be in Austin?" he said.

"I don't know. I'm not sure. Something's . . . come up."

"It's not your grandmother, is it?"

"No, she's fine. It's . . . something else."

"Not another man in your life, I hope."

"In Amethyst? Don't be silly." Rue laughed, but found herself looking at Juss Goodbody's card on the table.

"Good. Because I actually do have a reason for calling you, other than missing the sound of your voice. I'm flying to Austin tomorrow."

"To Austin? What for?"

He lowered his voice. "Well, I shouldn't be talking about this on a company phone, but . . . I'm in the middle of interviewing for a very high-level position with a certain Austin-based computer megagiant."

"Glenn Computer?"

"Shhh! Suffice to say, this is my second round of interviews. I was supposed to be seeing them tomorrow afternoon—they sent me the ticket and booked the hotel—but it seems that Mr. Glenn—who insists on conducting this interview himself—was called away at the last minute, and as a consequence, since said computer giant is too cheap to change my ticket, I'll be arriving in Austin tomorrow afternoon with nothing to do until the *next* day. So . . . I was hoping you'd come to Austin, too, and the two of us could spend the day together. Maybe take a run around Town Lake? You're always telling me how pretty the trail is. I'm staying at the Three Muses. I hear the restaurant on the top floor is the best in Austin. On me?"

Rue sighed. It was a sigh of relief, she realized. Hearing from Dylan, however unexpectedly, had lifted her spirits. Their conversation was pulling her back into her usual orbit, reconnecting her to the normal routines that gave her a sense of security and self-confidence. "A day with you in Austin is tempting," she said. "But . . . I can't leave my grandmother right now. Don't ask me to explain. It's . . . complicated."

"'Complicated.' I see. What's his name?"

"Dylan! I told you, it's nothing like that."

"If you say so. Okay, then, how about this—after I get into Austin tomorrow, I'll drive to Amethyst?"

"It's a ninety-minute drive."

"So? They're providing the rental car. I'll drive straight to Amethyst, and you and I can have dinner at the local *taqueria,* or wherever people go when they eat out in Amethyst."

"But—I'm not sure I can invite you to spend the night here."

"Is there a spare bedroom?"

"Yes. But the house is so small. And my grandmother—well, I don't think she'd understand."

"So? I'm sure they have a motel in Amethyst. And the next morning we'll have breakfast, and then I'll drive back to Austin in plenty of time for my interview."

She smiled. "I should warn you, Dylan, the motel in Amethyst is nothing like the Three Muses in Austin."

"No turn-down service? No mint on the pillow?"

"A cockroach on the pillow, more likely."

"Gross!" His laughter, so open, so uncomplicated, reminded her of what had first attracted her to him. "So, seriously, Rue—is it a plan?"

Why not? She had asked Reg to come to Amethyst, and he had refused. Now, out of the blue, Dylan was offering to come. He could meet Gran. Rue could show him her hometown. And she wouldn't be alone. "Yes. Yes, I'd like that, Dylan."

"Great! Listen, I'll call you when I arrive at the Austin airport. I'm taking the Nerd Bird nonstop. If I drive straight to Amethyst, I figure I should get there by three or three thirty."

"If you're sure it's not too much trouble. All that driving back and forth . . ."

"Hey, it was my idea, right? I'm looking forward to it. I'll see you tomorrow."

"Okay."

The boisterousness dropped from his voice and his tone was suddenly quiet, almost gentle. "Good night, Rue. Sorry I woke you."

"Good night, Dylan."

She hung up the phone, sank back into the overstuffed chair, and closed her eyes. Her head seemed to empty of every thought, leaving only a blank. Talking to Dylan had reassured her somehow, never mind that he was two thousand miles away. Tomorrow he would come to Amethyst. What good would that do? She didn't know. She was too exhausted to think about it rationally. She only knew that in spite of the day's terrible jolts, she had somehow arrived at a sense of well-being. Everything would be all right.

She dozed, aware that she dozed and fighting against it, thinking she needed to stay awake. But her exhaustion won, and she plunged abruptly into a deep dream. There was no story to the dream, only a vague sense of being elsewhere, not in the house in Amethyst but in a warm, safe, neutral place, a soft-edged, sleepy gray cocoon in which she lay very still while her conscious thoughts flitted about her head like butterflies just out of reach, never quite connecting to one another, caressing her mind with butterfly-wing softness.

And then the phone rang.

13

At first it was merely a phenomenon of her dream, a ringing in her ears that interrupted the flitting, half-formed dream thoughts, dispersing them like an onslaught of buzzing locusts. The persistent ringing grew louder, more insistent, vaguely menacing.

Rue opened her eyes and gave a start. Her sleep had been so deep that for a confused moment she couldn't remember where she was. She instinctively reached for the phone and lifted the receiver. The ringing stopped.

She was groggy, dazed, not even quite sure what to do with the phone in her hand. She stared at it through bleary eyes. She gave another start, because for an instant she imagined it was something other than a phone in her hand, something alive and snakelike. She fought the impulse to fling it away, gripped it harder, and slowly brought it to her ear.

She heard nothing. Had she only dreamed that the phone was ringing? No, because then she would hear a dial tone, not empty silence. Someone must be on the other end of the line. Why didn't they speak? Were they waiting for her to speak first?

Her mouth was dry, her voice hoarse. "Dylan?" she whispered.

There was no answer, only silence.

Even lower, she whispered, "Dad? Is that you?"

She heard something, a faint rustling over the phone line, and then the sound of shallow breathing. Then a whispering voice, hoarse and gruff.

"Bitch. Stupid bitch."

She felt frozen in place with the phone pressed hard against her ear. Her face turned hot. Her pulse pounded in her ears. From the phone there was only a long silence, then a harsh click, then the locustlike drone of a dial tone.

She slammed the phone down. The hard contact caused the bell inside to emit a single *ding* that reverberated in the room.

Outside the house, the wind howled. The tree branch scraped the roof, knocking against the tin like a banging fist.

Then she heard another banging. It came from the front door. Not like a fist, but a rattling, slamming noise. It was the screen door, being opened and slammed shut by the wind. Surely she had latched it, using the little eye hook screwed into the door frame. The wind couldn't possibly have lifted the hook.

She slowly rose from the chair and walked to the front door. She had left the porch light on. Yellow light entered through the little diamond-shaped pane of glass in the front door. Rue remembered an irrational fear that had given her nightmares as a child, a fear that some dark night, peering out that little diamond pane of glass, she would come face-to-face with someone else peering in, a leering face only inches away, just on the other side of the glass. Approaching the door, she flinched and pressed her hand to her breast, her heart was beating so fast. She stepped slowly to the pane of glass and looked out.

There was no face outside. She flinched nonetheless, imagining that one might appear at any moment. She saw only the pillars of the porch and the long walkway running from the porch to the driveway, away from the light and into the darkness. Her rental car was a vague, uncertain silhouette. Beyond the car, the tops of the nearest mesquite trees thrashed in the wind.

She gave a start as the screen door, which had been wide open, suddenly slammed shut. A gust of wind swept across the porch and the screen door swung wide open again, banging against the house. The wind held it there for a moment, pressing it hard against the wall, then flung it once more against the door frame. There was a peculiar violence about it, made even more horrible by its utter mindlessness, the way the wind held the screen door in its power and toyed with it, slamming it against the wall and then against the door frame.

If the ringing of the phone hadn't already awakened Gran, then the banging of the screen door surely would. Rue had to do something about it.

That would mean opening the front door.

She put her hand on the doorknob. The door had no dead bolt, no extra locks, only a flimsy little button lock built into the doorknob itself. She had only to press her thumb against the button and it would spring out, unlocking the mechanism, allowing her to turn the knob.

But how had the screen door come undone? Surely she had latched it. She had painstakingly secured every lock on every door and window in the house before settling in for the night. She was sure she had.

Or had she? No one in San Francisco had a screen door. No one in San Francisco had to worry much about flies or wasps or scorpions or snakes coming inside from the wild when they left their front doors standing open. She had forgotten about screen doors. Perhaps, she told herself, she had left it unlatched after all.

But even as she pressed her thumb against the button and unlocked the doorknob, she had a flash of memory and distinctly remembered latching the screen door. Even so, she turned the knob and pulled the front door open—and for a strange, terrifying moment something on the other side, outside the house, pulled at the door, almost wrenching the knob from her grasp.

Rue stifled a shriek—then realized that it was only a strong gust of wind that had sucked at the door, almost pulling it shut. She drew the door open and stood in the doorway, staring out at the porch and the darkness of the front yard and the driveway beyond. Nothing stirred except the treetops buffeted by the wind. She leaned out and peered right and left at both ends of the porch.

She reached for the screen door and pulled it toward her. When she tried to latch it, she saw the problem. The eye bolt that screwed into the door frame had been pulled from its hole. The wood in that spot was soft and rotted. The eye bolt had barely been screwed in place. The wind, catching at the screen door, had been strong enough to pull it free and set the door swinging. Tomorrow she would fix it.

In the meantime, something would have to be done to keep the screen door from banging. She needed something to prop the door open, flush against the house. She looked down and saw the yellow brick that for years had been kept on the porch for just that purpose; on the rare occasions Gran left the house, it was easier to maneuver her wheelchair in and out the doorway with the screen door propped open. Rue stepped out onto the porch, pushed the screen door against the wall, and slid the brick against it with her foot.

Her common sense told her to step back into the house immediately and shut the door behind her, but another impulse prevailed. Summoning the nerve to peer out the diamond pane of glass and then to unlock the door had given her a sense of power. She hated the idea of shutting herself away, of cowering inside a locked house, afraid of the dark. She had always resented the idea of letting fear rule her life. In San Francisco, she still ran alone when it suited her, even after dark sometimes, even though some of her friends had given up running altogether out of fear of muggers and rapists. Of course she was prudent; she kept away from certain areas, never wore headphones, almost always carried pepper spray. She should have brought her pepper spray with her, she thought, but it had never occurred to her that she might need it in Amethyst. Had Amethyst ever been the innocent place she imagined?

She stepped onto the porch, peering into the darkness beyond the reach of the porch light. Instead of feeling intimidated, she felt perversely emboldened by the wildness of the wind and the layers of darkness all around. For no logical reason, but with no less certainty because it was purely intuition, Rue felt absolutely sure that there was not another waking human for miles around. The whole world was asleep. Here, in this spot, there were only herself and the wind and the cold starlight above.

Somewhere, someone had made the last phone call to the house, but that person was nowhere nearby.

She stepped off the porch, onto the walk, and headed slowly, deliberately toward the rental car. When she reached it, she turned around and looked back at the house.

How small it looked, and how alone, with no neighbors anywhere nearby. How vulnerable. *Bitch,* the voice had said. *Stupid bitch.* Who was he? Where was he? If she left tomorrow, would that be the end of it? What did she know, after all? Nothing. She had seen a dead body, and then the body had vanished. What did Gran know? Even less. Surely Gran would be safe without her, perhaps safer than with Rue in the house. Rue would have to leave in a few days, anyway. If she had any sense, she would pack her things right now, get into the car, and drive straight to Austin.

She stood in the darkness, her arms wrapped tightly around her, shivering, until the cold became too much for her and she hurried back inside. She closed the door behind her and locked it.

Back in the living room, she found herself standing over the telephone, staring at Justice Goodbody's card on the table. The card lay facedown, showing the cell phone number he had written across the back. Rue glanced at the clock. It was after one. She picked up the card and ran her fingers over it.

Suppose she called him. Then what?

He was probably asleep. Would he be gruff? Groggy? Unexpectedly happy to hear from her at one in the morning?

He would want to know why she was calling. *Because I received a threatening phone call,* she would say.

Threatening?

Not exactly threatening. More like an obscene phone call.

Obscene?

Not exactly obscene. He called me a bitch. A stupid bitch.

And you are. I told you to get out of town. Now hang up and don't call back!

No, that was not what Goodbody would say. She replayed the fantasy, and in this version he insisted on coming over right away. When he arrived, in the middle of the night, would he still be wearing his Stetson? If Rue had any say in the matter, he would soon be wearing nothing at all . . .

Rue smiled and told herself she was much too tired to think rationally. Her mind was going off in all sorts of strange directions. What she really needed was sleep.

She put down Goodbody's card and found herself staring at the phone. Earlier, half awake, she had imagined that the phone was a snake in her hand. Sure enough, it had bitten her.

Bitch, the voice had whispered. *Stupid bitch.*

For the first time in her life, Rue found herself wishing there were a gun in the house. It was a stupid idea. She wouldn't have the first idea of how to use it. Still, she pictured herself dozing in the chair, a gun lying beside the telephone on the table. Half the women in Texas carried a gun. You could even carry a concealed handgun in Texas now, thanks to George W. Bush. She wondered if Ginger carried a gun in the glove compartment of her car, or in her handbag. Would she, with children around? Probably. Marty certainly had rifles in his pickup, and probably more guns in the house.

Marty . . .

Rue tried to remember every detail of the last phone call. Had it been threatening, or not? The caller said nothing about Dawn, nothing about keeping her mouth shut or getting out of town. The caller had spoken only three words, and those words constituted an insult, not a threat.

Could it have been Marty? She hadn't recognized the voice, but the caller had spoken in a low, gruff whisper. It *could* have been Marty, drinking after midnight, calling to insult her while Ginger slept, getting a puerile thrill from hanging up. It could have been Marty—not her father, not a stranger—who made the earlier hang-up calls, as well.

The more Rue thought about it, the more it made sense. Or was she just rationalizing, settling on the least threatening explanation she could think of?

She sighed and yawned, totally exhausted. Little by little her uneasiness gave way to exasperation. Every man she had talked to, or tried to talk to, on the phone that night had given her trouble—her brother, her father, even Dylan calling her after midnight because he couldn't keep his time zones straight. And Marty! She found herself reliving the moment she kneed him in the groin, wishing she had hit him even harder. Much, much harder . . .

Once again, sitting in the chair, Rue fell into a deep sleep. The phone did not ring again that night.

14

Rue woke to the smell of sizzling bacon from the kitchen. The living room drapes were dappled with morning sunshine. She glanced at the clock and saw that it was almost nine. She put her arms over her head and stretched. She was stiff from sleeping in the chair, but wonderfully rested.

For a brief, pleasant moment, her mind was a blank. Then the phone on the table beside her rang, and everything from the previous day and night came rushing back to her. She stared at the phone until it rang again, then lifted the receiver. "Hello?"

"Good, you're still here! I was afraid you might have up and left."

"Ginger?"

"Listen, I heard what happened yesterday. You and me have got to talk."

"Heard about . . . what?"

"What you saw, of course."

"Who told you?

"Does it matter? Horace Boatwright told Bertha, and Broadcast Bertha's been burning up the phone lines. Everybody in town knows about it. So when can you come over?"

"Well . . . Marty's not there, is he?"

"Of course not. It's Tuesday. He's at work."

"I guess I could come by in about an hour."

"Shit, you *were* asleep, weren't you? You are living the life of Riley, Rue Dunwitty. Snoozing till nine o'clock. Well, get over here as quick as you can. Bye-bye."

Breakfast was bacon with toast—the way Gran made it, spread with butter and broiled on the top rack of the oven—and eggs fried in leftover bacon grease. Rue would never have allowed herself to eat such rich food anywhere else, but this morning it seemed to be just what she needed.

She told Gran about her phone call from Dylan, and tried to explain who he was and why he was coming for a visit, but she made the explanation too complicated, mentioning Dylan's postponed job interview, and Gran became confused about whether Dylan was from San Francisco or Austin. It was too much to try to explain again from the beginning, so Rue didn't try. The important thing was to let Gran know that a stranger would be coming by the house that afternoon, that he was a friend of Rue's, and that Rue was expecting him.

She also told Gran about her call to Reg, but not about any of the other calls. It turned out that Gran had not heard the phone ring once the previous night. Nor had she heard the banging of the screen door. Did she sleep that soundly, Rue wondered, or was she losing her hearing?

"Did you know about this new job Reg has, going back and forth between Austin and San Antonio?" Rue asked.

Gran shook her head. "Maybe he said something about it over Thanksgiving, but I don't recall."

"I asked him to come to Amethyst."

"Good! What did he say?"

"He can't come."

Gran made a sour face. "He's not a bit of use, is he? Takes after his father, I reckon."

"Gran! Reg has to work."

"Even so, he ought to be here. You shouldn't be here in the house alone, Rue."

"I'm not alone. I'm with you."

Gran said nothing. She reached for the San Angelo paper and stared at the front page, though Rue knew she must have read it already.

After a long shower, Rue dressed and drove up to Ginger's house. When she turned off on the road to the new subdivision, she saw cars and pick-ups parked everywhere along the curb. More vehicles, including the deputy's patrol car, were parked among the prickly pears and scrubby mesquites in an unfenced patch of land past the last of the new houses. Rue pulled in alongside Ginger's Pontiac in the driveway, in the spot for Marty's black pickup.

Ginger had been watching for her. Before Rue could ring the bell, the door opened and Ginger pulled her inside.

"Thank goodness you're here!"

"Why are all those cars parked out there?" Rue asked.

"It's the search! They're all down there on that hillside behind the house, over on your dad's property. Closest way to get there is to cut through my backyard, cross that strip of wild land, and then climb over the fence."

Rue walked across the living room to the sliding glass door and looked out. "I guess it makes sense that they'd come down through here," she said.

Ginger walked up beside her. "So you *do* know what's going on! First clue we had was last night when Juss Goodbody came by, asking questions."

"What kind of questions?"

"Had we seen anybody coming or going? Did we ever see a parked car up here we couldn't account for? I told him no, and figured that was the end of it, but then this morning all these cars started showing up, and everybody started tramping across our yard. Goodbody rang the doorbell and told us they needed access to conduct a search of that hillside. Wouldn't say why, but I knew it must be something to do with Dawn Frady. Marty got all pissed off and started yelling at Goodbody, sayin' he was gonna tear him a new one, 'cause nobody could cross our backyard without permission. I told Marty to shut up and stop makin' a fool of hisself and get his ass to work. I figure he was just in a snit 'cause Goodbody didn't invite him to be in the search party. Marty wouldn't have been much use anyway, with that banged-up foot of his."

"Goodbody didn't tell you what they're looking for?"

"Acted like it was none of our business! So I got on the phone to Bertha, and she told me about you seein' the body. Oh, Rue, that must have been an awful shock! Why didn't you call me last night? Well, never mind. You're here now." Ginger guided her to the dining area, sat her down at the table, and put a steaming cup of coffee in front of her. Rue noticed that the television was on, with the sound muted. A TV judge was holding court, banging his gavel and glowering at the smirking litigants.

Ginger sat down across from her. "So tell me—did you really see something, or not?"

"Of course I saw something. I saw Dawn Frady." The memory flashed before her eyes and Rue felt sick in the pit of her stomach.

"But did you *really* see her?"

"I don't know what you mean," Rue said, with a sinking feeling that she knew exactly what Ginger meant.

"Well, it's just—from what Bertha told me, and according to some of the other women I called up—"

"Other women?"

"Rue, hon, *everybody's* talkin' about it. And some people figure, maybe—"

"Figure what? That I imagined it?"

"It happens. Hell, it could happen to anybody! Haven't you ever been driving at night, and the way the headlights catch something . . ."

"This wasn't like that, Ginger. It was broad daylight. I was wide awake. I saw . . . what I saw."

"And what *did* you see?"

"I wrote it all down in the report for the deputy. Didn't Bertha read it to you verbatim over the phone?"

Ginger missed her sarcasm. "No, she didn't. So tell me!"

Once again, as she had for Gran, Bertha, the sheriff, the deputy, and then Reg, Rue explained how she had found the body in the cistern.

"Completely naked," Ginger said, shivering. "Well, she would be, wouldn't she? And those rope burns around her neck and her wrists—you know what that means. She was tied up."

"I suppose. I don't really want to think about it."

"Poor Liz Frady!"

"Do you think she's heard?"

"I don't see how not," said Ginger. "If the deputy hasn't told her, somebody else will. I can't imagine which would be worse, to know for sure that's Dawn's dead, or to hear that somebody saw her but then the body disappeared. Not knowing for absolute certain, and people trying to make her feel better by telling her . . ."

"Telling her I only *imagined* it." Rue shook her head.

"Maybe they'll find her this morning," said Ginger. "Maybe they've already found her. Let's go look! I'll grab a cigarette."

Ginger led Rue across the backyard. Where the lawn abruptly ended, a wilderness of cactus, scrubby live oaks, and mesquite trees took over, blanketing the verge of the hillside. They followed a little path worn by passing wildlife; Rue saw deer and possum droppings, along with fresh footprints and cigarette butts left by the search party. The land tilted sharply down and the path vanished as the ground turned to the flaky, fossil-rich soil her mother had called caliche. It gave way easily underfoot and Rue slid a bit. A quick, sharp pain jabbed her sprained left ankle, and she stepped more carefully.

They came to a rusty barbed-wire fence. Between two of the gnarly cedar posts the wire had been pushed down and stretched so that it bowed and sagged. They stepped over one leg at a time, each holding the wire down for the other.

A little farther on, past a faded black-and-yellow No Trespassing sign like the one on the Dunwitty property near Gran's house, the land tipped down again and the foliage gave way to a view from the hillside. All of Amethyst was below, beginning with the pecan orchards and open fields of the Dunwitty property, then the cluster of barns and outbuildings around the abandoned Dunwitty house. Gran's house was across a field off to the far right. Farther away were the naked treetops and rooftops of

Amethyst, with the courthouse and the Texaco sign dominating the low skyline, and a far horizon of low gray hills in the distance. It was not a dramatic view—not to Rue, who had lived in San Francisco, with its precipitous hills and extraordinary panoramas—but it was charming nonetheless. It was the kind of view that realtors all over the Texas hill country dreamed of, and Rue wondered why the houses in Ginger's development hadn't been built just a little farther this way, so as to take advantage of it. That would have meant building on Dunwitty property, of course. Had her father ever been approached about selling this narrow strip of land? And had he refused, wanting no houses to overlook his property?

Rue and Ginger moved forward a few more steps and were suddenly able to see the hillside and the search party immediately below them. A large square of land for fifty yards on each side of the ruined cistern had been overlaid with strips of orange tape unspooled in rows three feet apart. The twenty or so searchers were walking up and down their assigned strips of land, peering at the ground, emitting clouds of steamy breath in the frigid air. For Rue, who had always thought of the hillside as a private, almost secret place, it was a surreal sight.

"So that's the cistern?" Ginger puffed on her cigarette. "Damn, that thing's not more than a couple of hundred yards from my backyard. Freaky!"

Rue spotted Goodbody, talking to some men at the bottom of the hill. Even at a distance and amid so many others, the deputy stood out. It wasn't just his tan uniform and the black Stetson and black gloves and green jacket, but his height and proportions, the narrowness of his hips and the width of his shoulders. He happened to glance up, saw them, and waved. Ginger waved back, then cupped her hands around her mouth.

"Y'all find anything yet?" she yelled.

Goodbody didn't answer, but started hiking up the hill toward them.

"Damn, but he is good-looking!" growled Ginger under her breath, watching him approach. "Even smells good—have you noticed that? Not that I've ever gotten close enough to sniff him the way I'd like to."

Goodbody drew closer, taking high steps as he ascended the steep area immediately below them. He stepped up beside them, only slightly out of breath. His big chest rose and fell, and steam blew from his lips. Rue caught a whiff of the musky scent Ginger had been talking about.

Goodbody tipped his hat. "Morning, ladies," he said. He looked at Ginger first, but his eyes settled on Rue.

"So, have you guys found anything yet, or not?" said Ginger. "And why didn't you tell me it was Dawn Frady you were looking for? If that girl was dumped this close to my house, I should think I have a right to know about it."

"I'm afraid we haven't found anything yet," said Goodbody, answering Ginger but keeping his eyes on Rue. "I'll be searching the rest of the property this morning."

"Did you reach my father?" asked Rue.

"Not yet. Doesn't seem to be answering his phone down in Corpus. If and when we do find anything, Miss Dunwitty, I'll be sure to let you know. You're still at your grandmother's house?"

Rue nodded. "At least for today and tonight."

"Alone?"

"Actually . . . a friend of mine is driving up from Austin this afternoon. He might spend the night at my grandmother's house."

"He?" said Ginger, raising an eyebrow. Goodbody also reacted, but with an expression Rue couldn't quite make out. Was he relieved that she had a male friend coming to stay with her? Or was it a twinge of jealousy that crossed his face?

Rue changed the subject. "Actually, Deputy, there's something I wanted to tell you. About a phone call I received last night. It wasn't exactly a threat. It may have been just a crank call."

"A male caller?" Goodbody looked concerned.

"Yes?"

"What did he say?"

"Just three words." Rue felt her face grow hot. "He said, 'Bitch. Stupid bitch.' Then he hung up."

"What time was this?"

"Late. After midnight."

"You should have called me." Goodbody lowered his voice and his gaze took on the same intensity as the day before, when he had been recalling his experience with the Corpus Christi murders.

"I thought about calling you. But then I figured . . ." Rue didn't want to mention her suspicions of Marty, with Ginger standing there. "I figured it was just a crank call."

"I think you should take this very seriously," said Goodbody. He raised his hand and touched her shoulder. Then he glanced at Ginger, who was watching the two of them intently, not missing a thing, and he drew his hand away.

"Well, I need to get back to work," said Goodbody. "Still got a lot of ground to cover this morning."

Ginger stepped on her cigarette and blew smoke from her nostrils. She hugged herself. "I don't know about you two, but my ass is about to get freeze-bit. What do you say we head back to my house, Rue, and let the deputy get on about his business?"

Rue nodded. Goodbody looked at her for a long moment, then turned and headed down the hillside.

15

R ue Dunwitty, you have been holding out on me!" snapped Ginger as they headed back to the house. She seemed more amused than perturbed.

"I don't know what you're talking about."

"Don't play innocent! What's going on between you and Juss Goodbody?"

Rue furrowed her brow. "Nothing."

"Oh, come on, Rue. It's plain as day. He practically grabbed you, right in front of me. If I hadn't been there, he would have kissed you."

Rue shook her head but wondered if Ginger was right.

"Well, if you can't see it—open your eyes!" Ginger pushed down the fence for Rue to step over, then Rue did the same for her. "And what's this about some boyfriend coming up from Austin to stay the night?"

"He's a friend from San Francisco, actually. He just happens to be coming to Austin for a job interview, and he's going to spend the night in Amethyst."

"I see."

"It's not what you think."

Ginger made a skeptical noise and lit another cigarette.

Back at the house, Ginger offered her more coffee, then excused herself to go to the bathroom. Rue paced the cluttered living room. She glanced at the stacks of magazines on the coffee table. Ginger read soap opera digests and scandal tabloids. Marty read hunting and sports magazines. The magazines on top doubled as coasters and were covered with coffee rings. There were two ashtrays, a smaller one full of Ginger's Salem Lights with lipstick traces, and a bigger one the size of a casserole, decorated with Budweiser labels and full of cigar butts.

She stepped over a yellow Pokémon doll on the floor and glanced at the muted television. The TV courtroom faded to black and a commercial came on. A series of quick camera angles showed a young man lathering himself in a shower. Waves of slippery foam slid across his muscular chest and ribbed belly. The camera zoomed in on his navel, then on a nipple. Stripped of its cheerful jingle, the commercial looked blatantly pornographic. Juss Goodbody might look like that, Rue thought. He had that sort of body, beautifully conditioned and developed. Did he lift weights? Was there a gym in Amethyst? Or would he do it at home, in his garage—and afterward take a hot, soapy shower?

Rue wandered into the little hallway that led to the bedrooms. Marty Junior's room was cluttered with toy trucks and guns. April's room was done all in pink, with stuffed animals scattered on the unmade bed. Rue reached the end of the hall and stepped into Ginger and Marty's room.

Nothing in the room matched. The big, dark dresser was a scruffy antique with some drawer pulls missing. The comforter lying at a crooked angle on the unmade water bed had a red plaid pattern, while the sheets were pink and floral. The drapes were paisley in garish shades of orange.

Ginger and Marty shared the big ashtray on the dresser, to judge from the mix of lipstick-stained Salem Lights and snuffed cigar butts. Next to the ashtray was a stack of Marty's underwear. Rue had trouble picturing him in purple-and-yellow polka-dotted Jockey briefs. She started to turn away, then noticed something else on the dresser and felt her heart skip a beat.

It was partly hidden behind the stack of underwear, but so out of place with every other object in the house, she wondered why she hadn't noticed it the moment she entered the room. It was also immediately, eerily familiar.

It was a small, beautifully styled art nouveau clock, eight inches high and four across, made of bronze. Two long-stalked calla lilies framed a round clock face. Rue reached out and touched it.

She gave a start and realized that Ginger was standing behind her. "Precious, ain't it?" Ginger said. "Doesn't keep time anymore, but it's still pretty to look at. Marty got it for my birthday back in July. Found it at a little antique store in Halleyville."

Rue shook her head. "It didn't come from Halleyville."

"What do you mean?"

Rue took a deep breath. "This was my grandmother's."

"What?"

"It's from the old Dunwitty house."

Ginger frowned. "No, you must be thinking of some other clock."

"This clock used to be on the mantel above my grandparents' fireplace. I'd forgotten all about it. But I remember now, how pretty I thought it was when I was a little girl. I'd ask Grandmother Dunwitty to take it down from the mantel and let me hold it, and she'd say, 'No, Rue, it's not a toy.' So one day I pulled a chair over to the fireplace and climbed on the seat and reached for the clock, but the chair tipped over. Grandmother came running, and when she asked me what I was doing, I told her I was trying to reach the clock. I thought for sure she'd let me hold it then. But she didn't. She said, 'I hope you've learned your lesson, young lady.'" Rue sighed, staring at the clock. "But I think she must have put the clock away somewhere, because I can't remember ever seeing it since that day. That was her way whenever there was a problem, to cover things over or put them out of sight. Probably she put it in a closet, or in a drawer . . ."

Ginger frowned. "Or maybe she sold it to somebody in Halleyville, and that's how it ended up in a secondhand store."

"I don't think that's what happened, Ginger. And neither do you."

Ginger stared back at her. The frown hardened on her face. "I think it's not even the same clock, that's what I think. They probably made thousands of those clocks and sold 'em all over Texas."

"When did Marty give it to you?"

"July twenty-seventh. My birthday."

"It was in July that Gran heard the alarm go off at the Dunwitty house. She called the sheriff and Goodbody to come check it out."

"Rue Dunwitty, I don't like what you're insinuating."

"Oh, Ginger! You and I both know that Marty has been trespassing on Dunwitty land. He goes down there to hunt possums or shoot tin cans or whatever he does when he plays with his rifles."

"My husband may be a lot of things, Rue, but he's not a thief."

Rue thought about the crude pass Marty had made at her, and about the ugly phone call he made to her later, and the hang-ups and the other phone call, which might have been from Marty. *Bitch. Stupid bitch.* She bit her tongue, afraid to say words she couldn't call back. "Where was it that Marty got his foot stuck in a trap?"

Ginger's face turned red. She reached for a pack of Salem Lights on the dresser and lit one. The odor of mentholated tobacco filled the air. "That's got nothing to do with anything."

"Was it on my father's land?"

"What if it was? What sort of crazy old man sets traps on his land when he doesn't even live on the property—when he doesn't even live here in Amethyst? What if some poor fox or rabbit got caught in one of those traps, and then just had to struggle there and suffer and starve to death? It's cruel and inhumane to set traps if you're not around to check on 'em and put whatever you catch out of its misery. What if some little kid went wandering on that property, innocent as can be, and lost a hand or a foot in one of those traps? Emmett Dunwitty would be in a hell of a lot of trouble then. It's irresponsible, that's what it is."

"But it wasn't an innocent kid, was it? It's Marty who's been trespassing on the Dunwitty land."

Ginger blew out a cloud of smoke. "Maybe Marty's gone hunting down there a few times."

"And maybe that's where he stepped in a trap?"

"Yes! You should've been here when he came limping in off the patio that day, dragging his foot and squalling like a baby. You should've seen the mess that trap made of his foot, all the blood and bruises—damned thing had teeth that tore right through his leather boots. I told him we ought to sue Emmett Dunwitty for every penny he's got, but Marty said there wasn't any point, because the law in Texas always favors property owners over trespassers, and he was likely to end up fined or in jail himself if we raised a stink. But it's not right, setting traps like that. Why on earth would your father do such a thing? You'd think he had buried treasure on that land, or something else he's hiding."

What *had* her father been thinking, to set such a dangerous trap on his property? If there were more traps, Rue herself might have stepped in one! She had never really known her father. Setting steel-jawed traps for trespassers didn't seem entirely out of character for him—he was crusty, individualistic, jealous of what was his—but was he also that reckless and uncaring? Had his eccentricities, in the ten years that Rue hadn't spoken to him, turned into genuine paranoia?

She drew a deep breath. "You're changing the subject, Ginger. This *is* the clock that was in my grandparents' house."

"Well, what if it is?" Ginger's voice broke. "Maybe somebody else stole it. Did you think of that? Anybody could come and go in that house. Maybe some Mexican stole it and sold it to that secondhand shop in Halleyville, and Marty just happened to buy it for my birthday."

The idea of Marty going antiquing, even to find his wife a present, was so ludicrous that Rue laughed. "Oh, Ginger! We know Marty goes hunting on the Dunwitty land. Gran heard the alarm go off in July, and Marty gave you the clock in July. You don't have to be a rocket scientist—"

"Oh, sure, just go ahead and insult my intelligence, Miss Computer Whiz! You think you're so much better than anybody else because you're so fucking bright. You always got straight A's, you went to college, you got yourself a smart-ass job out in California. Except I don't see you with a husband and a family. I suppose you're too smart to bother with any of that, like a normal woman."

"Ginger, I never meant—"

"I know exactly what you meant. My husband's a thief and I'm an airhead who got herself saddled with a crappy marriage and a couple of snot-nosed brats. And if I happen to have one nice, tasteful, *artistic* object in my house, well, it couldn't have got there on its own, so somebody must have stolen it. Oh, no, it's not the kind of the thing *Ginger* could ever own, she wouldn't know how to appreciate it, she buys everything at Wal-Mart, so it must have come from your grandmother's house." Ginger's voice grew louder and louder until she was yelling.

"I think you're overreacting," said Rue.

"Just take it, then, if you're so goddamned sure it's yours." Ginger picked up the clock and thrust it at her. "Take it and get out of my house, and don't ever come back!"

"Ginger—"

"Get out!" Ginger screamed.

Rue took the clock, turned, and walked down the hallway as fast as she could, bumping her shoulder against a wedding portrait on one wall and knocking it askew. She reached the front door, then hesitated and turned back. Suddenly Ginger emerged from the hallway with a look in her eyes that Rue had never seen there before. For an instant she thought Ginger might physically attack her.

"Get out of my house, you stupid bitch!" Ginger screamed.

Clutching the clock, Rue slipped out the door. Ginger slammed it behind her as Rue hurried to her rental car, limping slightly because her left ankle was throbbing.

16

On the drive back to Gran's house, Rue looked at her hands on the steering wheel and noticed how white her knuckles were. She willed herself to flex her fingers and loosen her grip. She consciously took deep breaths and exhaled as slowly as she could. But whenever she inhaled there was a catch in her throat, and she knew she was on the verge of tears. She gritted her teeth and fought them back.

Perhaps she *should* cry. Cry and let it all out. Pull off to the side of the road and give herself over to a full-out weeping jag. *Don't be ridiculous,* a voice in her head chided her, and she knew it was her mother's voice. Not once had Rue ever seen her mother cry, not after the divorce, when Rue was a little girl, not through all the years of raising Reg and her, not even during her bout with cancer, when every day brought bad news. Nor had Rue ever seen Gran cry. Once, back when Rue was small and Gran still used crutches, the two of them had been crossing the courthouse square and Gran had fallen. A group of men came rushing out of the courthouse to help. Looking back now, as an adult, Rue realized how embarrassing it must have been for Gran, how helpless it must have made her feel, on top of the pain of twisting her arm and bruising her hip. Yet Gran never cried, never complained. Even so, that fall must have affected her, because afterward Gran put away her crutches for good and resigned herself to using a wheelchair for the rest of her life.

How could Rue allow herself to cry now, considering all that her mother and Gran had endured without ever shedding a tear? She came from a line of strong, stoical women—Texas women. The thought made Rue smile, because ordinarily she dismissed that kind of thinking as sentimental and silly and provincial. Stress was making her muddleheaded.

She glanced at the antique clock on the passenger seat, and sighed. A falling-out like the one she'd just had with Ginger could go on for years, maybe for the rest of their lives. Should she have said nothing, and allowed Ginger to keep the clock?

Back at the house, Gran was waiting for her in the living room. She saw the clock in Rue's hand and wrinkled her brow.

"What's that, hon?"

Rue handed the clock to Gran, who ran her long, thin fingers over the smooth bronze. "Well, if that's not the prettiest thing! Where on earth did it come from?"

"The Dunwitty house," said Rue.

"Did you just come from there?"

"I . . ." She didn't want to lie to Gran, but she didn't want to have to explain about Ginger and Marty either. Fortunately, Gran didn't wait for an answer. "Well, it's a good thing you brought it back here. A thing as pretty as this, it's a wonder it was still there. I'd have thought one of you kids would've taken it already, or your dad. Or some thief—I told you about that break-in back in July. It's a wonder whoever was snooping around there didn't see this thing and take it."

Rue simply nodded in agreement.

"I'll bet this is worth something."

"Maybe," Rue said, though she couldn't imagine ever selling something that reminded her so strongly of Grandmother Dunwitty.

"You should take this back with you to San Francisco, Rue. I'll bet you could find somebody out there who could fix this up and make it run again, and then it would look real pretty on your dresser."

Rue nodded and smiled. The thought pleased her immensely.

She followed Gran into the kitchen and helped her prepare a lunch of cold ham and lima beans, with a Jell-O salad for dessert. They were in the middle of eating when the phone rang.

"Hello?" said Rue.

"Well, I'm at the Austin airport. Can you hear me? This pay phone's out of whack."

"Dylan!" Rue glanced at the clock, which showed a quarter to one. "How was the flight?"

"Bumpy—don't ask! The steward spilled coffee on me. Fortunately, I brought a different shirt for the interview tomorrow. So, anyway, I've got the rental car. I'll need to run by the Three Muses to check into my room and see if I have any messages, but then I'll head straight for Amethyst. I should be there in a couple of hours."

"Don't rush. Drive carefully."

Dylan laughed. "Rue, you *are* from Texas!"

"What do you mean?"

"Your accent. I never knew you had one, but boy, I can hear it now."

"Spending a few days in Amethyst brings it out, I guess."

"So how is the old town? More excitement than you can stand?"

She was nonplussed for a moment, then realized that she had told him nothing yet about Dawn. "More excitement than you might expect. I'll tell you all about it when you get here."

"Sounds mysterious."

"You have no idea."

"Then I'll see you in a couple of hours."

"Good. And Dylan—thanks for coming."

"Hey, how many chances does a guy get to rendezvous with you and your grandmother in Amethyst, Texas?"

After Rue hung up, Gran asked her who had called.

"My friend from San Francisco. The one who's coming to visit. He just flew into Austin, and now he's about to drive here."

Gran nodded hesitantly. Rue had tried to explain to her earlier about Dylan's visit, and Gran hadn't quite understood who he was or where he was coming from, much less why. Come to think of it, Rue herself was not entirely sure why Dylan was coming. Was it just to kill time because his job interview had been pushed back a day? He could as easily have spent the night in Austin, enjoying himself in the music clubs on Sixth Street. Surely it was more than that . . .

Rue put her hand on Gran's. How thin and cold it felt! "His name is Dylan."

"Like Marshal Dillon on *Gunsmoke?*"

Rue smiled. "Close enough. He's very nice. You'll like him."

"I'm sure I will, hon."

Rue's spirits lifted. Now, at least, the rest of the day had a structure. Once Dylan arrived, the hours would take care of themselves.

She spent a moment admiring the art nouveau clock. What other small treasures still remained in the Dunwitty house amid all the junk and clutter, beneath the dust and cobwebs or hidden in drawers? She felt an impulse to go there, despite the deputy's advice. Had he finished his search yet? Rue looked at his card on the table, picked up the phone, and dialed his cell number.

He answered after the first ring. "Goodbody here."

"Deputy, this is Rue Dunwitty."

"Hello, Miss Dunwitty."

"Do you have a moment to talk?"

"Certainly, Miss Dunwitty."

"You know, I think I'd prefer it if you called me Rue." Without those blue eyes looking into hers, Rue found it easier to talk to him.

"All right, Rue. You can call me Juss, if you'd like."

"Okay, Juss. I was wondering how your search of the Dunwitty property was going."

"As a matter of fact, I'm in your grandparents' house right now."

"Perhaps I should come over and join you."

"I'd rather you didn't." His voice shifted into deputy mode. "I haven't found anything yet. I'm beginning to think there's nothing *to* find. But as long as there's any chance of something dangerous . . ."

"I understand."

"Besides that, somebody's set traps on the property. I've almost stepped in a couple. Unless you know where they are, you could be seriously injured. *Do* you know anything about those traps?"

Rue hesitated. "Perhaps you should ask my father."

"I intend to, when I finally get hold of him. Did you have a particular reason for wanting to visit the house?"

Rue glanced at the antique clock. Should she tell him what she suspected about Marty? "I'm just restless, I guess."

"But you have company coming, don't you?" Over the phone Rue heard the sound of his booted footsteps on wooden stairs. She could picture him on the narrow stairway that led up to her father's old bedroom in the finished part of the attic.

"My friend's on his way, but he's not here yet."

"This friend—is he . . . ?"

Rue waited for him to finish the question: *Is he your boyfriend?* Why did Juss want to know? How would she answer?

But his voice trailed off and all she heard was the sound of his footsteps over the phone. It was Rue who finally spoke. "What were you saying?"

"Never mind. I should get back to work now. I'll let you know if I find anything, Rue."

"Thanks, Juss." She reluctantly hung up.

She remembered that the screen door latch needed fixing, and decided to tend to it. The only drill in the house was an old hand drill with a wooden handle and a gear mechanism not unlike an old eggbeater. It was rusty and hard to use, but it did the job. She moved the eye bolt to a spot in the door frame where the wood was solid, and repositioned the hook to a corresponding spot on the screen door. The empty screw holes were ugly, but at least the hook was secure again.

What she needed to pass the time until Dylan arrived was a good book to read, but she had left her copy of the latest Harry Potter on the airplane. All Gran had were some old *Reader's Digest* condensed books and a stack of paperback romances. Rue looked through the shelves in her mother's old bedroom. Her mother's taste had run to true crime, especially with a Texas setting. Rue had never seen much point in reading about Dallas millionaires who murdered their spouses, and she was even less interested in psychotic serial killers or professional hit men. That kind of thing gave her the creeps. Surely her mother had *something* other than true crime among her paperbacks. There were a few legal thrillers by Scott Turow and John Grisham, but Rue had already seen the movies. She skimmed the other titles on the shelf, running a fingertip from spine to spine until she abruptly stopped and sucked in a breath. There on her mother's bookshelf was a copy of *The Corpus Corpses,* by somebody named Hop Hollingshead.

She pulled it from the shelf. The front cover was a collection of black-and-white photos with the title of the book and the byline in blood red letters. The dominant photo showed a haggard-looking, middle-aged man with a mustache staring sullenly at the camera. He wore a dirty T-shirt, his arms were handcuffed in front of him, and he was flanked by two uniformed officers, each of them gripping one of the man's arms. Inset in a vertical strip that ran from top to bottom along the spine were high school class photos of teenaged girls. All the girls were smiling, some had braces, and a couple of them were wearing graduation mortarboards. There were nine girls in all. Rue looked at their faces one by one, then looked again at the man with the mustache staring sullenly back at the camera.

She turned the book over and looked at the back cover. It was mostly print, except for a single small photo that made her turn her eyes away. How could they put a photo like that on the outside of a book? The details were grainy, almost abstract, because of some process that heightened the contrast, but the photo was obviously of a female body lying in a contorted pose, apparently naked. She forced herself to look at the cover again and to scan the words.

A horrifying, true tale . . .
The crimes that shocked a city, a state, a nation . . .
Before the terror ended, nine girls would be dead . . .
The torture went on—not just for hours but for days and weeks . . .

There were a couple of blurbs as well, single emphatic words followed by exclamation points—"Stunning!" and "Shocking!" and "Horrific!"—from newspapers Rue had never heard of.

There was also a longer blurb from somebody named Nan Dingle at *Lone Star Monthly* magazine: "A super-duper thriller-chiller, and every word is true! Hop Hollingshead pulls out all the stops in this Texas-style true crime roller-coaster."

Rue made a face. Why would anyone willingly, much less eagerly, open such a book? Did people really want to be "stunned" or "shocked" or "horrified"? Did they really want to know any more than they had to about whatever terrible things had transpired between the sullenly staring man on the cover and the nine smiling girls in the snapshots? Apparently people did, her mother among them, because the spine of the book was cracked and the corners were dog-eared.

She opened the book and looked at the publication date. The paperback edition had come out the very month her mother had received her cancer diagnosis. How odd that her mother had sought out this particular book to read, after receiving such terrible news. Hadn't the diagnosis been stunning, shocking, horrific enough? People read for amusement and comfort and pleasure, Rue had always thought, so why had her mother, facing death, turned to this of all books? It puzzled her. But Rue had long ago given up on understanding the tastes of other people, even those closest to her. You had to accept the fact that someone like the reviewer for *Lone Star Monthly* could compare a book about serial murder to an amusement park ride, and that your own mother could receive vicarious pleasure from reading such a book.

Rue felt a sudden stab of regret, almost of grief. If her mother were still alive, this was something they could have talked about. She had never understood her mother's passion for true crime books, had disapproved actually, yet apart from an offhand remark or two, she had never really told her mother how she felt, had never asked her *why*. Perhaps, if Rue had asked, her mother could have explained. They could have talked about it—agreed or disagreed, argued or laughed, but at least had a discussion. But now . . . now that could never happen. Instead, this was the best she could do, the closest she could come to her mother, to hold in her hands the copy of a book her mother had held in her final days, to read the same words her mother had read.

At the center of the book there was an insert with several pages of photographs. Rue dreaded to think what she might see, but she turned to the insert nonetheless. The first photo she saw was the same as the one on the cover, showing Charlie McCutcheon flanked by two lawmen gripping his arms, but this copy of the photo was not as tightly cropped. It showed more of the surrounding details, including the faces of the two officers.

Rue sucked in a breath. One of them was Juss Goodbody.

17

New on the force, just starting out, pretty much still a kid . . .

That was how Goodbody had described himself at the time of the Corpus Christi murders. The photo backed him up. Rue was surprised at how young he looked, like a sober-faced boy dressed up to play policeman. If the photo showed a true likeness, he was actually better-looking now than he had been then. His looks had matured and his body had filled out considerably—in the photo he looked almost skinny, a size too small for his uniform.

She looked again at the book's cover. Yes, it was exactly the same photo, and that was Goodbody on McCutcheon's left, although you couldn't really tell because his jaw was partly hidden by the title, and the top half of his head was cropped.

Rue turned to the index at the back of the book, found the entries under *G,* and scanned the column until she came to "Goodbody, Justice." She was a little disappointed to see that there was only one citation.

It was on page 357, near the end of the book, in a final chapter titled "Aftermath: Picking Up the Pieces, Getting On with Their Lives." The chapter focused on various people affected by the Corpus Christi murders—relatives of the victims, the detectives who broke the case, the district attorney, news reporters, ordinary citizens—looking at how they had coped with the events and moved on. Rue found the passage about Goodbody:

And what about the lawmen who played only a minor role in the case, whose lives were only brushed by the horror? Some of them were also powerfully, and negatively, affected. One of those was Justice "Juss" Goodbody, a twenty-five-year-old rookie on the police force when the investigation first began to break. Officer Goodbody was present at some of the crime scenes, including the gruesome discovery of Brandy Littleton's body. Even more traumatic, the final victim, Trina Schaeffer, was a neighbor of Goodbody's, and only days before her abduction she and Goodbody had discussed the murders and the danger a girl like Trina faced. After the arrest, Goodbody had the dubious privilege of escorting Charlie McCutcheon to and from his cell on several occasions.

"Something like this changes you forever, whether you want it to or not," says Goodbody. "You sort of lose your innocence, real quick. I've done a lot of soul-searching. I've thought about getting out of law enforcement. I've thought about moving to a small, quiet town. So that's one result of this whole case—that I may leave town, may even change professions because of Charlie McCutcheon and the things he did. And that makes me mad, that McCutcheon is still messing up people's lives, even after we've sent him to death row in Huntsville."

Rue read the passage again, and felt a shiver when she came to the reference to the girl named Brandy Littleton and the "gruesome" discovery of her body. Which of the smiling girls on the cover was Brandy? One of the pages in the photo insert reproduced all the snapshots along with captions to identify each girl. Brandy was a blond with braces, a sweet-looking teenager who looked more than a little like Dawn Frady.

Rue turned back to the index and found the entry for Brandy Littleton.

There were quite a few citations, including "discovery of her body, 174." Rue turned to the page. What she read sickened her.

Only a few days after Brandy Littleton was reported missing, an anonymous tip led police to an abandoned warehouse. The source of that tip has never been discovered; some investigators speculate that it might have come from McCutcheon himself, but McCutcheon, who never confessed his guilt, has never verified that suspicion.

Whatever its source, the tip proved accurate, and of all the girls who disappeared over the course of the killings, Brandy was the quickest to be found—but those who found her still came too late. Combing the vast warehouse from top to bottom, officers came upon a shedlike structure in one corner, approximately ten feet by ten feet and constructed of corrugated aluminum. There was a padlock on the door. When police cut through the lock and opened the door, the first indication of what they would find was the odor that issued from inside.

"It wasn't the stench of death, like we had smelled before," remembers one of the officers. "It couldn't have been, because she hadn't been dead that long—the coroner's report said only a few hours. It was more like a caged animal smell—sour sweat, body fluids, human waste. And something else. The only way I can describe it is to say that the odor that came out of that shed was the smell of fear itself."

Inside the structure, officers found Brandy's nude body lying spread-eagled, facedown, on a metal bed frame that had no mattress, only a rusty set of box springs. Her wrists and ankles were secured to the corners of the metal frame by handcuffs.

She had also been gagged, and the gag was still stuffed in her mouth with the ends tightly tied and securely knotted behind her head. The officers released a collective groan when they recognized the peculiar fetish that they had encountered at each of the previous discovery sites. Brandy Littleton had been gagged with a small replica of a Texas state flag, of the sort available in hundreds of memorabilia and souvenir shops across the state.

Even without the coroner's report, Brandy's body bore abundant evidence of sexual abuse . . .

The book proceeded to pile on gruesome details. Rue scanned the following pages but couldn't bear to read any further.

Who was the unnamed officer who had been quoted talking about the smell? Could it have been Goodbody? Rue thought about the shadow that crossed his face when he recalled his days in Corpus Christi, and felt that now she understood.

She turned to the photo insert and found the snapshot of the final victim, Goodbody's neighbor, Trina Schaeffer. She was a brunette with short hair and perfect white teeth. With her long nose and high cheekbones she wasn't conventionally pretty, like Brandy Littleton, but she was striking nonetheless. She could have become a model, Rue thought—then realized with a start that Trina Schaeffer looked more than a little like Rue had looked at age sixteen.

Rue was abruptly distracted from the book by the sound of a car pulling into the driveway. She carried the copy of The Corpus Corpses with her to the front door and peered out the diamond pane. She half expected to see Goodbody's patrol car, and felt a slight twinge of disappointment when she saw a red Mitsubishi instead. Who would come to visit Gran driving such a sporty car?

The driver's door opened, and Dylan Jeffries stepped out. Rue looked at her watch, surprised to see that it was almost four. Dylan stretched his arms above his head, then peered about, taking in his surroundings. Rue opened the door and stepped onto the porch.

Dylan smiled and walked toward her. When they met on the walk, he put his hands lightly on her shoulders and kissed her on the cheek. It was an indeterminate sort of greeting; anyone seeing them would have assumed they were more than friends, but not quite lovers.

She leaned back and looked at him, and realized she was comparing him to Justice Goodbody. Dylan wasn't as big as Goodbody or as handsome, but he was certainly cute, especially when he grinned. After a long day of traveling, his chestnut hair was more unruly than ever. His hazel eyes lit up at the sight of her.

She was definitely glad to see him. After the spookiness of the previous night, it was a relief simply to have someone from back home in San Francisco standing next to her. She let out a pent-up sigh as they stepped apart.

"So this is the house where you grew up," said Dylan, nodding toward the porch.

"Be it ever so humble. But it keeps out the rain."

"I think it's great. So much space around you." Dylan gestured toward the Dunwitty property.

"My grandparents' land. My father's land now, actually. The fields, those barns, the big house you can see way over yonder. Grandmother and Grandfather Dunwitty are both gone now. But it was pretty special, growing up so close to them. And like you say, having so much space. It seemed even bigger when I was a girl. I can't imagine what it's like for kids to grow up in a big city." She smiled. "But how did you find the place? I thought you were going to phone when you got into Amethyst."

Dylan shrugged. "I just followed my nose." He grinned, then shook his head.

"What?" said Rue.

"Nothing. Just your accent. 'The big house you can see *way over yonder.*' Honestly, I never noticed it before last night, on the phone. And today, I do declare, if I was to close my eyes, you'd sound a mighty lot like the First Lady of these here United States."

"Watch it, buddy." Rue used the book in her hand to playfully poke him in the ribs. "Well, you know what they say: You can take the girl out of Texas . . ."

"What are you reading?" Dylan glanced down at the copy of *The Corpus Corpses,* then made a face. The playfulness left his voice. "Why on earth are you reading that?"

Rue wrinkled her brow. "You haven't read it, have you?"

"Unfortunately, yes. A couple of weeks ago on a plane. Somebody left a copy in the seat-back pocket. I picked it up and read it straight through, and then I wished I hadn't." He shivered. "Ugh! Really gross. Gave me nightmares."

"It'll probably give me nightmares, too."

"Then why are you reading it?"

Rue took a deep breath. "Oh, Dylan, it's all kind of complicated. Listen, I don't know about you, but I'm getting cold standing out here. Let's go inside and I'll introduce you to Gran. Then we can take a drive around town—and I'll try to explain what's happening in Amethyst."

18

Dylan's introduction to Gran went well. Rue found herself remembering the quality that had first attracted her to him—the completely genuine nature of his charm. Talking to an old lady in a wheelchair, most men Dylan's age might project a bluff, phony cheerfulness or, worse, use a condescending tone as if they were talking to a child. But Dylan spoke to Gran as he might to any other woman, and Gran clearly appreciated it, even though it seemed to Rue that Gran was still a bit unclear about what he was doing in her house. At one point Gran reached up from her armrest and touched Dylan's hand in a way that would have been flirtatious if done by a younger woman, and Rue had a flash of insight that touched her heart, a fleeting glimpse of Gran as she must have been when she was Rue's age or even younger.

Rue felt a bit self-conscious about how the house must look to Dylan. Gran kept it neat as a pin, but it still looked like what it was, a humble house with humble furnishings. For Rue the place was so full of nostalgia that her memories overshadowed the shabbiness. But what would an outsider make of it? Whatever he thought of the place, Dylan seemed completely at ease.

Gran told them to take a drive and not to worry about dinner. She would feed herself, and they could eat out if they wanted. Rue laughed and cautioned Dylan not to get too excited about the local cuisine.

They took Rue's rental car and she drove, figuring Dylan needed a break after the drive from Austin. Neither of them was particularly hungry yet, so Dylan suggested they take a drive around town first. "You can show me the sights while it's still light," he said, without a trace of irony in his voice. Rue wondered how her last boyfriend would have reacted to Amethyst, and could imagine him making one cutting remark after another. But Dylan seemed to take a genuine interest as they drove around the courthouse and the quaint old storefronts that surrounded it, then by the Methodist church and the little public library across the street, then by the yellow brick high school building. As they drove past the football stands, the stadium lights came on, and through the chain-link fence they could see the team practicing on the field.

Rue found herself slipping into the kind of sentimental reverie that a drive around Amethyst inevitably induced in her. Even the most mundane landmarks summoned up so many memories: the mesquite tree at the corner of the Bagwells' yard where Jimmy Bagwell had given Rue her first real kiss when she was fifteen; the patch of wilderness across from the grade school where Reg had once fallen backward into a stand of prickly pears—Rue had been no more than five or six, terrified by the catastrophe and fascinated that night while she watched her mother and Gran laboriously pluck the tiny, hair-fine needles out of Reg's back; the unpaved, rock-strewn stretch of Kline Street, which had seemed as steep as a mountain road when she was nine years old, where she and Reg overturned in Reg's red wagon and ran home crying with bloody elbows and knees. So much had happened to her in Amethyst that every corner of the town stirred a memory or evoked a mood. Back in San Francisco, she left all this behind, closed off in a box of forgetfulness, but when she was here, everything came back to her in a continuous rush, an engulfing ocean of childhood experiences.

As the twilight deepened, she willed herself back to the present. Somehow she had to explain to Dylan everything that had been going on. Keeping her eyes straight ahead, driving slowly down the residential streets around the high school, she started by telling him about her arrival in Amethyst and how she had seen the placard with Dawn's picture in the window at Schneider's.

Dylan listened intently, never interrupting except for an occasional exclamation, as when she told him about finding the body. When she told him about returning to discover that the body had disappeared, and the way Goodbody and the sheriff had reacted, Dylan shook his head and finally spoke.

"Jesus, Rue, why didn't you tell me all this on the phone last night?"

"Why? Would it have stopped you from coming?"

"Of course not! If anything, I'd have tried to catch an earlier flight. With something like this going on, it's crazy for you to be here alone."

"I appreciate that, Dylan. But—this isn't something that you ought to have to worry about. I mean, it's not like we're . . ." Rue shook her head. "I almost feel like I was dishonest, not telling you. You offered to come, and I . . . I wanted you to. But I can hardly be good company, can I? This thing with Dawn is all I can think about."

"Rue, for Christ's sake, I didn't come here looking for 'good company.'" He rolled his eyes. "No, wait, that's not right. I mean, I came here to be with *you,* good company or not. Damn! That's not right either, but you know what I mean. I came here to see you, and to meet your grandmother. And so that you could show me your hometown. And if this is what's going on around here, what's going on with you, then that's what I want to be here for. Does that make sense?"

She managed a faint smile. "I think so. Anyway, thanks for being here, Dylan. But if you want to turn around and head straight back to Austin, I'll understand."

"No way, if only because my butt's too sore from driving! And now I'm starting to get hungry."

She laughed. It felt good, releasing at least a bit of tension. "Let's eat, then. But maybe we should swing by the motel first. Not much chance they'll run out of rooms, but you never know."

"What, that skanky motel over by the park? No way, Rue. Not after what you just told me. I'm not letting you stay in that house by yourself tonight."

"The motel's not that 'skanky.' How would you know, anyway? We haven't driven by it yet. And I won't be by myself tonight. I'll be with Gran."

"Even worse, the two of you alone! No, I'm staying at your house tonight. Didn't you tell me there was a spare bedroom?"

"Yes, but Gran—"

"Your grandmother won't have a heart attack just because a grown man spends the night in her spare bedroom. Give her some credit, Rue."

Rue raised an eyebrow. A part of her bridled at his presumption that she needed and wanted a man in the house. But another part of her was glad that he was being so insistent.

Dylan smiled at her. "Hungry?"

"As a matter of fact, all of a sudden I'm starving."

"Well, I'm the visitor and you're the native. Lead me to your local Tex-Mex."

Rosita's Tamale House was located on the highway on the far side of town, in a big old house painted bright yellow with purple trim. The family that ran the place lived in the back of the house. The big, L-shaped front porch had been enclosed and turned into a dining room with long picture windows. There were only ten tables, and only two of them were occupied. Rue didn't recognize any of the diners, who looked like travelers passing through.

Other than the red-and-green tablecloths and a dusty piñata shaped like a burro that hung from the ceiling, there was not much of a cantina atmosphere. There were no decorative serving trays and neon signs for Mexican beers like Corona and Tecate; but of course, Rosita's wouldn't have those, because Amethyst County was dry. People had to drive thirty miles to Mayhew, just beyond the county line, to buy alcohol. She should have asked Dylan to buy some beer in Austin and bring it with him. Rosita's allowed people to bring their own beer.

Rosita's had been open for several years, but Rue had been there only once or twice. She could only vaguely remember the middle-aged woman who seated them—Rosita, she presumed—but the woman acted as if she remembered not just Rue but Dylan as well. Rue chalked it up to small-town friendliness and Mexican hospitality. The woman looked straight at Dylan and said, "So you liked my tamales last time, eh, señor, and you come back already?"

As the woman went to wait on another table, Rue had to stifle a laugh. "I think Rosita's got you confused with someone else," she whispered.

"Oh, I imagine she's just flirting," said Dylan, flashing his grin and studying the menu. "I forget—what's a flauta?"

The food was better than Rue remembered, or maybe it was just the company. Dylan could have pressed her with questions about Dawn, but he seemed to sense that what she needed most was a break from all that, and they talked mostly about the office back in San Francisco and the prospects for Dylan's interview the next day. If he got the job, it would mean a huge jump in salary, plus some hefty stock options, and of course a move to Texas. That led to a discussion of the relative merits of living in San Francisco and in Austin. Rue loved both cities, but she could see drawbacks to living in either place.

"In San Francisco you've got bone-chilling fog in the middle of August—that was the hardest thing for a Texan like me to ever get used to. And of course, a beautiful beach—where nobody can take a swim without a wet suit because the water's so damned cold. Gridlock traffic on the bridges . . . and road rage . . . all the usual big-city aggravations. And the real estate! Even after the dot-com bust, prices are unreal."

"And don't forget the earthquakes," said Dylan, biting into his flauta with a crunch.

"Well, Austin may not have earthquakes, but we do have tornadoes and hailstorms. And in the summer, the heat! Over a hundred degrees for days on end. You can get a blister from touching the hood of your car. And there's no public transit, so you have to drive everywhere, and all the shopping is at big-box stores and strip malls. Rush hour traffic is ridiculous! And real estate—housing was so cheap in Austin when I was a student, but now it's the most expensive in Texas. Used to be if you moved from the Bay Area to Austin you could trade in your two-bedroom bungalow for a mansion with a boat dock on Lake Travis. Now, maybe, you can trade a one-bedroom condo on Portrero Hill for a two-bedroom ranch house in Travis Heights, and fight traffic to get to the lake on weekends."

"Doesn't sound so bad."

Rue smiled. "It's not. Austin's a great place—if you can stand the culture shock."

"But it's cool, right?" He laughed. "I don't mean the weather. I mean, everybody says Austin is so hip."

"Sure it is. But drive thirty minutes out of Austin in any direction, and you're—well, you're here. In some place like Amethyst."

"What's wrong with that?"

She sighed. "Nothing. Unless you want to have a beer with your Mexican dinner. I don't know, I'm just not sure Texas is the right place for you, Dylan."

"You're just jealous."

"Of what?"

"Of my big fat job offer in Austin."

"Don't jinx yourself. You don't have the offer yet."

"But I will. And you're jealous. Because you'd love to move back to Texas. Admit it."

She knew he was just making light conversation, but his remarks suddenly stirred up strong, complicated feelings in her. She frowned and stared at the remains of the food on her plate.

"Rue! Hey, I'm sorry. I didn't mean to tease you." He put down his fork and reached across the table to grasp her hand. His touch felt good.

When they were finished with their meal, Dylan insisted on paying, since Glenn Computer was covering all his expenses for the trip. As they were leaving, Rosita opened the door for them.

"Everything was good, eh?"

"Very good," said Rue.

"And hey, which you like better, señor, my tamales last time, or my flautas?"

Dylan grinned. "Ask me next time, after I try your chalupas."

Rosita laughed.

As they were getting into the car, Rue smiled and shook her head. "She definitely has you mixed up with someone else."

Dylan just smiled.

19

Rue had never noticed before how dark it was in Amethyst on a moon-less night. The streetlights along Main Street were barely adequate, and after they turned onto a gravel road, taking a shortcut back to Gran's house, lights of any kind were few and far between. The houses along the road were simple wooden boxes with tin roofs, spaced well apart, with plots of grass or vegetable gardens or sometimes whole fields between them.

When Rue had first moved to California, one of the things that impressed her most was the giant scale of things—sweeping beaches, towering sea cliffs, hills that Texans would have called mountains, and especially the vegetation, the giant eucalyptus and redwood trees. Here in Texas, all the foliage was on a smaller scale—oak trees that seemed stunted compared to their California cousins, scrubby mesquite trees, small, shaggy junipers, prickly pears and yuccas and thickets and briars. But the vegetation was copious, nonetheless, and growing as it did, thick and low to the ground, it provided plentiful concealment to the small wildlife, the armadillos and raccoons and rabbits and rodents who shared the town with its human inhabitants. But what else might those tangles of ground cover conceal? Especially at night, with only scattered street-lights for illumination, Amethyst was honeycombed with patches of impenetrable darkness. Rue suddenly saw the town as a collection of little brick or wooden boxes shut up tight to keep out the cold in winter and the heat in summer. The pale light leaking from their drawn curtains was not nearly strong enough to bridge the gaps of darkness between them. Anything could be happening in those patches of darkness. Anything could be hidden among those tangled briars and thickets.

She shook her head, trying to dislodge such dark thoughts. She had never considered such things in Amethyst before, had never looked at the town and seen it as she was seeing it now. Sentiment had never clouded her vision; anytime she took a hard look at Amethyst she saw things she didn't like—pettiness, small-mindedness, smugness in the better parts of town, and simple ugliness in the poorer sections. But never before had she looked out at Amethyst from her car window and seen such darkness or felt such uneasiness. Something truly terrible was out there, and not far away. It was so close that she could probably see it despite the darkness, if only she knew where to look.

Suddenly the car was flooded with flashing red lights. Rue looked in the rearview mirror and saw the rotating cherry lights of a police car.

Dylan gave a start and looked over his shoulder. "What the fuck!" he muttered.

Rue raised an eyebrow, surprised. Dylan never talked like that. Even preschoolers said the F-word these days, but the harshest curse Dylan usually uttered was a "damn." As Rue slowed down and pulled over, she glanced at Dylan and saw a strange look in his eyes. Maybe it was just the weird glow of the flashing red lights that made him look so startled.

The lights went off. Looking into the side mirror, Rue saw a figure step out of the patrol car. Outlined by the faint glow of a distant streetlight, Goodbody's broad-shouldered silhouette was unmistakable.

Rue watched him approach. She lowered her window and heard his footsteps on the gravel. A moment later his face was in the window as he leaned over, resting one hand on the roof of her car. He touched the brim of his Stetson before he spoke.

"Evening, Rue."

"Good evening, Juss. Was I doing something wrong?"

"No, not at all. Hope I didn't startle you too much by flashing the lights."

"A little." Rue glanced at Dylan. Had he gone pale? His jaw was rigid and his mouth was a straight line. "Juss, this is Dylan Jeffries, a friend of mine from San Francisco."

"I'm Deputy Sheriff Juss Goodbody," said Juss, introducing himself but not bothering to tip his hat again. Dylan nodded, and the two men studied each other for a long moment. Rue looked from one to the other and sensed an almost palpable line of tension between them.

"What's up, Juss?" she said.

"I drove by your house earlier, meaning to drop in on you, but I saw that your car was gone. Saw another rental car parked there, a red Mitsubishi—I suppose that belongs to you, Mr. Jeffries?"

"That's right," said Dylan. His voice was curt.

Juss nodded. "Didn't want to disturb your grandmother if you weren't there, so I just drove on by. Just now I spotted your car and figured it might be best if I gave you a friendly flash to pull you over, so we could talk here, away from your grandmother's house. I appreciate that you want to keep her out of this as much as possible."

"Is this about the search?" said Rue.

"That's right."

Rue noted his frown. "Bad news?"

"No. But it's not exactly good news, either. Thing is, our search of that hillside didn't turn up a thing, and those fellas went over that ground like a pack of bloodhounds. I can't explain it. I don't doubt that you saw what you saw, but we didn't find one shred of evidence to indicate that anybody had been up on that hill lately."

Rue bit her lip. "And the rest of the property?"

"I looked in all the outbuildings—all those barns and sheds and lean-tos, even that overgrown chicken coop. I did a thorough search of the house, including the storm cellar and the attic. And I crisscrossed the entire property twice, looking for signs of anything unusual."

"And?"

He shook his head. "The only indications of any suspicious activity were a few spent rifle shells—and we already suspected that somebody's been hunting over there without permission. And of course the traps, which presumably were set by your father."

"Have you spoken to him yet?"

"Not yet. He's not answering his phone. I asked an old buddy of mine on the Corpus police force to have a look, and he tells me your father's place there appears to be shut up tight. Neighbors don't know whether he's out of town or not. I'll keep trying until I reach him." Goodbody lowered his eyes. The brim of his hat hid his face in deep shadow. "I don't know which is worse at this point, finding that poor girl's body—or not finding it."

Rue sighed heavily. "Juss, I saw her. I saw Dawn."

"I know you did. And if she *is* dead, believe me, I want to find her as soon as possible."

"But there's no question that she's dead," said Rue quietly, staring at her clenched knuckles on the steering wheel. "I know what I saw."

He sighed. "Then it's my job to find her. And that's what I intend to do. I'll just have to keep looking." He drew closer, near enough for Rue to smell his distinctive cologne, and he touched her lightly on the shoulder. Did Dylan see? He seemed to shift uneasily in the passenger seat. Rue felt a powerful impulse to reach up and touch Juss's hand on her shoulder, but instead she kept her fingers on the steering wheel.

"Thanks for telling me, Juss. And thanks for doing it where Gran wouldn't overhear. I appreciate that."

Goodbody's fingers tightened on her shoulder. "One other thing, Rue. Even though I didn't find anything, I still don't want you to go wandering over on your father's property. I set off the traps I came across, but I may have missed some. And maybe—maybe I missed something else. I want you to stay clear of the place until all this is over. Okay?"

"I understand." Even with Dylan watching, her urge to reach up and touch the hand on her shoulder was irresistible. She started to do so, but at the same moment Goodbody drew back and pulled his hand away. Rue felt a stab of disappointment.

"I still think the best thing would be for you to head to Austin, Rue, as soon as you can."

Rue nodded. "I'll think about it."

"And I apologize again if flashing my lights gave you a bit of a start." He glanced past Rue at Dylan, who gazed back at him with a cold stare.

Goodbody tipped his hat and turned away. Rue watched him in the side mirror. He got back into his patrol car and started the engine, then pulled slowly past them, waving as he did so.

Beside her, Dylan let out a noise of disgust. "What a pompous jerk!"

"Juss Goodbody?"

"That *can't* be his real name."

Rue smiled. "You don't know the half of it—literally. Juss is short for Justice."

"Justice Goodbody?" Dylan grunted and shook his head. "What a walking, talking stereotype of a small-town Texas lawman, except he hasn't got a big beer gut. Yet."

"No, the one with the beer gut is Horace Boatwright, the sheriff. His gut is big enough for both of them."

"That attitude!" Dylan snorted. Rue had never seen him so agitated. "Flashing his lights to pull us over, just so he could chat you up."

Rue pursed her lips. "It wasn't just a chat, Dylan. I've been waiting to hear from him. I'd have been upset if he *hadn't* made an effort to fill me in on what happened today."

"Not much, by the sound of it. What sort of amateurs are in charge of this town? You found a dead girl's body, and the best they can do is to poke around and then shrug and say, 'Aw shucks! Sorry, lady, but I don't see nothin.'"

Rue gritted her teeth. "You know, Dylan, there's no call for you to make fun of the way people talk here. This *is* my hometown."

He didn't apologize, which surprised her, but crossed his arms and stared at the dark patch of road ahead. The taillights of Goodbody's patrol car were still visible for a moment in the distance, then he made a turn and disappeared. Rue started the engine and pulled back onto the gravel road.

"What was that look on your face when he flashed his lights?" she said. "I thought you were about to jump out of your skin." As soon as the words were out, she knew she had no business talking to Dylan that way, grilling him. But her anger was getting the better of her. Who was she angry at? Not Dylan. Not Goodbody or the sheriff, for that matter. She was angry at the situation, at her own frustration and the confused feelings that were stirring in her.

"I'd say that's a normal reaction when some power-happy cop flashes his lights at you in the middle of nowhere," said Dylan.

No, Rue thought, *it was more than that . . .*

Dylan seemed to sense her doubt. He sighed. "Okay, I guess maybe I was a bit rattled, because . . ." His voice trailed off. "If I tell you something, will you promise not to ever repeat it?"

His tone was suddenly so serious that it gave her a shiver. "Of course," she said quietly. "What is it, Dylan?"

"When I was younger—damn, this is hard to talk about! When I was sixteen, back in Minneapolis, I did something really, really stupid. A buddy and I stole a car and we went joyriding. I don't know what we were thinking. We weren't even drunk or stoned, we just did it for a thrill. I wasn't driving, he was, but I was just as guilty, because it was my idea. I still remember the instant the red lights started flashing behind us—the car lit up all red inside, just like tonight. The cop was right on our tail, there was no way we were going to outrun him, but there's a kind of chase instinct that takes over. It's like, every mile per hour you go up, your IQ goes down a notch. First we had one police car chasing us, then two. We drove a hundred miles an hour until we ran out of gas, somewhere on the other side of Saint Paul." Dylan fidgeted, not looking at her. "I guess the cops were pretty wired by that point. It was dark. We were in the middle of nowhere, on a country road. No houses around. No witnesses. They pulled us out of the car and they beat the shit out of us."

"Dylan, that's awful. Were you badly hurt?"

He shrugged. "Bruises and a black eye. No broken bones. I remember one of the cops twisting my arm behind my back and pounding my head against a tire. Maybe that's part of their training, ways to knock a guy around without actually cracking his head open. But the worst thing was when one of the cops pulled out his gun. He actually fired it, right over my head. Scared the shit out of me. And then he pistol-whipped me with it. Just once, across the face. You can still see the scar across my cheekbone if the light hits it just right."

"Dylan . . ." Rue didn't know what to say.

"My parents were completely freaked out. On the one hand, the cops beat up their little boy. On the other hand, their son was a car thief. It was a big mess—lawyers and court appearances and stories in the newspapers. At least they never used my name, since I was a minor. It seemed to drag on forever, and it cost my dad a fortune. I still feel guilty about that, even though I eventually paid him back. I don't know who took it harder, him or my mom. When it was all over, the cops got off and so did I. But ever since, I don't even step in a crosswalk against the light. And I hate cops. Can't help it. Especially when I see those red lights flashing." He shook his head. "Jesus, Rue, I can't believe I'm telling you all this."

Rue reached over and put her hand on his. He laced his fingers between hers and smiled wanly. "Now you know my deepest, darkest secret." He let out a long sigh. "So what's going on between you and the deputy?"

"Me and Juss? Nothing . . ."

"Are you sure about that?"

Rue didn't answer. He gripped her hand more tightly, then released it so that she could return it to the steering wheel. They crossed the highway and turned onto the drive to Gran's house.

"Well, there is *one* thing the deputy said that makes sense," said Dylan.

"What's that?"

"You should leave Amethyst. You're not safe here, Rue."

20

When they reached Gran's house, there was another car in the driveway, parked behind Dylan's red Mitsubishi. It was a dinged, funky-looking little Toyota.

For a moment Rue thought the car was empty. Then a bump in the drive caused her headlights to illuminate the interior, and she saw that someone was sitting in the driver's seat. The driver turned around. For just an instant, captured by the headlights, she saw the face of Dwayne Frady, wide-eyed and drained of all color by the glaring white light.

"Someone you know?" said Dylan.

"Yes. Dawn's brother."

Rue pulled past the car and parked alongside Dylan's rental. In her side mirror she saw Dwayne get out of his car. He was wearing his black-and-orange letterman's jacket. He hugged himself and shivered as he walked toward her car. How long had he been sitting there, waiting for her to show up?

Rue opened her door. Before she was halfway out of the car Dwayne was hovering over her. There was a wild look in his eyes.

"You saw her!" he said. "Is that right? Did you see her? That's what everybody says. Did you see her, or not?"

She was taken aback by the sheer intensity of the way he loomed over her, shifting nervously from foot to foot, staring at her, hugging himself, thrusting his face too close to hers.

Dylan stepped out of the car and circled around. "Excuse me, buddy," he said, walking up beside Rue.

"Who's he?" said Dwayne. The two of them sized each other up.

"A friend of mine from San Francisco. Dylan, this is Dwayne Frady—"

"Did you see her, or not?" Dwayne's voice went high on the last word, breaking like an adolescent's.

"Dwayne, calm down, okay?" Rue laid her hand on one of his arms. "Let's go inside where it's warm."

He shook off her hand. "I don't want to go inside!"

"Look, buddy, calm down." Dylan stepped between Rue and Dwayne.

Dwayne backed away. He sniffled and wiped his nose against the wristband of his jacket. By the pale white light from the porch Rue could see that his eyes were red and puffy.

"What did you hear, Dwayne? Who told you?" she said quietly.

"Everybody! At lunch, everybody at school was talking about it. They say you saw Dawn somewhere in those fields over there, but then you couldn't find her again. Like either she must have got up and walked away, or else—" He swallowed hard. "They say a bunch of men searched the place where you saw her, but they couldn't find her. Where did you see her? How did she—what did she—"

"Christ!" muttered Dylan, turning to Rue. "Shouldn't it be the sheriff's job to talk to the family? This isn't your responsibility, Rue."

Rue agreed, but at that moment Dwayne Frady was standing in front of her, shivering from the cold and trembling with agitation.

"Dwayne," she said, "surely the sheriff or the deputy spoke to your mother, either last night or today."

"She's out of town. She drove to Temple last night, to Scott and White Hospital, to see some specialist. She had to go, the appointment was scheduled weeks ago. She's not back yet. If the sheriff tried to get hold of her at the house, she wasn't there."

Dylan shook his head. "What a mess."

"Oh, Dwayne." Rue was at a loss. How could she possibly describe to him what she had seen? "Surely you didn't stay at school today, with everybody talking about it?"

"Where else could I go?" His voice broke again. He was close to tears. "I just got off football practice an hour ago."

Rue wanted to scream. Only in Texas would a boy feel compelled to do his duty to the football team when something like this was going on in his life. Only in Texas would a coach have allowed it.

"Listen," she said. "You've got to come inside. It's too cold out here. Have you eaten?"

"No."

"Come inside, Dwayne."

"No! Just tell me what you saw."

"Dwayne, I—"

"She was dead, wasn't she?" Suddenly his voice lost its hysterical edge. The words were as cold as the air biting at Rue's ears.

She bowed her head, unable to look him in the eye. She felt Dylan's hand on her shoulder, offering comfort and support. But who was going to comfort Dwayne?

"Dwayne, I'm so sorry."

A noise came out of Dwayne, a sound like nothing Rue had ever heard before. It erupted from his throat, shattered the frozen air, and then was sucked back into his lungs—a stillborn scream of despair.

"Show me!" he wailed. "Show me where you found her!"

"Oh, Dwayne! It's too dark. It's too cold. There's no way we can go tramping across those fields right now. There's no point."

"But I want to see it! I have to see the place where you found her!"

"Tomorrow, Dwayne. Skip school tomorrow and come over here first thing. We'll go over together."

"No, *now!*" he shouted.

"Hey!" said Dylan. "Calm down, buddy. You've got no business yelling at Rue."

Dwayne swallowed hard. He clamped his jaw. A jet of steam shot out of his nostrils into the frigid air.

"Then come here," he said, his voice no longer hysterical, but still not quite under control. "Come here, I want to show you something." He headed back toward his car. When Rue didn't follow, he turned back, reached past Dylan, seized Rue by the wrist, and pulled her after him.

"Hey, buddy, watch it!" Dylan said, but he was left behind as Rue hurried to catch up with Dwayne, making no effort to resist him. They reached the little Toyota. Dwayne let go of her wrist and opened the door. He reached under the driver's seat.

"Jesus Christ!" Dylan gave a start and jumped back.

Rue put her hands to her mouth. "Dwayne, where did you get that thing?"

It was a pistol. Rue had no idea of the make or caliber, but the long barrel gleamed dully, catching the glow of the porch light. Dwayne held it in his right hand, pointing the barrel straight up. "It's my mom's," he said.

"What on earth are you doing with it?" She took her eyes from the gun and looked over her shoulder at Dylan, who remained behind her, his face drained of color and his eyes wide.

"Don't worry, she has another one," said Dwayne. "She took it with her to Temple. She says a woman alone has to have a gun these days."

"For God's sake, put that thing away," said Rue. "Surely your mother doesn't know you're driving around town with a gun in your car."

"I don't care whether she knows or not. This is going with me everywhere until I find out what happened to Dawn. And when I do . . ."

He raised his arm and pointed the gun straight up. Rue realized he was going to fire. She started to reach for his arm, then flinched and drew back. At the same time Dwayne lowered his arm, keeping his elbow straight, and clasped the gun with both hands. He pointed it past Rue and Dylan, who scrambled back, and aimed it into the dark fields of the Dunwitty property.

"No!" Rue cried, but her voice was drowned out by the sudden crack of the pistol shot.

An instant later, Rue heard the sound of the bullet striking something solid over on the Dunwitty land, a tree trunk or the side of a shed. A series of echoes followed, carried on the cold, crisp air. They seemed to come from everywhere and then abruptly died away, leaving behind utter silence.

Dwayne lowered the gun. The look on his face was a mixture of pain and anger and confusion. "That's what I'm going to do," he said, his voice eerily quiet. "When they find out who did it—when they catch the motherfucker—that's what I'm going to do."

He stepped into his Toyota and slammed the door. Before Rue could stop him he backed recklessly out of the driveway, making the engine roar and going so fast that he almost went into the shallow drainage ditch. Where the drive met the road he executed a sharp turn and peeled out. A moment later he was out of sight.

Rue stood in the cold, hugging herself. Suddenly she felt Dylan's hand on her shoulder, then his arm encircling her and his body next to hers. She leaned against him. As he tightened his arm around her, she realized that she was shaking. Neither of them spoke for a long moment, then Dylan said, "Let's get you out of the cold."

Gran wasn't in the living room. Had she gone to bed already? The wall clock indicated it was only eight, but it seemed to Rue that it had to be later than that. She felt utterly exhausted.

Rue looked in the kitchen. Gran was at the table in her wheelchair, her hands holding an open library book, but her head was slightly bowed and her eyes were shut. She was dozing.

Thank goodness, Rue thought. She had been worried that the shouting and the gunshot might have frightened Gran, but she hadn't heard any of it. As Rue stepped into the room, Gran stirred and opened her eyes. She seemed confused for a moment, then looked at Rue and smiled. There was nothing in the world as sweet as Gran's smile, Rue thought. So loving, like a mother's, but also so utterly innocent and trusting, like a child's.

Gran cleared her throat. "How was your dinner, honey?"

"It was good."

"Did you see anybody you know?"

Rue hesitated. "Not at the restaurant."

"Where's your friend?"

Dylan stepped into the room. "Here I am, Mrs. Lee."

Gran smiled. "Well, what do you think of Amethyst, Texas?"

"It's a pretty little town."

"Dylan's birthstone is amethyst," said Rue, to make conversation. Her heartbeat had finally slowed to normal and she was able to take a deep breath.

"Is that right? When's your birthday?" said Gran.

"April seventeenth," said Dylan.

Gran frowned. "But amethyst is the birthstone for February."

Dylan looked blank. "I don't think so."

"Oh, I may look old and addled, but there's a few things I know for sure, and that's one of 'em. Anybody who grows up in Amethyst knows that amethyst is the birthstone for February. Isn't that so, Rue?"

Now it was Rue's turn to frown. "I don't know if it's written in stone, so to speak."

"Well, I know when my birthday is, and I'm pretty sure about my birthstone," said Dylan. "But hey, I could be wrong. It wouldn't be the first time."

Gran laughed. "Where are you from originally?"

"Now, *that* I can tell you for sure. Minneapolis, Minnesota."

Gran nodded as if the city's name actually meant something to her, though Rue knew Gran had never been outside of Texas.

Rue sat at the table and touched Gran's wrist. Gran put aside her book and squeezed Rue's hand. She was always quick to show affection.

"If it's okay with you, Gran, Dylan is going to spend the night here. In the spare room. I thought, with everything that's going on—"

"Well, of course it's all right! That bed's already made, with clean sheets on it. I made sure Reg's wife made it before they left after Thanksgiving."

"Thanks, Mrs. Lee. I appreciate your hospitality." Dylan smiled. Rue noticed that the color had returned to his face. Poor Dylan, thought Rue. This had become his night for confronting old demons, with the deputy flashing his cherry lights and Dwayne brandishing his pistol. Surely he hadn't anticipated this much excitement from a side trip to a little Texas town. Should Rue have told him beforehand about Dawn, and warned him not to come? Perhaps, but at that moment, in the warm kitchen with Gran, it felt right to have him in the house.

"Were you asleep when we came in?" said Rue.

Gran smiled sheepishly. "Maybe I was dozing."

"Then it must be time for bed."

Gran nodded. "You go to bed, too, honey. You need your rest. You look tired."

Gran said good night and wheeled her chair down the hallway to her room. Dylan and Rue stepped into the living room and collapsed side by side onto the sofa.

"You see?" said Dylan. "No problem. I think your grandmother likes having me here."

"I think you're right." Rue smiled. "I'm glad you're here, too, Dylan. Thanks for coming."

They both sighed and sank deeper into the sofa. Rue felt the warmth of his thigh press gently against her own.

"We should report that kid to the sheriff," Dylan said. "Or to that deputy friend of yours."

"Report Dwayne?"

"He's out of control, Rue."

She shook her head. "I don't want to get Dwayne into trouble. With all that he's going through right now—"

"Hey, I feel as sorry for him as you do. And I realize the attitude about guns is a little different down here in Texas."

"That's not the point, Dylan."

"But it *is* the point. He's going to hurt somebody with that gun. Maybe himself."

Rue raised an eyebrow. "You don't think he's suicidal, do you?"

"Who knows? Dawn was his twin sister, right? Twins are usually really close, aren't they, in some special way? That's got to make it even worse for him. And from what he said, his mother has some kind of health problem, and right now she's out of town. He's just a teenager. How's he supposed to cope with all this? Plus . . . I suspect he has even more on his plate."

Rue frowned. "What do you mean?"

"Well, I mean . . . who knew?" Dylan shrugged.

"Knew what?"

"That there were gay teenagers in Amethyst? But I guess gay people come from everywhere."

Rue wrinkled her brow. "What are you talking about? His *earring*? That doesn't mean anything. All the kids pierce and tattoo themselves these days, and dye their hair. Even in Amethyst. Even football players."

"No, it's not the earring."

"Then what?"

Dylan sighed. "Rue, I haven't been a straight man living in San Francisco for the last five years without learning to tell when a gay guy is checking me out—and Dwayne was checking me out."

"What! When? He hardly even noticed you. He was talking about Dawn the whole time, mostly to me, or staring out at those fields."

"Not the whole time. When he first looked at me, he gave me the look."

"'The look'?"

"Yeah."

"Oh, Dylan. Dylan Jeffries! I had no idea you were so vain." Rue laughed, but she also rearranged herself on the sofa so that her thigh was no longer touching his.

"Vanity has nothing to do with it," he said.

"Oh, I think it might."

Dylan sighed. "Dwayne gave me . . . the look. Any man knows it when he gets it. Or when he gives it, for that matter. I only mentioned it because it must be hard for him already, living in a town like this, and having a secret like that. And with everything else that's happening right now . . ."

Rue shook her head. She picked up one of the pillows from the sofa and playfully hit Dylan with it. It was the right thing to do. Dylan laughed and so did she.

155

She yawned. "I don't know about you, but I'm exhausted. And you've got to get up bright and early tomorrow and drive to Austin for that interview. We'd both better go to bed."

"Okay." He looked at her steadily, no longer smiling. In his eyes she saw an invitation, not pressing, not lascivious, but open to the possibility that something might happen in the next moment, the next heartbeat. Rue hit him with the pillow again and got to her feet.

"The bathroom's down the hall. Don't worry about waking Gran. She sleeps like a rock. Me too, usually, when I'm in this house. There's an electric blanket on your bed, and an alarm clock on the night table."

Dylan nodded. "I'll just get some things from my car. Kiss?"

Rue bent down and put her lips to his. The contact felt good, but she was glad that Dylan didn't try to turn it into something more. She drew back, smiled, and headed toward her room.

"Rue?"

She turned back.

Dylan had spotted Justice Goodbody's card by the phone. He picked it up and looked at the handwritten number on the back. "Are you going to call the deputy? Somebody needs to take that gun away from Dwayne."

Rue sighed. "Maybe tomorrow. Good night, Dylan." She went into her room and shut the door.

21

Rue tossed and turned. Her mind refused to shut down. Her thoughts kept circling. As soon as she managed to banish one image from her mind, another took its place. The sight of Dawn in the cistern was replaced by the anguish on Dwayne's face when he pulled the trigger. Trying to push both images from her mind, she found herself thinking about her mother—not pleasant thoughts, but memories of her mother's final, agonizing months.

At last she sat upright and turned on the bedside lamp. She got up and searched her suitcase for the medicine bottle that contained her sleeping pills. She had obtained the prescription when her mother was dying. Since then she had used the pills only rarely. She disliked the idea of needing a drug to get herself to sleep. But tonight there seemed to be no other way to make sleep come.

She got into bed and turned off the light. As the medication kicked in, her free-floating thoughts abruptly took an erotic turn. It was all the tension built up inside her, she thought. She began with a fantasy of stealing into Dylan's bedroom and sliding naked and warm beneath his blanket. She had never had sex in this house. On the rare occasions she had brought a boyfriend home from college to meet her mother, they always had slept in separate beds. There would be something delicious about having sex for the first time in the house where she grew up, and also having sex for the first time with Dylan . . .

But the fantasy refused to stay focused. In Dylan's place she suddenly found herself imagining that it was Juss Goodbody in the next room, naked beneath the sheets, awake and restless, impatiently waiting for her, his body hard and warm, his sex stiff and eager. When she tried to imagine Dylan without his clothes, no clear image formed in her head, but an image of Juss naked stole into her mind without effort, as clearly as if she had seen him naked already. His body was the perfectly chiseled body you saw modeling underwear in magazine ads . . .

The sleeping pill jumbled her thoughts and opened a Pandora's box in her head. Suddenly her simple erotic scenarios with Dylan and Juss were invaded by terrible images from *The Corpus Corpses*. Rue thought of Brandy Littleton, the girl who had been bound spread-eagled and naked on a set of rusty box springs with a Texas flag stuffed into her mouth, her helpless terror a source of amusement for the man who had abducted her . . .

The book had poisoned her mind, Rue thought, as she struggled against the images. But as her fantasies deepened into dreams beyond her control, her excitement only grew, magnified by an exquisite terror more forbidden than any waking daydream she ever would have allowed herself.

Gradually, groggily, Rue was drawn back to consciousness. It was a muffled, distant voice that pulled her back. At first it seemed to be a voice from a dream—a bad dream, because there was something about the voice that made her uneasy, even frightened. But as Rue slowly woke, she realized the voice was coming from somewhere in the house.

She opened her eyes and lay still, listening. Above the sound of her own heartbeat, she could barely hear the voice. It was a man's voice, but whose? And what was he saying? Rue couldn't make out any words, but something about the voice carried a bad association in her mind.

It seemed to be coming from the living room. Was Dylan still up? It wasn't Dylan's voice, of that Rue was sure. She glanced at the bedside clock and saw that it was after midnight.

She got out of bed, pulled on some sweatpants and a pullover, and stepped into house shoes. She stepped to the bedroom door and quietly opened it, peering out toward the living room. No lamps were on, but the room was lit by a cold, flickering light. The voice was coming from the television.

She stepped into the living room and saw that Dylan was lying on the sofa, stripped down to a T-shirt with a blanket pulled over him. His eyes were shut and he was gently snoring. He must have fallen asleep watching the television with the volume turned very low.

In the unlit room the glare from the television hurt Rue's eyes and made her squint, but she instantly recognized the bland features and snow white hair of the TV evangelist who called himself Brother Zack. As before, he was standing in front of rose-covered lattices, clutching a scrap of paper in one hand—another letter from a lost soul in torment?—and gesticulating with the other hand. He raised his eyebrows and stared at the camera with a fierce gleam in his wide-open eyes. The volume was turned so low that even standing in front of the TV, Rue had to strain to hear him. "Pray for his soul, brothers and sisters! Pray for an end to his torment, and the torment he inflicts on the innocent, and always remember that sin is a disease and any one of us could fall prey to it. You—yes, *you*—could find yourself outcast from the body of Christ just like this poor, fallen sinner."

Rue looked for the remote and spotted it in Dylan's hand. He must have been channel surfing when he fell asleep. Rue studied his face by the flickering television light. Asleep, he looked even more boyish than usual. Rue thought of the story he had told her about the trouble he got into when he was a teenager in Minneapolis. He looked hardly older than a teenager now. She reached down and brushed an unruly lock of hair from his forehead. Dylan stirred slightly but didn't wake. He clutched the remote control tightly and hugged it to his chest.

Rue sighed and stepped to the TV, but as she reached to press the Off button she was distracted by a noise from outside. It was the sound of a car coming up the driveway in front of the house. Rue heard the low purring of an engine and the crunching sound of tires rolling very slowly over gravel, more slowly than anyone would normally drive. The tires slowed even more, then came to a halt, and the car engine died. All was silent again except for the murmur of the television, Dylan's gentle snoring, and the pounding of Rue's heart in her chest.

She stepped to the front door and peered out the diamond pane, then felt a flood of relief when she saw Juss Goodbody's patrol car parked behind Dylan's red Mitsubishi. His headlights were off and Rue could see him only as a deep shadow among other shadows inside the car. He seemed to be just sitting behind the wheel, not moving.

Stepping quietly, Rue hurried back to her bedroom and slipped on a long cashmere coat that had belonged to her mother. She went back to the living room, and careful not to wake Dylan, she opened the door and stepped onto the porch.

She stepped onto the walk, clutching the coat lapels beneath her chin. The driver's door opened and Juss stepped out of the patrol car. His familiar, broad-shouldered silhouette gave her a sense of comfort even as it stirred more unsettling feelings in her. His face was entirely in shadow beneath the brim of his Stetson. He moved toward her, taking long strides. There was such a sense of purpose and resolution in his gait that Rue suddenly expected him not to stop until his arms were around her and his body was pressed against hers. At the last moment he seemed to catch himself and he stopped short, not quite touching her but so close that Rue could smell his cologne and feel the warmth of his breath against her forehead.

Rue tensed, fearing he had something terrible to tell her. Juss seemed to read her thoughts. His voice was hardly more than a whisper. "Nothing's wrong, Rue. I was just out driving on patrol, and I thought I'd . . . I just wanted to check on you. Make sure everything's all right."

"We're fine, Juss. Everyone's asleep. I'd ask you inside, except . . ."

"That's okay. I know it's late. I just thought I'd pull into the drive and sit here for a while, make sure everything looked okay. I didn't expect you'd still be up; didn't think I'd actually see you. But getting to see your face one more time tonight is just a bonus, I guess." Despite the shadow that covered his face, Rue could see that he smiled, but the smile faded and his voice turned serious again. "But seeing as you are up, there is something I need to say to you."

"What, Juss?"

"I wanted to apologize again if I gave you a start tonight. When I flashed my lights at you and pulled you over, I mean. It wasn't exactly professional of me. I acted on impulse. That was stupid."

"I don't understand."

"I recognized your car and I saw that you were driving. Then I saw there was a man in the passenger seat, and . . . I got a cold feeling in the pit of my stomach."

"But it was only Dylan."

"I didn't know that. For all I knew, it could have been. . . . hell, I don't even want to say it out loud."

Rue drew a breath and nodded. "I think I understand. You thought it might have been a stranger in the car with me. The same man who. . . ."

Juss nodded. "I had this flash of . . . panic, I guess. I felt kind of shaky when I walked up to your window. Did it show?"

"Not at all."

"Not shaky because I was afraid," he added hastily, as if she might think otherwise. "But because . . . all of a sudden I was so worried about you. All of a sudden I realized . . ."

"Realized what, Juss?"

He didn't answer immediately. "Since I moved here, I haven't exactly . . ." He shook his head. "I guess I've always been kind of a loner. Back in Corpus, it didn't matter so much. I knew lots of people at work, always had plenty of work to keep me busy. But ever since I moved to Amethyst, I've been kind of lonely. I haven't really connected with anybody here yet. Hell, I can't think of the last time I felt a—a spark, if you know what I mean. I'd almost forgotten what that felt like, until . . ."

"Until when, Juss?"

"Until the other night at the ball game, when I looked up and saw you in the stands. Was I just imagining it? Or did you feel it, too?"

Rue smiled and lowered her eyes. "I'm not sure what I felt. But I do remember that moment."

"And then, the other day, when I came over here to respond to that call from Bertha, it ended up the call had come from you. What were the chances of that happening, that I'd end up seeing you again? You don't even live here. You might have come and gone and I'd never have even laid eyes on you, but instead I saw you at the game, and then. . . . I know it's awful of me, trying to find something good in all this. That was a terrible thing for you, finding Dawn's body like that. But because of that, I saw you again. And talking to you that day only made me more certain that there was some kind of spark between us. Only it's crazy, because you *don't* live here. I shouldn't be telling you any of this, because there's no point. Pretty soon you'll head back to San Francisco, and it won't matter whether that spark I felt is real or not."

Rue looked into his eyes, so dark beneath the brim of his hat that she could barely make them out. "You're the one who keeps telling me I should leave Amethyst, Juss."

"Do you think I like telling you that? It's the exact opposite of what I want to say. But a part of me thinks, What if Rue stays . . . one day too long? What if she stays and something awful happens? I could never live with that. I'd go out of my mind!"

His sudden vehemence startled her. "Juss, don't talk like that."

"You don't understand. Back in Corpus . . ."

Rue nodded. "Maybe I do understand. I read some of that book today—the one about the murders. You were there when they found one of the girls."

He nodded. "Brandy Littleton."

"And wasn't one of the girls a neighbor of yours?"

"Trina," he said. "Trina Schaeffer. She was the last."

"The book said you talked with her not long before she disappeared. About the murders."

He nodded.

"You warned her about the danger."

Juss bit his lip and shook his head. "No. I mean, yes, I told her to be careful and watch out for herself. But I also told her . . ." He took a deep breath and threw back his head. For a brief moment, by starlight, Rue thought she saw the glint of tears in his eyes. "I told Trina that she didn't really have anything to worry about, because she didn't fit the profile. Most of the other girls had long blond hair, like Brandy, but Trina had short brown hair. Her mother had told me that Trina had practically stopped eating, and was having nightmares so bad she couldn't sleep. I just wanted to set her mind at rest a bit." He lowered his eyes. "I looked Trina in the eye and I told her she had nothing to worry about. I told her mother the same thing. And a few days later, Trina disappeared, and her mother never saw her alive again."

Rue drew a deep, cold breath and clutched the coat lapels more tightly beneath her chin. "Juss, I'm sorry. I had no idea."

He was silent for a long moment. "So that's why I sort of panicked tonight, when I saw someone in the car with you. And that's why I keep telling you to leave town—even though I wish you could stay."

Rue felt her face flush hot, even while the rest of her shivered.

"What am I thinking, keeping you out here in the cold?" said Juss. "You must be freezing." He stepped forward, and the next moment Rue felt his arms around her. As her shivering subsided, she lowered her arms and returned his embrace. He felt just as she had imagined he would, big and strong and solid. Before she knew what was happening, his mouth was on hers.

The kiss was long and deep and took her breath away. When it was over, his lips were still touching hers, brushing against her as he murmured her name.

"Rue! You don't know how badly I've been wanting to do that."

He was taller than she was, but during the kiss her forehead had bumped the brim of his Stetson and pushed it back a bit from his face. She looked up and smiled. "Don't you ever take that thing off?"

The grin on his face was a relief to see, after the pain she had seen there only moments before. "The hat comes off for only one thing," he said.

"To take a bath?" she ventured.

Steven Saylor

He shook his head. "Oh, Rue! Damn, I knew that spark was real. If only . . ."

"What?"

"Just a crazy idea. I wish I could take you home with me right now."

"I'm not dressed."

"Doesn't matter. We could take the patrol car, be at my place in five minutes."

She raised an eyebrow. "What would my grandmother think?"

"I'd have you back before she wakes up."

She looked into his eyes. "You're serious, aren't you?"

He gazed steadily back at her. "Maybe."

For just an instant, Rue allowed herself to be tempted by the idea, and she felt a thrill of excitement. Then she looked over her shoulder, back toward the front door. Almost without thinking, she began to extricate herself from his embrace. She frowned. "I'm sorry, Juss. This probably isn't a good idea. Not here. Not now."

"It's not because of your grandmother, is it? It's because *he's* here."

"Maybe. I don't know."

He sighed. "I've offended you, haven't I? I didn't mean to imply that you were the sort of woman—"

"No, Juss, it isn't that. It's a lot of things. It's all . . . so complicated." She stepped back and hugged herself.

"You're starting to shiver again, Rue."

"I should go inside."

He nodded. The two of them stood facing each other for such a long moment that Rue felt obliged to speak again. "It was good of you to come by—to check up on us, I mean."

"It was nothing."

"And I'm glad you told me . . . what you told me."

He merely nodded.

She opened her mouth to speak again, but Juss turned away and walked quickly to his car, not looking back. He started the engine and slowly backed out of the driveway, leaving as quietly as he had arrived.

Back in the living room, Dylan was still fast asleep, but the remote had slipped from his hand and fallen to the carpet. Rue picked it up and aimed it at the television. Brother Zack was still clutching the letter. "God shall cast the sinner into the flames of hell, never to see His face again!" Rue heard him say. She took grim satisfaction in pressing the button and sending Brother Zack's image to oblivion.

In the darkness, she navigated her way back to her bedroom, stripped off the coat and the things she was wearing underneath, and slipped back into bed. She thought she would be up for the rest of the night, tossing and turning, but she fell into a deep sleep almost instantly.

22

The smell of frying bacon woke her.

Dylan was already up and showered and dressed, sitting at the kitchen table with Gran. Rue excused herself to wash her face, and was surprised to see in the bathroom mirror that she looked quite rested. She brushed her teeth, threw on some clothes, and joined Gran and Dylan in the kitchen.

"Aren't you running late?" asked Rue.

Dylan looked at his watch. "No. Got plenty of time. Especially for a breakfast as good as this." He smiled at Gran, who smiled shyly back. "Listen, I've been thinking. Are you coming to Austin today?"

Rue hesitated for a moment, then shook her head. "I just don't see how I can leave right now."

Dylan nodded. "Then I'd like to come back and stay here again tonight."

"Well . . ." Rue felt torn. A part of her wanted Dylan to be there, but another part of her wondered what might happen if Dylan wasn't there and Juss came to call on her again. In her confusion, she looked to Gran, as if the decision rested with her.

"I don't see why not," said Gran. "But tonight you'll have to let me cook you dinner, instead of eating out."

"That's a deal," said Dylan.

"Are you sure, Dylan?" said Rue. "What if they want to take you out for drinks or dinner after your interview?"

Dylan smiled. "They're not that sort of crowd. All business, no play."

"And all that driving."

"It's no problem."

"What about your return flight to San Francisco?"

"They sprang for a full-fare ticket. I can take any flight I want. Really, it's no problem."

"Okay, then. We'll expect you for dinner," said Rue, covering her uncertainty with a smile.

Excited by the prospect of cooking for two guests, Gran made a shopping list right away. Rue cleared the table, then stepped into the living room. Dylan followed her. "If you want to go shopping right now, I'll go with you."

"Are you sure you have time?" said Rue.

He looked at his watch. "Positive."

"Only—what if Dwayne Frady comes by?"

"I doubt if he will, Rue."

"He wanted to see the cistern. I told him to come back this morning."

"After the way he left here last night, I don't think he'll be showing his face this morning. Come on, let's go shopping. It'll take your mind off things."

Rue poked her head into the kitchen to say good-bye to Gran, then followed Dylan onto the porch. He looked at the Dunwitty fields and frowned. "And Rue, while I'm gone today, I think you should take the deputy's advice. Don't go wandering over on your father's property."

Rue looked toward the fields. By the bright morning light it suddenly seemed impossible that she had actually seen Dawn in the cistern. The memory began to seem strangely unreal. No wonder the sheriff had doubted her. "What if Dwayne *does* show up, and he wants me to show him the place where I saw Dawn?"

"Don't do it, Rue. Don't go over there. *Especially* not with Dwayne. You saw how crazy he got last night."

Rue sighed. "I guess you're right."

"You know I am. If Dwayne needs to go over there, let the sheriff or the deputy take him. Surely they're competent to do at least that much." He pulled out his keys. "Let's take my car. After we do the shopping, I'll swing back here to drop you off, and then head for Austin."

Driving through town, Rue again felt the sensation she had when looking at the fields, that the crisis over Dawn was something she had only imagined, that it couldn't really be happening. The winter light was too bright, the town was too sleepy, the people on the sidewalks were too ordinary. The town that had seemed so uncharacteristically menacing the night before, with its pockets of impenetrable darkness between lonely houses, was its placid, prosaic self again.

But when they pulled into the parking lot at Schneider's, Rue's eyes went immediately to the handwritten sign in the window, and she felt a shiver. HAVE YOU SEEN DAWN? the sign asked.

Yes, she thought. *Yes, I have.*

They got out of the car and walked toward the entrance. Dylan noticed the placard and stopped for a moment to study the picture of Dawn, but neither of them spoke. Rue pulled Gran's list from her pocket and they stepped through the automatic doors into the warmth of the store.

Dylan wheeled the big cart up and down the aisles while Rue did the shopping, trying to remember the brands and sizes Gran preferred. It seemed to be a slack time at the store, and they saw hardly any other shoppers except for a few elderly people whom Rue didn't recognize.

Then they turned a corner and almost ran into another cart, pushed by a woman with a little girl in the baby seat and another toddler trailing behind her. Rue smiled as she recognized DeeDee Botner, who'd been a year behind her in school.

"Rue! Rue Dunwitty, is that you? I heard you was in town, visiting your grandmother. How is she doing? And, oh, hon—I was *so* sorry about your mother. I was living off in Port Arthur at the time or else I would have come to the funeral. That must have been just awful for you. And who is this?"

That had always been DeeDee's way—no tact, no holding back, and seldom letting anyone else get a word in edgewise. "Take no prisoners" was the way Rue's mother had described DeeDee's conversational style.

Rue ignored every question except the last. "DeeDee, this a friend of mine, Dylan Jeffries. We work for the same company in San Francisco. Dylan's out here to interview for a job in Austin."

DeeDee raised an eyebrow. "Amethyst is a long way from Austin!"

Rue realized it must be obvious, given the early hour, that Dylan had spent the night. She changed the subject. "And who are these two?"

"Just my brats. I think you must have met the older one back when she was about the size of Shawna here, with the drool on her chin. Shawna, what a mess! That's her older sister, Cherie, back there, wandering off toward the candy aisle—Cherie, you get back here, honey! No! It's way too early in the day for you to start stuffing yourself with Tootsie Rolls!" She lowered her voice. "Tootsie Rolls are her favorites, the little individually wrapped ones. She *lives* for those things. I always thought they looked like little turds!"

Suddenly Cherie halted, turned, and hurried back to her mother, but from the way she kept looking over her shoulder, it wasn't on account of her mother's scolding. Someone else was coming up the candy aisle. A moment later another shopping cart rounded the bend.

It was a woman who looked to be in her early forties. She had fair hair and pretty features, but she appeared run-down, with a lackluster, almost furtive manner. When her cart accidentally bumped against Rue's, she muttered an apology and hardly glanced up.

"Well, hi there, Liz!" said DeeDee. "You back from Temple, hon? Lord, I hope those doctors at Scott and White gave you some good news! Liz Frady, this is Rue Dunwitty. Rue's an old friend of mine, lives way out in San Francisco now. And this fellow is Rue's friend from California—now darn it, don't tell me. I am the *worst* when it comes to remembering names . . ."

DeeDee was yammering even faster than usual because she was flustered, Rue thought. Who wouldn't be, in Liz Frady's presence?

Rue felt a cold chill pass through her as Liz Frady stared at her. The woman's face was expressionless. "Rue Dunwitty," she finally said.

"Yes," said Rue.

"You're the one who . . . the sheriff just spoke to me. He told me . . ."

DeeDee frowned. "Oh, Lordy, that's right. That *was* you, wasn't it, Rue, who thought you saw . . ." Her voice trailed off. "But they went lookin' yesterday, didn't they? And they didn't find nothin'. That's what I heard, that it was all a false alarm. Oh, cheer up, Liz! They're gonna find Dawn, and she's gonna be perfectly okay." DeeDee reached out to touch her arm, but Liz shrank back. She must have been a pretty woman under normal circumstances, thought Rue, robust and active—she trained the drill team and organized the grade school aerobics. Was it Dawn's disappearance that had drained the life from her? Or was she ill?

"Is that what it was?" Liz Frady looked steadily at Rue. "A false alarm?"

Rue's mouth was dry. "I only wish it was. But I know what I saw . . ."

Suddenly Dwayne Frady appeared, stepping up behind his mother. Liz began to tremble and weep. Dwayne gave Rue a hard look, then put his hand on his mother's shoulder. "Come with me, Momma," he said gently. "I told you it was no good, you coming to the store. I'll take you home now."

He put his arm around her and they turned away, leaving the shopping cart behind. Rue stepped after them.

"Just leave us alone!" snapped Dwayne.

Dylan put a hand on Rue's arm, holding her back. "Let them go," he said quietly.

"Poor Liz Frady!" said DeeDee. "This business with Dawn runnin' off, and now they say Liz might have cancer. And there's something just plain odd about that boy of hers, don't you think?"

Rue took a deep breath. "I think Dylan's going to be late for his interview in Austin if we don't get out of here. Take care of your little girls, DeeDee."

"Oh, don't worry about them. They pretty much run the show around my house. Sometimes I call 'em Princess Number One and Princess Number Two . . ."

Before DeeDee could elaborate further, Rue gripped Dylan's elbow and pushed the cart around the bend into the next aisle.

She didn't stop pushing until they arrived at the checkout counter. Maybelline Schneider was at the register, reading a tabloid with an unflattering photo of Hillary Clinton on the cover. She looked up, recognized Rue, and smiled. Then she saw Dylan, and her smile widened. It was the same smug, I-know-a-secret smile that Maybelline had flashed at Rue on Friday when she arrived in Amethyst, after asking if she had a boyfriend in San Francisco. "Not exactly," Rue had said, and Maybelline had acted as if Rue were hiding something. Now Rue had Dylan at her side, and some suspicion of Maybelline's was apparently confirmed. That was the only explanation Rue could think of for the woman's smug look and her knowing glance at Dylan.

Rue imagined the trail of gossip forming in her wake—the girl who had abandoned Amethyst for the big city and Texas for California, who cried wolf about Dawn Frady, who invited strange men from San Francisco to spend the night at her grandmother's house—and suddenly she was weary of being back in Amethyst.

All the time Maybelline was checking the groceries, Rue kept waiting for her to ask a question about Dylan or Dawn. But Maybelline instead made small talk about the tabloid she was reading. "I just can't stand that Hillary Clinton, can you? Why can't that awful woman just crawl back under a rock? Now, Laura Bush—there's a *real* lady . . ."

Rue paid for the groceries and headed for the automatic doors, feeling rattled. Behind her, Dylan gathered up the two bags. When Rue turned back, she happened to catch the parting glance that Maybelline and Dylan exchanged. For just an instant, a disturbing intuition flashed through her mind, but it faded before she could make sense of it.

23

Back at Gran's house, Dylan insisted on carrying the groceries to the porch.

"Set those down," said Rue, opening the door. "I'll take them inside. You'd better get going, hadn't you?"

Dylan looked at his watch. "I guess." He smiled. "I kind of hate to leave. Are you sure you'll be okay?"

"Of course I will. Listen, Dylan—put all of this out of your mind. Me and Gran, and Amethyst . . . and Dawn. You've got an important interview today. That's what you need to be thinking about."

He hummed and nodded. His eyes never left hers, but he didn't seem to hear what she'd said. There was a look in his eyes Rue had never seen there before. He stepped toward her. Involuntarily, she gave a small start. Then his arms were around her and his mouth was on hers.

If anything, the kiss he gave her was even more passionate than the one Juss had given her the previous night. Despite the confusion she was feeling, Rue found herself drawn into the kiss, as all the pent-up erotic tension of the previous day and night suddenly welled up inside her. Dylan wrapped his arms more tightly around her, as if he mistook her trembling for fear and wanted to quell it. There was a strength in his arms that she hadn't anticipated.

She pulled back from the kiss. Dylan gradually released her. The look was still in his eyes.

"So . . . I'll be back for dinner," he said quietly. "Okay?"

Rue nodded, a bit dazed, and watched him walk to his car with a boyish spring in his step. He backed out of the driveway and onto the paved road. Rue waved. Dylan waved back, then drove off. Rue crossed her arms and hugged herself and exhaled a long sigh.

She took the bags inside. Gran was in the kitchen. Rue put away the groceries in a kind of trance, smiling vaguely at Gran's rambling chatter. Her body was still reacting to the kiss. That was what she needed, she thought—to be with a man again. To become completely physical. To have sex. It was her body reacting, not her mind, and that confused her. Was it Dylan himself she was responding to, or merely Dylan's touch?

At least she had something to think about, something to keep her mind off more unpleasant things, such as her encounter with Liz Frady at the grocery store, and Maybelline Schneider's smug smile at the checkout—

Suddenly, Rue knew what Maybelline's smile had meant. She had met Dylan before, and that meant that Dylan had been to Amethyst before.

The realization was so overwhelming that Rue had to sit down at the kitchen table. Gran was still talking to her, chattering happily on, but she couldn't hear the words over the sudden pounding in her ears. Her palms were suddenly sweaty. Her face felt hot. She told herself to take a deep breath and to calm down.

Why had she realized the truth only minutes after Dylan left, when it was too late to confront him? Briefly, she considered getting into her car and trying to catch up with him on the highway to Austin. But Dylan had a twenty-minute head start and would be driving fast to get to his interview in time. Trying to catch up with him was a crazy idea.

She could call him on his cell phone—but then she realized she didn't have the number with her. It was on her speed dial back home in San

Francisco. And was Dylan even carrying his cell phone? He hadn't used it to call her from the Austin airport; he had specifically told her he was calling from a pay phone—but was that the truth? How did she know where he had been calling from? With a cell phone, he might have been calling from anywhere. Suddenly everything was thrown into doubt, because Dylan had been deceiving her. But why? And was everything a lie, everything he'd told her?

Did she even know for certain that Dylan really had an interview scheduled in Austin? How could she check? She could call Glenn Computer—but they wouldn't give out that sort of information over the phone. Dylan had said he was registered at the Three Muses in Austin. She could call the hotel, make sure he had actually checked in the previous day—

But this was crazy, she told herself. She was getting carried away. There had to be an innocent explanation. But what? And why had he deceived her?

She would simply have to wait until Dylan phoned later in the day to tell her how the interview went; then she could confront him. But that was hours away! Waiting and wondering would be intolerable. She had to know if her suspicion was correct, and she had to know *now*.

As much as she hated the idea, there was only one way to know for sure. Gran watched her get up from the table and put on her coat. "Where are you going, hon?"

"Back to the store."

"Did you forget something? You got everything on the list."

"It's something . . . something I didn't think of until just now."

"Okay, hon. You come right back."

How strange it was that the character of the town could change again so completely, back into something unfamiliar and unsettling. Everything looked the same as when she and Dylan had gone to the store before; if anything, the sun was brighter and there were more people on the sidewalks. Yet she felt a stranger again in Amethyst, out of step, not just with the town but with the whole world. All the comforting rules of normalcy, the reasonable expectations of decent behavior that make the world a livable place from day to day, were obsolete, not just in Amethyst but everywhere, because if life could become so unpredictable here, then no place was safe.

She pulled into the parking lot at Schneider's. There were more cars than before. That meant more customers. If she had to stand in line and wait to speak to Maybelline, fretting and holding in her emotions, she might scream.

But Maybelline wasn't at the checkouts. Rue walked past the row of registers, peering up and down the aisles. A pair of old ladies pushing shopping carts smiled and waved, and Rue managed to smile back. She came to the produce aisle and spotted Maybelline at the far end, talking to Milton. Rue took a deep breath and walked toward them. She felt her heart racing and told herself to calm down; the last thing she wanted was to sound shrill and demanding. It took all her control to smile as she approached the Schneiders and keep her voice light.

"Maybelline Schneider!" Rue said. Did the grin she was forcing look as phony as it felt?

Maybelline turned and automatically smiled back, and then, realizing it was Rue, her smile gradually assumed the same smug character as before. "Well, howdy, Rue. You back already? You bring your fellow back with you? You can introduce him to Milton."

Milton chuckled, showing off gold-capped teeth. The laugh was spontaneous and friendly, but it made Rue cringe. She had the feeling that Maybelline and Milton had just been taking about her and Dylan.

"Listen, I think I know a little secret." Rue managed to keep the grin on her face.

"What's that, hon?" Maybelline inclined her head, clearly amused. Milton chuckled again.

"I think . . . I think this morning wasn't the first time that Dylan has been in the store." Rue raised her eyebrows, trying to look arch. Maybelline raised an eyebrow in response.

"Well, now, Rue." Maybelline pursed her lips, looked at Milton, then let out a laugh. "You're right on target, hon! Oh, am I the worst at keeping a secret, or what?"

"You *are* the worst," Milton agreed good-naturedly.

"Rue, your fellow was in here a couple of weekends ago—Thanksgiving weekend," said Maybelline. "He and I struck up a little conversation at the checkout and the two of us hit it off right away. That one's a charmer, Rue. If I was you, I'd keep a close eye on him until he's got a ring on his finger."

"Thanksgiving?" said Rue, her grin fading.

"That's right. I said, 'Howdy, stranger,' because he obviously wasn't from around here. I figured he was here for the holidays, so I asked him who he was visiting, and he said nobody, and I said, 'What, you're just passing through?' And he said, 'Not exactly,' and I said, 'Well, then what on earth brings you to our humble little corner of heaven?' And then he told me about knowing you, out in California. 'You're a friend of Rue Dunwitty?' I said. 'Well, then, you're A-okay in my book.'"

"But—what was he doing here?" Rue could no longer keep the smile on her face, but Maybelline didn't seem to notice.

"Said he'd been down in Austin for a job interview. Oops! That's the part I wasn't supposed to tell you, or at least he made me promise not to, if I should happen to see you anytime soon, and I told him I understood, because I know how it is when people are looking around for a new job, sometimes you don't want *anybody* to know what you're up to. I promised him I wouldn't blab, even to you. But I guess it's okay for me to tell you now, now that he's been here to visit you. Anyway, he said he was finished with his first round of interviews in Austin and had some time to kill over Thanksgiving weekend waiting for his plane to leave on Sunday, so he said to himself, Hey, I think I'll just drive up and have a look at Rue's hometown. And I said, 'You're sure you and Rue are just *friends?*' And I swear, he blushed like a schoolboy. Made him even cuter. And I thought, Well, if that's not mighty sweet, for a fellow to come all the way to Amethyst from Austin alone and on a lark, just to have a look at his sweetheart's hometown. I'm telling you, Rue, this one's a keeper."

Milton suddenly hunkered down and got in her face. "Somebody's sweet on Rue-oo!" he said in a singsong voice. When Rue was a teenager and had worked at the store, Milton had always enjoyed teasing her. It had never particularly bothered her, but at that moment his puerile behavior struck her as grotesque.

"But I don't understand," said Rue, keeping her voice even. "When Dylan was with me in the store this morning, why didn't you mention seeing him before? You deliberately didn't say anything, like you were still keeping it a secret."

"Well, he asked me not to tell you, didn't he?" Maybelline laughed. "And besides, Rue, when you got into town last Friday, I asked you specifically if you had a special fellow back there in San Francisco—you remember me asking you?—and you said no." She wagged her finger. "So who was keeping secrets from who? You keep a secret from your old friends in Amethyst, and don't be surprised if they keep a secret from you, missy!" The smug smile reappeared on her face, and now Rue understood the secretive parting glance Maybelline had exchanged with Dylan behind her back that morning.

So Dylan's little deception was innocent after all. Wasn't it?

She managed to disengage from the Schneiders, saying that Gran would be missing her. She maintained a cool, indifferent smile as she walked through the store. Finally, back in the car, she gripped the steering wheel and let out a long, pent-up breath. From the placard in the store window, the image of Dawn Frady stared back at her.

No wonder Dylan hadn't stopped to call and ask for directions to Gran's house when he got into Amethyst—"I just followed my nose," he had told her, but in fact, he had already been to Amethyst, and must have already figured out where Gran's house was. How? It wouldn't be hard; he could have asked anybody around the courthouse square to point him to the house where Rue Dunwitty's grandmother lived. Perhaps he had even asked Maybelline.

Now she understood why Rosita at the restaurant had acted so familiar with Dylan. It wasn't a matter of small-town friendliness or Mexican hospitality—Dylan *had* been there before, and he had charmed Rosita just as he had charmed Maybelline. That meant he had been in Amethyst long enough to eat a meal. Had it been lunch—or dinner? Was it possible he had stayed the night in Amethyst? Rue suddenly remembered something Dylan had said in passing about the motel in town—"that skanky motel over by the park," he had called it. Something about the comment had struck Rue as odd at the time, but there had been more important things to discuss, and she had forgotten about it. "Skanky" was a strong word; how could anybody have such a strong opinion about a place unless he had actually been there? And how had he known it was by the park? Rue hadn't driven him by the park when they had toured the town.

Dylan had told Maybelline he was in Austin for a job interview. Over the four-day Thanksgiving weekend? That seemed unlikely—or did it? From what Rue had heard about the go-getters at Glenn Computer, it wasn't impossible that they might have been back at work on the Friday after Thanksgiving. And the long holiday would have been a perfect time for Dylan to fly to Texas and back without anyone at the San Francisco office knowing or even suspecting. It actually made sense that Glenn Computer might have arranged the interview for that Friday, and that Dylan had chosen to stay over in Austin until Sunday. Left to his own devices in a town he didn't know, over a holiday weekend, out of boredom and curiosity he had decided to drive up to Amethyst and back, just to have a look at the little town Rue was always talking about.

What exactly *had* she told him about Amethyst? She had talked about Gran, surely. Had she also talked about the Dunwitty property and the abandoned house? Probably; but her mind was cloudy and she couldn't remember.

What Dylan had done was perfectly innocent, perfectly natural—wasn't it? Maybelline and Milton Schneider had thought so. They thought his behavior was charming. But why hadn't Dylan told Rue about his previous visit to Amethyst?

"A keeper," Maybelline had called him.

But Rue thought of a far less pleasant word. *Stalker.*

24

As she pulled out of the parking lot and headed toward the center of town, Rue kept thinking of little discrepancies in things Dylan had said. He had told her that amethyst was his birthstone, and that was why he could remember the name of her hometown, but Gran had refuted that. Which of them was right? And if Dylan was wrong, had he been lying, or merely mistaken? Why would he lie merely for the sake of lying? Unless he had some ulterior motive.

And he had been strangely mistaken about the time, when he called her Tuesday night from San Francisco—he had said it was nine thirty California time, when it must have been ten thirty. That was an innocent mistake, surely—or was it? How could Rue know for sure that Dylan had actually been calling from San Francisco? What if he had been calling from somewhere else? What if he was *already* in Texas on Tuesday night?

Why had he reacted so strongly when Juss flashed his cherry lights, and when Dwayne brandished his gun? Did he have some particular reason to be afraid of Juss or Dwayne? Of course, Dylan had explained to her about the joyriding incident when he was a teenager, and his fear of guns—but was that story true?

Her imagination was running away with her. Still, how much did she really know about Dylan? How much could you ever actually know about another person? At the beginning, everyone judges others based on the most superficial aspects—how they look and dress, what they sound like, whether they're attractive or ugly.

You can't ever tell by looking. In her head, Rue heard her mother's voice so clearly that it seemed as if she were actually speaking to her inside the car. Rue remembered the circumstances. They had been talking about men and how to judge character. Her mother had specifically been talking about the mistake she made when she picked Rue's father to marry all those years ago, because she was young and naive. "I married Emmett Dunwitty for just one reason, because I thought he was good-looking and I figured the two of us would have good-looking kids." Her mother had actually said that. At the time, Rue had been speechless, unable to think of a reply.

She found herself driving aimlessly around town, or so she thought, until she realized she had arrived at the little park. The trees were naked. The grass was a field of gray littered with brown leaves. There was no one in the park. The day was too cold. She pulled into the empty little parking area, turned off the ignition, and found herself staring at the motel across the street.

Dylan had called it skanky, but it was merely a typical two-story motel with a small parking lot and no extras—no pool or play area, no restaurant attached, and nothing flashy to attract attention, just a small wooden sign by the road that read MOTEL AMETHYST with a Vacancy/No Vacancy indicator in neon. It had been built in the 1960s, but a few haphazard remodelings since then had stripped it of any period character it might once have possessed. In its current incarnation the exterior was a nondescript sandy beige. The doors were white. The metal railings were pink. There were twenty rooms in all, ten above and ten below. The office was in a separate building with living quarters in the back. An ice maker and some vending machines were outside the office. Rue knew it was the office because the clear glass door said so, in black capital letters printed on yellow metallic plates. The letters were slightly tilted and not quite centered.

The motel had changed hands several times over the years. Rue had never known any of the owners. They were usually out-of-towners who'd been talked into buying a business the locals knew could never make much money.

She took a deep breath, got out of the car, and crossed the street. The neon Vacancy sign was on, and she heard it buzzing quietly as she pushed open the office door. A cowbell attached to the door made a sudden clanging. Inside, there was a small waiting area with a bright green sofa. Behind a registration counter there was a little office with a desk and a computer monitor. An open door beyond the desk appeared to lead to the living quarters. Rue could hear the sound of a television turned to a talk show with a cheering audience.

She wasn't quite sure what she would do when the manager appeared. Would he tell her outright if Dylan had stayed there on Thanksgiving weekend, or let her look at the guest register? Did motels still even have guest registers? They kept that kind of information in a computer nowadays. In old movies, motel managers always put up a fuss if they were asked about their guests, or had to be bribed to tell. Rue felt a bit absurd, and almost turned around to leave. Then she saw what looked like an old-fashioned guest register lying right on the counter.

The register looked old, perhaps as old as the motel itself, with well-worn black leather covers. On the front, beneath gilt letters that read REGISTRATION, MOTEL AMETHYST, there was an old black-and-white postcard inserted into a slot. The photo showed the motel as it must have appeared when it first opened, not much different but with a few design touches that had long since vanished, such as a neon sign with a Sputnik-style satellite on top.

Rue opened the cover, expecting to find a sort of time capsule, but new pages had been inserted into the binder. On the top sheet, written in fountain pen, were the words "Motel Amethyst, Dub & Patty Ireland Proprietors Since 1999." She knew who Dub Ireland was; he had been a grade ahead of her in high school. Was Patty Ireland the Patty she had known, Patty Kline, who had dated Dub the year that Rue and Patty were seniors?

The registration pages that followed began with entries from July 1999. As Rue began to turn the pages, she looked furtively toward the open door behind the registration counter. Added to the sound of the television, she thought she could also hear a baby crying. There was no indication that anyone had heard the clanging cowbell when she entered.

Her heart sped up as she turned the pages, even though she was doing nothing wrong. The registration book was there on the counter for anyone to look at, a kind of nostalgic flourish, Dub and Patty Ireland's idea of how motels were run in the good old days. If and when someone appeared at the counter, it would simply look as if Rue had been leafing through the register to kill time. But then what would she say? What excuse would she give for being there in the first place?

She turned the pages until she located the most recent entry, dated the night before, then turned the pages back one by one, looking for the weekend after Thanksgiving.

Then, with the turn of a page, she found what she was looking for. Staring at it, she felt a kind of numbness, a sensation of unreality. Dated the Saturday after Thanksgiving, there was an entry with Dylan's name, his San Francisco address, and his signature.

Until that moment, a part of her had been hanging back, suspending judgment, almost amused in a perverse kind of way and ready to laugh at herself when she discovered just how far from the mark she had let her imagination carry her. Now she felt a rush of blood to her head, as if she had been standing on a trapdoor that had abruptly given way.

That was how Patty Ireland found her when Patty suddenly appeared at the counter, a nursing baby in her arms.

Rue looked up, one hand holding a page of the registration book, the other hand hovering over Dylan's signature. For a moment she stared blankly at the woman who had appeared silently from nowhere. It *was* Patty Kline, she realized. Now Patty Ireland, Dub Ireland's wife, proprietor of the Motel Amethyst.

Patty looked at her sidelong, rocking the baby gently and readjusting him to give better access to her nipple. She looked puzzled for a moment, then smiled. "Rue! Well I'll be darned. Haven't see you in a coon's age. That *is* you, isn't it?"

Rue looked at her dumbly, managing what she hoped was a smile in return.

"Looking through the guest register for the rich and famous? Oh, we've had all the big names stay here—George W., and Garth Brooks, not to mention the Judds. That Naomi was a hoot."

Rue looked at her blankly.

Patty laughed. "Rue, I'm funning you! That old register was here when we moved in. Had lots of fresh paper in it, nobody had signed it in years, so Dublin said, 'Why don't we just put it out on the counter and have folks sign in.' Like this was the Ritz-Carlton! But you know, people seem to like it. Course, we do get our share of folks signing in as Mr. and Mrs. John Doe, if you know what I mean, and that's *not* the name on their credit card. You see it *all* in this business! People from Halleyville and Mayhew drive all the way here to do their naughtiness. Makes you wonder where folks from Amethyst go. But mostly we get salesmen and truckers and visiting relatives. But listen to me, talking a blue streak! Guess it's 'cause things have been kind of slow and I don't have nobody to talk to except little Oscar here, on account of Dub's gone most of the day working for the highway department." Patty adjusted the baby in her arms. "So, I guess we know which John Doe you're looking for," she said.

Rue felt an impulse to turn and leave. After all, she had found what she was looking for. But what was Patty talking about? What did she mean?

"John Doe?" Rue said quietly.

"This one's yours." Holding the baby with one arm, Patty used her free hand to turn the pages in the register to a more recent entry. "There, that one. Got in Friday night."

Rue stared at the page, where Friday's date and the name "John Doe" had been filled in. On the address line, the same hand had written, "Corpus Christi, TX."

Patty laughed. "Of course, he's not always John Doe. Last time, he was Alan Roe, and before that he was Harry Toe, or something like that. But he always puts Corpus; don't know why he's not more creative about that. I don't know why he makes such a secret of being here, either, but that's the way he wants it. Dub says he must be doing some shady business deal and doesn't want anybody to know—but good luck keeping your business a secret in Amethyst! Sooner or later everybody knows everybody else's business around here. But if he says he doesn't want just any old stranger to know that he's staying here, well, Dub and I *do* know how to keep our mouths shut. That's one thing you definitely learn in the motel business."

Rue looked at her helplessly. "Patty, what on earth are you talking about?"

"Well, your dad, silly! Isn't that who you came here to see?" Then Patty saw the look on Rue's face. Her smile faded. She clucked her tongue and pursed her lips. "Uh-oh. Looks like I put my foot in it. You didn't know he was staying here, did you?"

Rue shook her head.

"Well, shoot! When he said to keep it quiet he was up here, I never would have thought he meant family. He should have said so. Well, damn! I hope I haven't opened a can of worms."

"He's stayed here before? Recently?"

"Well, now, I'm not sure I ought to . . ."

Rue turned back the pages in the register until she came again to Dylan's name. Seeing it still gave her a start, but stranger still, on the very same date, the Saturday after Thanksgiving, there was another entry on the line just above Dylan's: "Joe Bloe, Corpus Christi, TX."

The lettering was the same as the later John Doe entry. Strange, that she didn't know her father well enough to recognize his handwriting. "How did you—how did you even know that he was my dad?"

"His last name, of course. Dunwitty's what's on his charge card, even if that's not what he signs in the register. I guess I must have asked him the first time he stayed here—oh, months ago—if he was related to you, and he said yes, he was your dad. He never made any secret of that. That's why I figured, with you showing up here today, and him being here, it had to be okay to . . ." She shook her head and lowered her voice. "Listen, if you two are feuding or something, don't do it here. Take it elsewhere."

"Feuding? Of course not. I just . . . I just didn't realize he was in town . . . today."

Patty wrinkled her brow. "So, if you didn't come here to see your dad, what brings you—"

But Rue was already at the door, making the cowbell clang as she pulled it open.

"Oh, and hey!" Patty called after her. "Somebody was telling me that you saw a dead deer or something out in a field, and thought it was that Frady girl. What on earth made you think—?"

Rue stepped out of the office. The late-morning light, cold and bright, hurt her eyes. The neon Vacancy sign overhead seemed to send its quiet buzzing straight into her brain.

She hurried across the street. As she opened her car door, she heard a noise from the direction of the motel rooms, and turned to see one of the upper-floor doors swing open. A man wearing khaki pants and a green ski jacket stepped out of room 210. It was her father.

She hadn't seen him in years. His hair was grayer and he looked much older, but Rue recognized him at once. She would have known him even if Patty hadn't told her that he was staying there. What a shock that would have been, to have simply spotted him out of the blue. But it was even stranger seeing him like this, after reading the false names he had put in the guest register, knowing that he had cajoled Dub and Patty Ireland into keeping quiet about his visits. What on earth was he up to?

While Rue watched, her father walked to the stairwell, covering his mouth to cough. Did he have a bad cold, or was it a smoker's cough? His footsteps clanged down the concrete-and-metal steps. He stepped into the parking area and walked to a dark green Oldsmobile. Was this the handsome man whose looks had dazzled her mother? To Rue he looked stooped and haggard. He opened the trunk and fiddled with something inside. It was long and thin and made of leather, like a carrying case for pool cues, or for skis—or for a rifle . . .

On a sudden impulse, Rue stepped away from her car and began to cross the street, not bothering to look for traffic. She walked straight toward her father, her heart pounding in her chest. She reached him just as he was slamming shut the trunk of his Oldsmobile. He gave a small start when he saw her.

"Ada," he whispered, and for a moment he looked as if he had seen a ghost.

"It's me, Dad. Rue. Your daughter."

"Well, of course it's you, Rue. Did I call you by your mother's name? You look so much like her, especially now that you're older."

"You look older, too, Dad."

He nodded. "I guess that's what happens when people don't see each other for a long time. Kind of a shock when you see how much they've changed."

If she could see him now, would Rue's mother still have considered Emmett Dunwitty a good-looking man? It was hard for Rue to spot any vestiges of the smiling youth she had seen in old photos of her father. Here was a stern-looking man with weathered features and salt-and-pepper hair. He coughed into his fist. When he looked back at her there was a weariness in his eyes that, for the moment at least, softened the animosity she was feeling toward him.

"You're still in California, aren't you?" he said.

"Yes. I'm just back for a while to visit Gran. Maybe you could visit her every now and then. You seem to be up here often enough."

He flashed a thin smile. "I'm not sure your grandmother would appreciate a visit from me."

Rue shrugged. "Did the deputy ever get hold of you?"

"What deputy?"

"Juss Goodbody. Horace Boatwright's deputy."

Her father looked at her with a blank expression.

Rue sighed. "Even if Juss hasn't tracked you down, you must have heard about it by now, from people in town."

"Heard about what, hon?"

"Don't call me that! I'm talking about . . . what I saw in the cistern, and the search Goodbody conducted."

"Rue, I don't have a clue what you're talking about." He began to cough again.

Her animosity returned in full force. "Dad, don't you even talk to anybody when you come up here, or do you just hide out in your motel room like a hermit? How could you not know about Dawn? And what do you think you're doing by setting all those traps on the Dunwitty property? Somebody's going to get hurt, and you're going to get slapped with a nasty lawsuit. And if I suddenly look older, it's because you haven't seen me in years, and whose choice was that? If you'd come to Mother's funeral—" She caught herself. She was all over the map. Rue wasn't sure what she had intended to say when she walked up to him, but it wasn't this unfocused tirade.

From the direction of the office she heard the clanging cowbell. Patty Ireland emerged around the corner, holding little Oscar and scowling at them. Had Rue been speaking so loudly that Patty could hear her even inside the office?

"Maybe this isn't the best place to have a talk," her father suggested.

"Maybe not."

He coughed. "I suppose I could come by your grandmother's house this afternoon."

"Don't put yourself out."

"Rue . . ."

"I'm sorry. I shouldn't have said that. What time?"

"It'll have to be later. Right now I have to drive to Mayhew, but I'll come right back."

What was her father up to? She looked at the lid of the trunk, but didn't ask. She looked one last time into his weary eyes, then shrugged and started back toward her own car across the street, feeling Patty Ireland's eyes on her.

When she got into her car, she looked into the rearview mirror and saw her father's Oldsmobile in the parking lot. He was idling the engine to warm it up, sending clouds of exhaust into the air. Finally he shifted into reverse, backed out of his space, and pulled into the street. He drove past Rue but never looked her way.

Rue watched until the car disappeared around a corner. Then she looked back at the motel. Patty had gone back inside. Rue felt an impulse to return to the office and look through the register again. Why? To check all the dates her father had been in town. But why should she do that? What was it she suspected?

Then she thought of Patty's scowling face, and instead of heading back to the office, Rue started her car and drove away as quickly as she could.

25

Lore confused now than before, Rue did what she always did when she needed to think in Amethyst. She drove.

But driving didn't seem to help. The passing sights only seemed to burden her brain with jumbled memories that had nothing to do with her current confusion.

As she drove down one of the streets that ran parallel to the railroad tracks, she saw a familiar car. It was Dwayne Frady's beat-up little Toyota, parked alongside another car, an equally dinged, equally old Ford, in the driveway of a drab little house—the Frady residence, Rue realized. Passing the house, Rue felt as if the gloom inside seeped out and palpably touched her, sending a cold chill through every part of her body.

She drove on, paralleling the railroad tracks, then took a right turn, back toward Main Street. As she crossed the tracks, the tires thumping over the steel rails and cross ties, she realized that she was once more headed in the direction of Schneider's Grocery, and felt another chill. This must have been the route that Dawn took on the day she disappeared, when her mother sent her on an errand to the store. But Dawn never arrived at Schneider's.

It was only a few blocks from the Frady house to the store. Only a few blocks, Rue thought, feeling her guts twist inside her, and yet Dawn had never made it to the store. What had happened? Who had met her along the way? Someone she knew? Or a stranger, offering her a lift? Had she gotten into the car willingly, or had she been forced? *Where* had it happened—and why had no one along the route seen anything, heard anything, suspicious? Paralleling the railroad tracks, rows of low warehouses blocked the view from most of the houses set farther back. Was this the very spot where Dawn had been abducted?

Rue kept driving. A couple of blocks farther on she came to the rear entrance to the grocery store parking lot. She stopped and sat for a moment with the engine idling, then turned the car around to retrace the route back to the Frady house. How many houses would she pass along the way? She counted them, driving slowly, peering at every door and window. Had no one been looking out a window on the day Dawn disappeared? Had no one been in their front yard? Probably not. No one peered back at her from those houses now. No one was outside. For all the evidence of life in the houses or the yards, the stretch of road from the store to the Frady house might as well have passed through a ghost town.

She felt an impulse to pull the car over, to retrace Dawn's route on foot, to stop at every house and knock on every door, to ask everyone along the route: *Did you see Dawn?* But surely that had already been done. Dylan had insinuated that the sheriff and his deputy were incompetent, but surely they had questioned everyone who might have seen or heard anything along the route of Dawn's last known steps.

The gloom that had reached out to her from the Frady house seemed to follow her all the way back to Gran's house, like a lengthening shadow.

Walking up to the house, she realized that the front door was open. She hesitated for a moment, sensing something amiss, then saw that Gran was sitting in the doorway, her wheelchair pulled up to the screen door.

"Gran, what are you doing with the door open? It's cold outside."

"I was worried about you. You said you were coming right back. I couldn't imagine—"

"Oh, Gran, I'm sorry. How long have you been sitting here? Let's get you back inside and shut this door."

She pushed Gran back from the doorway, turning her wheelchair around and pushing her toward the kitchen.

"What were you doing all this time?" said Gran. Her voice sounded thin and reedy.

"Just driving around. I'm sorry. I lost track of the time."

"I was worried. I thought . . ." Gran left the sentence unfinished.

"It's almost lunchtime. Are you hungry?"

"Not really."

"Well, I am. I'll heat up some stew." Rue reached into the refrigerator. Walking to the kitchen counter, she looked at Gran and frowned. She thought she saw something in Gran's face that hadn't been there before, a pinched look and a slight pallor. "Are you feeling okay, Gran?"

"I guess I'm a little cold from sitting at that open door."

Rue pressed her palm to Gran's forehead. "You don't feel hot. Maybe you just need to get something warm in you." She squeezed Gran's shoulder, thinking how bony it felt. Was Gran looking more fragile suddenly, or was it just Rue's black mood coloring everything around her? She busied herself preparing the stew and brewing a fresh pot of tea.

Gran protested that she had no appetite but managed to eat a little stew anyway. Afterward she pulled her chair close to the floor furnace in the living room, where she fell asleep in her chair, her library book lying unopened in her lap.

Rue paced the living room. She reached for the phone. She would have to keep her voice down so as not to wake Gran.

She dialed Reg's home number in Austin. The phone rang so many times that she was about to hang up. Then there was a click.

"Dunwitty residence."

"Cathy, this is Rue. Is Reg—?"

"Rue! When are you coming down to Austin?"

"I—I'm not sure. Is Reg there?"

"No. He's at work, of course."

"Can you give me his work number?"

There was a pause. "He's down in San Antonio again today."

"What's the number there?"

There was another pause. "I don't have it. Not on me, anyway."

"But . . . how do you reach him if you need to?"

"He calls me. Always calls when he's on his way home, to ask if there's anything he should pick up on the way. Why, is there some sort of emergency?"

"No, nothing like that. I just wanted . . . to talk." Reg had mentioned running into their father in Amethyst over the Thanksgiving holidays. Did he know any more than Rue did about their father's visits to Amethyst? Probably not, but still, she felt a need to talk to him. "What's the name of the company Reg works for?"

Cathy told her, then started to make small talk. As soon as there was a break in the conversation, Rue said good-bye and hung up.

She called information in San Antonio, got a number for Reg's employer, and had it dialed automatically. Voice mail finally gave her an option to speak to a company operator.

"I'm trying to reach an employee, Reg Dunwitty. I'm not sure if he has a regular extension at the San Antonio office—"

"Hold, please."

The line rang twice, then someone answered—not Reg, but a man with a gruffer voice and a much thicker Texas accent. "Howdy?"

"I'm trying to reach Reg Dunwitty," she said.

"Reg's not in today."

"Are you sure? This is his sister, Rue Dunwitty. I'm calling long distance."

"Sorry, but he's not here. Hold on a sec." He placed her on hold. Rue sat and stared at Gran, asleep in her chair, her head gently nodding as her slender chest rose and fell. The library book was within an inch of slipping off her lap. Finally the man came back on the line. "You still there, Miss Dunwitty?"

"Yes."

"I'm sorry, but Reg phoned in sick today."

"Sick? Are you sure?"

"That's what the secretary says. She took his call this morning."

"Oh. I see."

"You got his home number in Austin? That's where he'll be."

Rue hung up the phone with a sinking sensation. Nothing seemed to make sense anymore. It was as if she had fallen down a rabbit hole. What was going on with Reg? There must have been a simple misunderstanding—but how? If Reg wasn't at home and wasn't at work, then where was he? And why didn't Cathy know?

She found herself staring at the phone, as if it might abruptly ring and someone, somewhere, would be able to explain to her everything that was going on with Dylan, and her father, and now Reg.

She paced the length of the living room one more time, then wandered into the bedroom—aimlessly, she thought, until she found herself standing in front of the bookcase, her forefinger reaching out to tip back the spine of *The Corpus Corpses.*

She lay on the bed, opened the book to the first chapter, and started reading, not dipping and skimming as she had before, but reading quickly and deliberately, learning the names of all the victims, reading the interviews with their friends and families, plowing through the digressions about the colorful personal habits of the investigating detectives, forcing herself through the more gruesome passages.

When it came to the parts that discussed why anyone would commit such crimes, the book contained an awful lot of what her mother would have called psychobabble. Rue had never been much impressed by the little she knew about profiling, the attempt to create composite psychological profiles of serial killers. So-called experts had always been eager to step forward and explain why criminals commit crimes. A hundred years ago, people had taken quack science like phrenology seriously, thinking you could spot a deviant by the shape of his head. Now it was all talk about childhood trauma and abuse.

Rue remembered a radical feminist in San Francisco—the woman had been part of a book-reading group she'd belonged to—who had claimed that every man carried inside him the capacity to rape and murder, that all any man needed to set him off was the appropriate circumstances, that the atrocities committed in wartime by otherwise ordinary men proved as much. "Socialization dampens it down, makes most of them suppress it almost completely," the woman had told her, "but put them in a situation where society actually encourages their aggression—like torching an enemy village—and there's no limit to what they'll do. The psychological establishment—men—will tell you that torturing and raping women is totally deviant, a sickness. But the fact is that any given man is just as capable of doing it as any other."

Rue had argued with the woman and finally dismissed her ideas about men. But reading *The Corpus Corpses* and thinking about Dawn, she couldn't help remembering what the woman had said, and wondering now if there'd been some truth to it.

The same woman had also believed in recovered memories. She claimed her father and her brother had molested her for years when she was a child, and she had repressed the memories so completely that they had returned to her only after months of therapy. Rue had never been able to accept that disturbing notion, either.

Whether or not the profilers had the answers, it did seem that a lot of serial murderers had traits in common, including a fondness for mocking the authorities. "Cheekiness," Hop Hollingshead called it in his book. They liked to play cat-and-mouse games, not just with their victims but with the people trying to stop them. The book went all the way back to Jack the Ripper to make the point, citing letters the killer had apparently sent to the press, taunting them. The Zodiac Killer in northern California had done the same thing back in the 1970s. Some serial killers left "calling cards"—idiosyncratic tokens—at the scenes of the crime, or on the bodies of the victims. "Catch me if you can," the killers seemed to say, laughing at the press and the police and a terrified public from a safe distance, gloating over the power they possessed, not just to inflict pain and death but to cause panic and fear and confusion, and to get away with it.

Serial killers often hoarded trophies, as well—photographs of their victims in torment, or pieces of their personal property. Even when the police began to close in on them, some serial killers would hold on to these incriminating souvenirs rather than destroy them.

Such killers experienced no remorse. They could look straight into the eyes of a victim's grieving loved ones and feel nothing—or worse, feel a kind of smug superiority, even a sense of pleasure at the pain they had inflicted, while showing nothing on the surface.

Rue quickly read a hundred pages straight through, then slowed down. Her mind felt weary and overloaded. She found herself reading the same paragraph over and over; the words seemed to slip out of her consciousness the moment her eyes scanned past them. She closed her eyes to rest them and let the open book drop onto her chest.

Suddenly she heard the door to her room swing open. For some reason, Rue couldn't move or even open her eyes, but she knew that someone was in the room because she could hear his footsteps and his steady breathing, and then the quiet rustle of the dresser drawers being slowly opened and shut, one at a time. She lay paralyzed on the bed, listening, until the booming of her own heartbeat drowned out every other sound. She tried to open her mouth but she couldn't. She sensed a presence beside her, looming over her. She heard him breathing, very close and coming even closer, and then with a shock she felt his breath against her face, warm and moist. *Bitch,* he whispered. *Stupid bitch . . .*

Rue sprang upright on the bed, so abruptly that the book lying on her chest catapulted forward, tumbling over her knees and off the bed. It made a noise as it struck the floor that must have awakened Gran, because a moment later, in a feeble, throaty voice, Gran called out, "Rue? Are you in your room? What was that noise?"

"Nothing," Rue called out, clearing her throat. Her head was full of cobwebs and her skin was clammy, despite a chill in the room. She got out of bed and walked into the living room, stumbling when her toes caught on the edge of the rug. Sleeping in the middle of the day always left her groggy and disoriented.

"Be careful, hon," said Gran, her own eyes narrow and puffy from sleep. Rue had not been imagining it; Gran's color wasn't good. She looked pale and haggard.

Rue was about to say something about Gran's color when the phone rang, making them both jump. Feeling irritable and confused and worried about Gran, Rue reached for the phone and picked it up.

26

"Hello?" she said.

"Rue?" It was Dylan. "Damn, this is a lousy connection. Is that you, Rue?"

She tried to take a deep breath, but it caught in her throat. "Yes." She covered the speaker and spoke to Gran. "It's Dylan."

Gran nodded, then looked away and seemed to lose interest.

"Wow, there's so much crackling on the line," said Dylan. "Is there noise at your end?"

"No." The connection sounded crisp and clear to Rue, though somehow Dylan's voice seemed very far away. "Where are you calling from?"

"I'm on my way back to Amethyst. Calling on my cell phone."

"I didn't think you had it with you. When you called from the Austin airport, you said you were on a pay phone."

"I was. Cell phone battery was dead. Had to recharge it. Listen, I'm afraid I have bad news."

"Bad news?"

"About the interview. They really screwed me. Somehow, somebody at Glenn Computer found out about that arrest for joyriding when I was sixteen. There's no way they could have gotten that information legally. I was a minor. The records were sealed. But they asked me about it today, and what could I tell them? I wasn't going to lie. And they're not going to hire me. Can you believe it? Probably just as well. That place is run by a bunch of right-wing jerks."

"Dylan, why didn't you tell me you'd been to Amethyst before?" Rue glanced at Gran, who was staring at the book in her lap, paying no attention.

There was a long, hollow silence on the line.

"Dylan? Are you there?"

"I'm here."

"Did you hear me?"

"Yes."

"And?"

"How'd you find out?" His voice was quiet and almost too calm. "I suppose that lady at the grocery store told you?"

"She didn't have to tell me, Dylan. I figured it out. Why didn't *you* tell me?"

There was another long pause, so long that Rue thought she had lost the connection. Dylan finally spoke. "I was going to, Rue. But when I first got there, the moment didn't seem right, and it's one of those things, if you don't say it right off, the longer you wait, the more awkward it gets."

"It's more than just awkward, Dylan." She fought to keep her voice steady. "You were in Amethyst the Saturday after Thanksgiving, weren't you?"

"Yes. Look, I was down here in Austin that Friday for the first round of interviews—"

"You're telling me they scheduled you to fly in from San Francisco for a job interview on the Friday after Thanksgiving?"

"They never stop working at that place, holiday weekend or not. It actually made sense, because I didn't have to miss any work, and I wasn't planning to go home to Minneapolis for Thanksgiving anyway. I did the interviews that Friday, and the ticket didn't have me leaving until late Sunday morning, so on Saturday I thought, What the heck, why don't I drive to Rue's hometown just to have a look at the place? You always said it was friendly and quaint."

"I don't remember saying that. I wouldn't use that word. I've never in my life called Amethyst 'quaint.'"

"Okay, maybe not quaint, but whatever."

"And you simply took it in your head to drive up here—and what? Scope the place out?"

"Rue! You don't have to sound so . . . Listen, maybe I should hang up and call back. This line is really bad."

"No, don't hang up! I want to talk about this. Why did you come to Amethyst? And why didn't you tell me?"

"Like I said, it was on a whim. I got into town and I met that lady at the grocery store. I mentioned that I knew you, and we had a friendly conversation."

"About me?"

"Mostly, I guess. After that, I drove around the town for a while—"

"And what about Rosita's? You'd eaten there before, hadn't you?"

"Yes. I was surprised she remembered me."

"Yet you pretended you had no idea why she was acting so friendly. Why, Dylan? Why didn't you tell me then that you'd been to Amethyst before?"

"Like I said, I felt awkward. I just didn't know how to bring it up. We were having such a good time and I didn't want anything to spoil it."

"Did you think I'd never find out?"

"Rue, I don't know what I was thinking, except that it felt good to be with you."

"And what about the motel? When you were here before, you checked into the motel, didn't you?"

"It was getting dark. I didn't feel like driving all the way back to Austin. Yes, I checked into that dumpy motel."

"And then what happened, Dylan?" Rue felt her heart speed up.

"Jeez, Rue, what do you think? I watched a movie until I fell asleep. And the next morning I got up really early and drove to Austin and caught the flight home."

"You never told me at work that you had visited Amethyst."

"It never came up. Look, I know how feeble that sounds, but the whole trip was on the QT. I didn't want anybody at work to know that I'd been to Austin for an interview."

"Not even me?"

"I thought it would be best if I didn't mention it to anybody. You included."

"Even though you'd been to Amethyst?"

"And what if I *had* told you, Rue? What if, on the Monday after Thanksgiving, I'd come into your office and said, 'Hey, guess what? I happened to be in Texas over the weekend and I took a two-hundred-mile round trip just to have a look at your hometown.' You probably would have thought that was a little . . . odd."

"A *little* odd, Dylan? I would say *very* odd."

"Except that it's not." His tone was suddenly heated. "I drove to Amethyst that day because . . . I wanted to know more about you."

"That's creepy, Dylan."

"No, it's not. Rue, you must know how I feel about you."

"Do I, Dylan?"

She heard him draw a deep breath and expel it. "How can you *not* know?"

"I'm not sure what I know anymore."

"Listen, I'm on my way. I'll be in Amethyst in an hour. We can talk about it when I get there."

The thought of Dylan staying in the house suddenly sent a chill through her. "I don't want you to come here."

"Oh, Rue, don't make me turn around and drive back to Austin! We can talk this out, face-to-face."

He kept speaking, but Rue didn't hear. A thought had suddenly occurred to her, and the implications of it set the blood pounding in her head. She remembered the two entries, one just above the other, in the Motel Amethyst guest register for the Saturday after Thanksgiving, the very day Dawn disappeared. Dylan and her father had checked in on the same day, at virtually the same time. Was it just a coincidence?

"Dylan, when you stayed at the motel . . . did you meet my father?"

"What?" The question seemed to throw him off balance.

199

"You were both there on the same day, at the same time. Tell me the truth, Dylan. Do you know my father?"

"Rue, I can barely hear you. I think I'm about to lose you. It's this damned cell phone battery—won't hold a charge anymore. Rue, can you hear me? All I can hear is static . . ."

The line went dead.

Rue held the phone in her hand, staring at it. She glanced at Gran, who was dozing in her chair.

Rue dialed information for Austin. An operator came on the line. Rue asked for the number for Glenn Computer and had it automatically dialed.

A woman answered. "Glenn Computer. How may I help you?"

Rue cleared her throat. "This may sound like an odd question, but . . . were your offices open on the Friday after Thanksgiving?"

"I believe we were, ma'am."

"Are you sure?"

The woman laughed softly. "Glenn Computer is a twenty-four/seven operation. No such thing as a four-day weekend around here! Why do you ask?"

"Would the right people have been there that Friday to conduct an interview? This would have been for a—"

"I'm afraid I wouldn't know that, ma'am."

"I'm not asking for any details."

"We never discuss job applicants or interviews over the phone with third parties."

Rue sighed. "Of course not."

"Can I help you with anything else, ma'am?"

"No, I guess not."

"Then you have a very pleasant day, ma'am."

Rue hung up and sat back, trying to think, but her mind was in a fog. She watched Gran sleeping, studying the slight rise and fall of her bony shoulders. Gran suddenly looked very, very old to her.

The house was utterly quiet. Dark, too, she realized. While she was on the phone, a thick layer of clouds had blown in from the north, casting a premature twilight over Amethyst. Rue sat unmoving in the gloom.

Everything Dylan had said made sense. She couldn't fault the logic of his explanations. And yet . . .

She picked up the phone, dialed information again, and placed a call to the Three Muses in Austin. The hotel operator asked, "How may I direct your call?"

"I need to know if someone is registered there."

"Certainly. Would you like me to put you through to that guest?"

"No. I just need to know, do you have a Dylan Jeffries staying there?"

"One moment, please. No, I'm afraid we currently have no guest with that last name."

"Are you sure?"

"Yes, ma'am."

"I see. No, wait! Maybe he checked out. Would you be able to tell—"

"I'm afraid I can only tell you whether we currently have a guest staying here or not."

"But he may have checked out only in the last hour or so."

"Perhaps, but right now, there's no Mr. Jeffries staying here." Did the operator think that Rue was a suspicious wife trying to check up on an errant husband?

"So you can't tell me if a Dylan Jeffries was registered there yesterday?"

"I'm afraid that would violate our privacy policy."

"That's ridiculous!"

"Is there another guest at the Three Muses to whom I can connect your call?"

Her hand shaking, Rue slammed down the phone. Gran stirred in her chair but didn't wake up. Nor did she wake when there was a knock at the front door, even though the sudden banging almost made Rue jump out of her skin.

27

Rue sprang up quickly, rushing to reach the door before another round of knocking woke Gran. Through the little diamond-shaped pane of glass she saw Dwayne Frady's peering, anxious eyes.

She steeled herself for the encounter, then opened the door and stepped onto the porch. Dwayne was like a live wire. His every movement, even the simple act of stepping back to make room for her, bristled with tension. Some part of his body was always in motion—his jaw grinding, his eyes shifting, his hands clenching and unclenching. It made Rue nervous just to look at him. He looked more haggard than any teenager should, as if he'd been ill or hadn't slept for days.

"Dwayne, shouldn't you be in school?"

"School?" His voice broke like an adolescent's, grating on her ears. "You've gotta be fucking kidding. School!" He suddenly whirled in a circle, dancing like a boxer, and struck the palm of one hand with the fist of the other. The loud crack and the sudden violence made Rue jump.

She shook her head. "Oh, Dwayne . . ."

"So are you going to show me, or not?"

"Show you . . . ?"

"The place where you fucking saw her!" His voice broke again, and suddenly he was in her face. He gripped her arm, squeezing it painfully hard. "You've got to show me!"

"All right, Dwayne. All right! I will. Just—let go of me."

He loosened his grip but didn't let go. His eyes were wide open, staring into hers, yet there was a blankness in his stare. What was he seeing inside his head? Rue shivered.

"Just let me go inside for a minute. Okay, Dwayne? To get my coat."

He finally released her arm. His shoulders slumped and he lowered his eyes. "Okay," he mumbled, his voice no longer shrill. Instead he sounded dull and defeated, as if all the fury had suddenly drained out of him.

Rue slipped into the house. Gran was still asleep in her chair. Rue had never known her to sleep so soundly in the middle of the day. She grabbed her coat, then went to the phone. Hurriedly, she searched for Juss Goodbody's card and dialed his cell phone.

"Juss Goodbody here."

Rue let out a sigh of relief. "Juss, this is Rue."

"What's up, Rue?"

"Dwayne Frady's here, at my grandmother's house. He's really keyed up. I think . . . I think he might be carrying a loaded gun. He's so wound up—"

"I'll be there as quick as I can, Rue. I'm clear the other side of the county right now, so it's gonna take a few minutes. Just try to keep him calm and don't do anything to set him off."

"Set him off? He's already acting crazy. I don't know that anything I do will make any difference."

"I'm on my way."

"Thanks, Juss. Oh, and we'll be—" Rue needed to tell him they would be at the ruined cistern, but Juss had already hung up. She started to dial again, then jumped. Dwayne was peering in through the diamond pane, banging on the door so hard it sounded like he was hammering a nail.

Gran stirred and lifted her head. "Rue? Who's that at the door?" Her voice was plaintive and confused.

Rue hung up the phone and put her arm around Gran's shoulders. "It's Dwayne Frady, Gran. He needs me to help him with something. I have to go out for a minute. I'll be back as soon as I can."

Gran nodded, but the look on her face showed no understanding.

"If the deputy shows up while I'm gone, tell him I'll be at the cistern. Okay?"

Gran cocked her head, looking puzzled. Dwayne pounded on the door again. Gran jumped in her chair and a look of alarm pinched her features.

"Oh, Gran, you poor thing! Don't worry. You just stay right here. I'll be back soon, I promise. Gran—I love you, Gran." Rue squeezed her shoulders and kissed her forehead, then hurried to the door.

On the porch, she closed the door behind her, then turned toward Dwayne, angry at him for scaring Gran. But the look on his face was so intense, so wild, that she kept her mouth shut. He grabbed her arm. "Show me!" he said.

Where was the gun? In his car, as it had been last night? Or was it pocketed in his letterman's jacket? Rue looked for a bulge but couldn't be sure.

He pulled her down the walk until she managed to yank her arm free. "You don't have to handle me like that," she snapped, rubbing her arm where he had hurt her. "I'll take you there, okay? Just . . . calm down."

She cut ahead of him, leading the way, walking fast to let off steam. It was colder than she had expected. The same cloud cover that cast a strange twilight pall over the gray fields had caused the temperature to plummet.

She was wearing cotton socks and running shoes, the wrong kind of footwear for walking in the fields. After striding only a few feet into the high grass, her shoelaces and socks were covered with grass burrs. She glanced back and saw that Dwayne was more suitably dressed, wearing jeans and cowboy boots. She again looked for the outline of a gun in his jacket, but he had thrust his hands into his pockets, pushing the jacket away from his body. His demeanor had gone from wild and out of control to unnaturally rigid. His lips were compressed and his jaw was clamped shut. He didn't return her glance but kept his eyes straight ahead, peering beyond her at the open fields.

They walked past the dilapidated barns and storage sheds and the abandoned beehives, then veered toward the left, trudging up the hillside that led to the cistern. Rue looked over her shoulder in the direction of Gran's house, but it was out of sight now, blocked by the barns and the trees. Would Juss Goodbody be able to figure out where she had gone?

As they drew closer to the cistern, Rue began to shiver despite the exertion of the climb. She should have worn gloves and a scarf. She glanced back at Dwayne to see if he was feeling the cold as well, but the expression on his face was so disturbing that she quickly looked away.

She had a premonition that something terrible was about to happen. But what? What was the worst possible thing? That they would reach the edge of the cistern, she thought, and gaze down—and Dawn would be there again, just as Rue had seen her the first time, and all the times since then in her dreams and waking memories, twisted and naked and dead.

The premonition was so powerful that she slowed her steps, almost certain, despite the illogic of it, that what she most dreaded was waiting for them ahead. Dwayne seemed to feel it as well. He slowed his pace to match hers and made no effort to hurry her. Her heartbeat sped up, pounding in her ears.

The low, curving wall of the cistern came into sight. A few steps more, drawing nearer, and Rue was able to see the emptiness beyond the upper rim, where the dome of the cistern had fallen in, and then the curve of the wall on the opposite side. She felt dizzy. Panic swept over her, causing her skin to prickle and her hands to tremble. At the same time she shivered from the cold—then gave a start when she felt Dwayne's hand on her shoulder.

She suppressed a little cry of alarm and turned to look at him. His face had softened from the hard, grim countenance that had been there when they began the walk to the cistern. His eyebrows were drawn together. His eyes were narrowed. His lips were parted and his jaw trembled. He didn't look at her, but kept his hand on her shoulder and gave it a squeeze. There was nothing menacing in his touch. He had seen her shivering, and had merely reached out to comfort her, to empathize. Or was he holding on to her for support, like a frightened child wanting to cling to someone? Suddenly he looked very much like a child to her, and she felt foolish for ever having been frightened of him.

"Dwayne—"

"This is it?"

"Yes."

"Down . . . in there?"

"Yes."

He stepped ahead of her, and she braced herself, making her hands into fists, clenching her teeth, a part of her preparing for the absolute horror of what her rational mind knew was impossible—that Dawn would be there. But when Dwayne reached the edge of the cistern and peered in, he simply stood still, saying nothing, showing no visible reaction, and Rue knew that there was nothing to see after all, only an emptiness where Dawn's body had been. She stepped up beside him.

"Down there?" he said quietly. "That's where you saw her?"

"Yes."

"Where, exactly?"

She didn't want to answer. She wanted to say that she couldn't remember, that it was all jumbled and blurred in her memory. But that would have been a lie. Gazing down at the piles of broken concrete and twisted rebar, she remembered exactly where the body had been located and exactly how it had looked—the splayed limbs, the tangle of blond hair, the wide-open mouth full of braces. The image seemed to hover just above the empty spot. When she closed her eyes it became more visible, not less, like a ghost image burned onto her retinas.

"Where?" Dwayne said again. The hysterical edge had crept back into his voice. Rue shivered and cringed. She raised her arm and pointed.

Before she could stop him, Dwayne climbed over the low cistern wall and jumped down inside, stumbling and almost falling when he landed on an unsteady slab of broken concrete.

Rue rushed to the wall and called down to him, "Are you all right?" Dwayne didn't answer. He walked toward the spot she had pointed to, keeping his eyes on it and stepping slowly over the jumble of debris, moving like a zombie. As she watched, Dwayne reached the spot and knelt down, touching the cold concrete with his fingertips. She couldn't see his face, only the back of his head, but from the way he suddenly trembled, she realized he was weeping. Rue hugged herself, feeling the misery that radiated from him, the same cold darkness that had reached out to her when she drove by the Frady house.

Rue suddenly realized that the old ladder she and Juss had used to climb in and out was no longer propped against the cistern wall. At some point—after the organized search of the hillside?—it had been removed. She scanned the ground nearby and spotted it lying only a few feet away, the weathered gray wood camouflaged amid the low grass. She shook her head. Could Dwayne get out of the cistern without the ladder? Rue couldn't see how. She would have to lift it over the wall and pass it down to him. But the ladder was heavy; perhaps she would wait until Juss showed up. Had he arrived at Gran's yet? She looked toward Gran's house, but the view was blocked by treetops farther down the hill.

She hugged herself, trying to stop her shivering. The view of the Dunwitty property below—the outbuildings and sheds, the neglected orchards, the overgrown fields, her grandparents' house in the distance—sent a strange mixture of emotions through her. Even at a moment like this, the somber, rustic beauty of the place called out to her. Over the years, this patch of land had been a bottomless well of nostalgia for her, brimming with memories, shadowed by the ghosts of her grandparents and what might as well have been the ghost of her father, for all the closeness that existed between them. On balance the memories had been more sweet than bitter, drawing her back time and again, but would it ever be the same after this trip, after what she had seen in the cistern, after what was happening at that very moment with Dwayne? Her well of nostalgia had been poisoned. Dawn's killer had poisoned it.

Something told her that she had not yet felt the full effects of that poison. Something began on the day she saw Dawn's body, and it wasn't over yet. Rue felt in her bones that her discovery of Dawn had set something in motion, an invisible chain of consequences that had not yet run its course.

Suddenly the hair on the back of her neck stood up. Her skin prickled and her heart boomed in her chest. Her body was reacting to the sound that abruptly rose up out of the cistern, a keening echo that was stranger than any sound she had ever heard before. It didn't sound human, yet it had to be coming from Dwayne.

She ran back to the cistern's edge and looked down. Dwayne was in a rage, staggering from one block of fallen concrete to another, picking up smaller pieces and hurling them against the sides of the cistern. The noise that came out of his mouth was something between a scream and a moan. It was almost unbearable to listen to. Rue covered her ears.

"Dwayne! Dwayne, stop it!" It was useless to shout at him. He didn't hear her. But shouting at least drowned out his screaming. "Dwayne! Please!"

He pulled the gun from his jacket. Rue instinctively jerked back, and almost tripped.

Dwayne was still screaming and spinning around in a mad circle, staggering over the rubble, his face twisted with rage. He held the gun with both hands and his arms fully extended. Every time the gun spun around toward her, Rue flinched and jerked back.

She started to cry. She couldn't help it. Suddenly her face was wet and her nose was running. She wiped it against her sleeve, feeling like a child.

Instead of slowing down, Dwayne spun about faster and faster, screaming louder and louder. Then the gun went off.

The shot wasn't in Rue's direction. She saw the little explosion on the far side of the cistern where the bullet struck. But the noise was so startling that she staggered backward and fell. A stabbing pain shot through her left ankle. She was shaking so violently that she had a hard time getting back to her feet. When she was finally upright, she didn't head back toward the cistern but in the opposite direction, limping down the hillside as fast as she could, wincing at the pain in her ankle.

She would head back to Gran's house. Maybe Juss would be there. If he wasn't, she would wait for him—outside, she thought, despite the cold, so that Gran wouldn't see her this way. When Juss arrived, they would go back to the cistern together, and once Dwayne calmed down, if he didn't kill himself first, they would lower the ladder to him. Then Dwayne could be on his way, and Rue would owe him nothing more, having shown him what he wanted. Rue could finally leave Amethyst and head for Austin and then back home to San Francisco.

It was over. She had had enough.

28

$\mathcal{S}$he hadn't gone a hundred yards before she began to feel guilty. And worried.

Dwayne had a gun. He was out of control, crazy with grief. What was to stop him from turning the gun on himself? Every time she stepped on a twig and heard it crack, she jumped, imagining the sound of a distant gunshot. If Dwayne shot himself, and she hadn't been there to stop him, how could she live with herself?

But *could* she stop him? Maybe. Not from the rim of the cistern, but what if she managed to get the ladder over the edge and climbed down to join him? If she could touch him, hold him, physically calm him down, maybe she could convince him to put the gun away and go back to the house with her quietly.

Or maybe not. Twice now she had seen him fire the gun, both times irrationally, without reason. Dwayne was dangerous, and not just to himself.

At the bottom of the hill she turned to look back. From here, she couldn't see the cistern at all; the low wall was set back from the verge of the hillside, out of sight. Nor could she hear anything—no screaming or weeping, no gunshots. Perhaps Dwayne had spent his fury. She imagined him huddled on the spot where she had seen Dawn, crouching down, hugging himself, quietly weeping. Tears welled in her eyes and she blinked them away. The tears made her suddenly aware again of the cold.

She walked on, uncertain about whether to turn back, until she was almost halfway to Gran's house. Her ankle was aching and she paused for a moment to rest it. She turned her gaze to a nearby shed, and something caught her eye. She stepped closer. In the midst of the weathered, gray wood there was a hole the circumference of her forefinger ringed by tiny splinters. It was the bullet hole made by Dwayne's gun the previous night. Rue imagined a bullet ripping with the same force into human flesh and put aside all thoughts of returning to the cistern alone.

Passing the shed, she caught sight of Gran's house in the distance. She could see her blue rental car in the driveway, along with Dwayne's green Toyota. And there was another car. Not Juss's patrol car, but a dark green Oldsmobile—her father's car. He had said he would come by to see her, and so he had, but Rue had absolutely no stomach for dealing with him. The last thing she needed at that moment was another confrontation with her father!

Suddenly, everything was too much. Rue closed her eyes and took a deep breath. With her eyes shut she was suddenly conscious of the stillness and empty space around her. There was no sound—no cars on the distant highway, not even the noisy birds rustling in the underbrush; they had already migrated on. No other people, only herself and this patch of cold, unpopulated earth. She felt alone—utterly alone, as if no one else in the world existed. No Dwayne, no Dawn. No Gran—a painful thought, but a reality she would eventually have to face. No Reg, with his clueless wife and his hidden porn magazines. No father, turning old and gray out of sight. No mother—she was gone already. No Ginger turning on her, and no Marty leering and grabbing at her. No Dylan stalking and deceiving her. No Juss pulling her toward him even while telling her to leave Amethyst.

None of them. All banished from the face of the earth. Only her, and the patch of land she had known from the very beginning of her consciousness. Rue opened her eyes and turned to face the heart of the Dunwitty land.

The pain in her ankle had subsided, but it still hurt a little as she stepped through the high grass, feeling the burrs snag and tug at her socks and shoelaces, delighting in the sensation because it reminded her of her childhood. The trees and the barns and sheds suddenly seemed bigger, taller, as if she had physically dwindled to the size of a little girl. Why was this place so magical to her, so comforting, despite its bittersweet memories? This was what she had been needing, craving—a walk on the Dunwitty property, unfettered by any thoughts of the present, immersed completely in the past. Yet it was the one thing she hadn't been able to do—Juss had warned her against it, and wisely so, she had no doubt.

She came to the biggest of the outbuildings, a long, high structure open at one end. She stepped inside. Even on a day as still as this, the air in the long shed was thick with suspended motes of dust. The walls were filled with shelves and cubbyholes crammed with every imaginable kind of tool and piece of hardware—bundles of rusted barbed wire and baling wire, shelves crammed with glass insulators, huge wrenches and pliers and ball peen hammers, glass jars filled with nails and screws, bundles of rubber washers turned brittle from years of exposure. There were cans of paint with drips running down the sides, glass jars of turpentine, tarpaulins and drop cloths, paintbrushes covered with spiderwebs. And there were work hats and bonnets and raincoats hung on nails and covered with so much dust that Rue couldn't tell what color they were, and a pair of old-fashioned gardening gloves with pink rubber dots on the palms for traction—those belonged to her grandmother, who had loved all things pink.

On the dusty floor, bundled lengths of rusted rebar nestled amid piles of bricks and cinder blocks. Above her head, hanging from the rafters, were rusted barrel hoops and lengths of chain, and cages for catching possums and armadillos.

What would a stranger make of this place? Would they see priceless relics, or a collection of junk? When Rue was a girl, the actual, intended uses for all these things hadn't mattered; in her child's mind, they had become whatever she imagined them to be. The big, rusted pieces of farm machinery had become spaceships and time machines. The big barrel hoops were magical rings—to step through one was to be transported to some enchanted kingdom. The iron vise mounted on one of the shelves had been a giant instrument of torture straight out of a James Bond movie—Reg had once used it to slowly crush the head of her favorite Barbie doll, pushing Rue away when she protested, and sent her screaming and crying back to the house. Her mother had given Reg a whipping with a belt that day. Rue shook her head. She had forgotten all about that ugly memory until this moment.

She stepped out of the long shed. There had once been a wide drive leading all the way to her grandparents' house, but weeds had encroached on either side until the drive was now hardly more than a footpath. Surrounded by outbuildings and trees and high grass, unable to see beyond them, Rue was in the heart of the Dunwitty property.

She kept walking until she came to the house. When she was a child, it had been kept freshly painted and in good repair, and the lawn and hedges and trees were well maintained. Even as an old man, her grandfather had been tirelessly enterprising, always fiddling and puttering and taking care of small jobs for her grandmother. Now the paint was blistered and worn. The window screens were rusty, some of them hanging askew. The tin roof had rusty patches and missing sections. The yard was wildly overgrown, a tangle of weeds and high grass.

Her grandparents' house had become the kind of derelict property that frightened small children. There had been such houses around Amethyst when she was a girl; Reg had told her they were haunted. She hadn't known then what ghosts really were, or about the power they still wielded over the living. What was it Reg had said about their father the other day on the phone? *He told me that he can hardly stand to go there anymore. Too many ghosts.* Rue understood. Now, when she thought of ghosts, she thought of her dead grandparents. She thought of her mother.

Rue headed toward the house, taking high steps through the tall grass. Her foot touched something hard, something that felt wrong—that was all she had time to think before she heard a whoosh and a sharp metallic clang. Rue instinctively jumped back, her heart booming in her chest, so startled she let out a stifled cry.

Once she caught her breath, she bent down for a closer look. It was a simple, hinge-jawed trap with a trip plate. She had jarred the trap with the side of her foot, just enough to set it off. She hadn't stepped directly on the plate, or else her foot would have been caught. The jaws had sharp teeth, and from the way the trap had leaped into the air, the spring mechanism was quite powerful—strong enough to cause terrible pain, maybe even strong enough to break a bone.

Juss had warned her about the traps. He said he had disarmed the ones he came across, but he had missed this one.

It seemed insane that her father had set them, but who else could have done it? What was he thinking? She remembered the aging man she had seen at the motel, so addled he had called her by her mother's name, and she shook her head, feeling more alienated from him than ever. He had always been emotionally distant, and then literally distant, moving hundreds of miles away after the divorce. She had never really known him. What sort of odd eccentric had he become, setting traps on a property he seemed to care nothing about, lurking in a shabby motel in the town where he had grown up?

She took a deep breath. Stepping very carefully, she entered the wildly overgrown yard. The grass and weeds were so high she felt like a swimmer wading through waist-high surf. The yard was unrecognizable, yet this was the place where she and Reg had played hide-and-seek, where she had helped her grandmother water flowers and pull weeds, where every Fourth of July her father had come to visit and they had all sat in metal chairs under the pecan tree, eating watermelon and counting fireflies as twilight fell.

She reached the sidewalk, glad to be clear of the high grass. Concrete steps led up to the screen door that opened onto the little porch. The screen door was never locked. Rue pressed the latch button with her thumb and pulled it open.

The porch was essentially a small, narrow anteroom, a transitional space between the outdoors and the house proper. Covering the left-hand wall, a collection of bonnets and brimmed caps hung on nails. Below the hats, her grandfather's workbooks and the old sneakers her grandmother had used for gardening were lined up against the wall. Her grandfather had built shelves into the opposite wall. Rue saw a copper watering can, pruning shears, hedge clippers, and a cardboard box full of sunglasses—all kinds of sunglasses, from vintage models with pink rhinestones to the World War II aviator glasses her grandfather had favored, some with broken stems or a lens missing. Rue sighed. Her grandparents had never thrown anything away. No wonder her father had never been able to face the job of rummaging through all these things, sorting the treasures from the junk, because every object, no matter how mundane, conveyed a memory. So many objects, so many memories, it was overwhelming— and she hadn't yet even entered the house.

She lifted one of the hats that hung on the wall—a shapeless work hat made of khaki that had been her grandfather's favorite—and found the door key in its usual place, hanging on a nail. She fitted it into the keyhole and opened the door, bracing herself for the shrill alarm. The battery-operated alarm was in two parts, one mounted on the inside door frame and the other on the door, so that the alarm went off when the door opened and the parts broke contact. For a brief moment the ear-splitting alarm pierced the silence, then Rue quickly reached inside and turned it off.

She stepped into the house and closed the door behind her.

29

Over the years since her grandparents had died, various objects and pieces of furniture had been removed from the house. Reg had taken some things, Rue others. Probably her father had taken some things as well. But no one had ever cleaned the house. Years of dust had settled on every surface. Cobwebs had accumulated in the corners. Mice had nibbled at the threadbare rugs and left droppings on the floors. Nor had anyone cleared out the dresser drawers and cabinets and closets.

The result was a house that seemed neither lived in nor totally abandoned. Not much furniture was left in the living room. There was a broken TV sitting on an old metal stand, a few rickety chairs, a half-empty bookcase, and a water-stained side table with a pink porcelain lamp too ugly for anybody to want. The rug on the floor was crooked. The nicer pictures—framed photographs and a couple of oil paintings—had been taken, leaving pale rectangles on the walls. The pictures that remained were the ones nobody wanted, including an old photo of her father, taken when he was just out of high school, looking impossibly boyish and flashing the handsome smile that had persuaded Rue's mother to marry him.

Anyone could tell at a glance that no one lived there anymore. And yet, if Rue were to open one of the built-in drawers, she knew she would find a cache of pencils and pens and pale pink stationery with her grandmother's monogram, and old stamps, and utility bills bundled with rubber bands, and postcards that Rue had sent to her grandparents long ago from Girl Scout camp. If she were to open the door to the little hall closet, she would find a whole collection of moth-eaten coats and wraps, and on the top shelf, stacks of pink hatboxes, because her grandmother had always worn hats and gloves to go to Sunday services and to weddings and funerals.

Clearly, no one had lived here for years, and yet the signs of those who had lived here were everywhere, as if they had just stepped out and might still return. Rue always found the atmosphere in the house slightly eerie, and yet at the same time, it comforted her.

The house had a musty, dank smell. It was cold, even colder than outside. Her breath formed white clouds in the air.

She walked into the dining room. Reg had taken the dining table and chairs, but the sideboard was still here, filled with her grandparents' second-best china; Rue herself had claimed the good china. On top of the sideboard there was a pink crystal candy dish that still held peppermints, which had long ago softened and rehardened into a single mass. Above the sideboard were two tall, framed pieces of fifties-era art—a pink poodle and a black poodle so kitschy that even now Rue had to smile and shake her head when she looked at them. Her grandmother had thought they were lovely.

"Lovely"—that was the exact word Grandmother Dunwitty had once used, sitting at the dining table with Rue and gazing at those pictures. Had they been having afternoon tea? How old was Rue at the time? She couldn't remember. She closed her eyes and tried to recapture the exact timbre and tone of her grandmother's voice saying that single word, "lovely," but memory failed her. Her grandmother's voice had receded beyond recollection. Rue could still recapture her mother's voice, could hear her speaking if she put her mind to it. But would even that voice, the first voice she had ever heard, fade to silence as the years passed?

She walked from the dining room into the kitchen, tripping a little because the linoleum on the floor was so badly buckled. The shelves were crammed with jars of homemade preserves. The window over the sink admitted only a feeble, filtered light. Vines had grown up the side of the house, covering the screen.

She walked from the kitchen into the little hallway with a built-in phone nook, where an ancient black phone with a rotary dial, long disconnected, sat atop an old Amethyst phone book. The little spiral notebook beside it was filled with jottings in her grandmother's handwriting. Over the years, Rue had pored over those jottings again and again, and had never been able to make out more than a word or a numeral here and there. Toward the end, her grandmother's handwriting had become unreadable to anyone but herself. It was as indecipherable now as the hieroglyphs of a lost civilization.

From the hallway, a narrow flight of stairs ran up to the second floor, but for the moment Rue passed them by and walked on, into her grandparents' bedroom, at the back of the house.

An image flashed through her mind, the same image she saw every time she stepped into this room. It was nighttime, and her grandmother was seated in front of the dresser, almost ready for bed, wearing her flannel nightgown and combing her long, silver hair.

The dresser was still there, with its tarnished mirror. So was the little stool with its frayed upholstery. Inside the dresser drawers, and filling the jewelry boxes atop it, were treasures that had fascinated Rue from her earliest childhood—gold and silver lipsticks, jars of rouge, compacts, hand mirrors, and a lifetime's accumulation of costume jewelry. Her grandmother had favored gaudy necklaces and clip-on earrings, the kind a little girl could borrow and play with.

During the day her grandmother had always worn her hair up, coiled and held in place with tortoiseshell pins. That was how Rue always pictured her, well turned out and a bit formal, even if she was only going out to shop at Schneider's.

But once, as a small girl—for a reason she could no longer remember—Rue had been in the house after dark, past her own bedtime, and she had seen her grandmother getting ready for bed. Never before had Rue realized that her grandmother's hair, unpinned, was so long, and that image of long silver hair had registered indelibly in Rue's mind. It was like a secret her grandmother had shared with her, not even intending to, unaware of how potently the sight would dwell in Rue's memory. Why did it haunt her? Because of what it suggested, she thought: that there was a part of her grandmother that existed beyond fancy coats and hats and coiffed hair and rouged cheeks and pink clip-on earrings, beyond gardening bonnets and gloves, beyond the twilit evenings when they would gather on the lawn to eat watermelon and count fireflies. There had been a part of her grandmother that was simply a woman, with appetites and desires and memories like any other woman, who slept each night in the same bed with her husband, whose body and let-down hair was seen and shared by him alone.

Rue stepped no farther into her grandparents' bedroom. Even though they had both been gone for years, it still felt like snooping. She backtracked to the phone nook and turned toward the stairway.

The stairs were narrow, tucked into the smallest possible space, like servants' stairs in a grand house. Halfway up, she reached the tiny landing, where a window looked out on the windmill in the backyard. She felt a twinge of pain in her ankle and paused, then turned and followed the rest of the steps to the top, her hand skimming just above the banister railing, covered with dust.

The upstairs of the house was nothing more than a partially finished attic, a single long room with a high ceiling and windows on either side set into the mansard roof. This had been her father's room when he was a boy. It was still furnished with his old bed and a child's dresser with a mirror. After her father was grown, her grandparents had stored their odds and ends in this room; mementos and bric-a-brac filled the built-in shelves along the walls.

When Rue was small, the upstairs had become a playroom for her and Reg, and some of their old toys and dolls were still scattered about. The Barbie whose head had been crushed sat cross-legged on a long shelf filled with *National Geographic* magazines. One of Reg's war toys—some kind of mobile missile launcher—lay on its side against the wall. A pack of Mother Goose cards was scattered on the floor.

Suddenly, it was all too much. So many memories, so much loss—

there was no way to take it all in. There never was. And yet she returned here over and over, trying to come to terms with the past.

Not for the first time, she had a fantasy of gathering all these odds and ends, repairing what was broken, cleaning what was filthy, scrubbing the whole house until it was bright and shiny, putting everything right again, with every item accounted for and in its proper place. But what purpose would that serve? Nothing would bring her grandparents back to life. Nothing would make her a girl again, trusting and innocent, not yet aware of death and decay. Better, she thought, to simply burn down the house and everything in it. Purify this place with fire, destroy these useless artifacts once and for all, turn away from the dead past.

She closed her eyes and took a deep breath. The air was musty, tinged with a sour odor and a whiff of something fetid. Vermin had had the run of the house for years. They lived in the house and presumably died there as well. Was that what she smelled?

She seemed to remember reading something recently about a bad smell. But where? The memory eluded her.

Another memory came to her instead, of the time when she was very small and Reg had tricked her into going into the unfinished part of the attic. She had stepped through a little door, she remembered, and then Reg had shut the door behind her. She had screamed until her grandmother came and rescued her. Grandmother Dunwitty had scolded Reg, but she had also scolded Rue. "Don't you know it's dangerous up there? There's electrical wiring, and wasps and yellow jackets! You could fall through the ceiling, you silly girl!"

After that incident, the little door into the unfinished attic space had vanished. How could that be? Had her grandfather sealed it up? Or had it simply been covered over somehow?

She remembered that the little door had been at the far end of the room, in the wall that ran across the center of the house. In the spot she was thinking of, a dresser with a mirror stood against the wall. But the dresser had always been there—or had it? Had her grandmother solved the problem of children in the attic in the simplest way possible, by having Grandfather Dunwitty place something across the door too heavy for a child to move?

But not too heavy for a grown-up to move. In fact, as Rue stepped closer to the dresser, examining the space around it, she saw scuff marks on the soft pine floor. The marks were faint, and she never would have noticed them if she hadn't been looking for them. It looked as if the dresser had been pulled away from the wall and pushed back again, not once but several times.

Rue gripped the left edge of the dresser. It was heavy, but she managed to pull that side away from the wall, exposing a wedge-shaped space behind. The scraping of the feet against the floor made a noise that set her teeth on edge.

Behind the dresser she saw a small plywood door set in the wall. It was less than two feet wide and no more than five feet high.

Juss Goodbody had searched the house. He told her he had looked everywhere, including the attic. But by attic, did he simply mean the finished room? Had he missed the hidden door? Had he failed to look in the space beyond?

The odor she had noticed before was stronger now. Suddenly Rue remembered where she had recently read about a smell—in the book about the Corpus Christi murders, in a passage that quoted one of the lawmen who had discovered the body of Brandy Littleton. *It wasn't the stench of death. . . . It was more like a caged animal smell—sour sweat, body fluids, human waste. And something else . . . the odor that came out of that shed was the smell of fear itself.*

She also noticed another smell, something familiar that had a more pleasant connotation, but it was so mingled with the other, ugly smell that Rue couldn't quite place it.

The door's latch had been removed—long ago, so no child could get trapped inside again?—and now there were just a couple of nails with a loop of string attached, holding it in place. She put her finger into the loop and pulled. There was just enough room for the door to clear the dresser. Rue pulled it flush against the wall, and the doorway was wide open.

The awful smell grew even stronger, like a fetid breath issuing from the dim, gray space beyond. It was unlike anything Rue had ever smelled before. She could imagine no words to describe it.

The room behind her was dim, lit only by overcast daylight from the windows, but the space beyond the open door was even dimmer. Rue squinted, but could discern only the vague outlines of posts and rafters.

The doorway was low and narrow. Rue had to make herself as small as she could to slip through. She hated dark, confined places. She had a sudden flashback to the time when she was a little girl and Reg had tricked her into going into the attic; she experienced a prickle of panic and suddenly felt small, helpless, childlike. It took all the courage she could muster to step across the threshold.

The surface beneath her feet was solid but slightly wobbly. Someone had laid sheets of plywood over the ceiling rafters, creating a makeshift floor. The air was thick with dust, and inside the room the fetid smell was so strong she thought she might faint. To steady herself she reached out to the nearest post, then drew back her hand when she touched something cold and metallic. It was a short length of chain attached to the pillar with a heavy-duty eye bolt. Dangling from the chain were a pair of handcuffs.

As her eyes slowly adapted to the dimness, she saw a set of rusty box springs lying on the makeshift floor. Handcuffs were attached to each corner. Beneath the box springs, patches of some dark liquid had stained the plywood.

She bumped against another post and turned her head. Thumbtacked to the wood at eye level were three wallet-sized class photos. Rue instantly recognized Dawn's picture. The other two girls were not as pretty, but they were just as young. Brittany Sumpter and Kandy Keegan, Rue thought—the girls who had gone missing in August. Nails had been driven into the wood below each picture, and pieces of jewelry were hung on the nails—a bead necklace, a charm bracelet, earrings. There was also a silver signet ring with the letter *D* in onyx. Dwayne had a signet ring like that; Rue had noticed it the first time she saw him, at the grocery store. This was a smaller, more delicate version. Marty Sutherland had told her that Dwayne and Dawn sometimes wore matching clothes. Apparently they wore matching rings as well.

Her foot struck something. It was a small metal strongbox. Rue opened the lid with her foot. Among the jumbled objects inside she saw a box of disposable plastic gloves and a box of condoms . . . a coiled whip . . . a girl's barrette made of purple plastic . . . a pair of alligator clips connected by a thin chain . . . a cheap lipstick in a shade only a teenager would wear . . . a leather dog collar.

And something made of cloth, like a handkerchief twisted and tied into knots at either end. The colors were red-white-and-blue—like the miniature Lone Star flags the killer in Corpus Christi used to gag his victims.

A smell issued from the box. It was the smell she had noticed before but couldn't quite place, mingled with the fetid odor. A good smell, like a perfume, but not like any scent her grandmother would have used.

The elusive association conjured by the smell nagged at her and seemed about to surface when she detected a noise from downstairs. It penetrated to the attic, muffled and indistinct. Rue might not have heard it if the house had not been utterly silent.

It was the sound of the front door being quietly opened and closed. She held her breath, listening intently. There was a pause, then slow, cautious footsteps wandered from room to room below her, until they arrived at the foot of the steps. Slowly, one by one, the footsteps ascended the stairs.

30

Who was on the stairs?

Rue felt an impulse to pull the little door shut, but what good would that do? The door had no lock and the dresser would remain pulled away from the wall, making it obvious that someone had been there and had discovered the secret space.

Time stopped. The whole world contracted to the dim, confined space around her. A cold chill settled over her. She glanced at the handcuffs hanging from the eye bolt, at the dog collar in the box, at the box springs with handcuffs at each corner.

Peering out the low, narrow entranceway, past the edge of the dresser mirror, she could see the top of the stairway. Whoever was on the stairs reached the little landing and stopped. Rue's heart pounded in her chest. The footsteps began again, sharp and heavy against the wooden steps.

Sheer terror consumed her, obliterating everything else. She opened her mouth, but she couldn't scream. She was frozen by panic.

Rue saw his black Stetson first, then his face—and the relief that swept over her was so overwhelming she let out a gasp and almost wept. A knot in her chest seemed to loosen and unfurl, and she realized just how frightened she had been.

She stepped out of the attic space, slipped past the dresser, crossed the room, and rushed into his arms. "Juss! Thank God you're here!"

Juss had his pistol drawn and he embraced her awkwardly at first. As she pressed herself against him, he held her more tightly. His body remained rigid, on alert, but to Rue he felt warm, strong, and solid. She wanted to disappear into his embrace and hide there forever.

At last she pulled back. He gradually released her. She wiped tears from her face. The fear she had just experienced was unlike anything she had ever felt before, and it left her feeling weakened and dazed.

"Where's Dwayne?" said Juss. He looked past her, his face grim. He still held the pistol.

Rue shook her head. "Not here. He went crazy. He jumped into the cistern. We'll have to lower the ladder before he can climb out."

Juss visibly relaxed. He holstered his gun inside his green jacket. "I just got to your grandmother's house a minute ago. She seems confused. Said you'd gone up to the cistern. But then I heard the alarm go off over here, so I headed straight over." He frowned. "I saw your car and Dwayne's in the drive, but who does that green Oldsmobile belong to?"

"My father," said Rue. "He's here in Amethyst, staying at the motel. Wasn't he in the house with Gran?"

"No. She was alone."

"Then I've got to go to her! She's not well, something's wrong with her."

"Calm down, Rue." Juss gently gripped her arms and nodded toward the far side of the room. "Who moved that dresser?"

"I did."

"What's through that door?"

Rue shuddered. "Oh, Juss! It happened here. He brought them here, to this house! Not just Dawn, but the other girls, too. This is where it happened, where he—"

"*Who* brought them here?" Juss looked at her intently.

"It must have been . . ." She shook her head. "I don't know—not for sure."

"If you suspect somebody, you have to tell me, Rue."

She bit her lip. "It had to be someone who knew about this house, and about that attic space. Someone who was here in Amethyst when the girls disappeared—oh, Juss, you can't imagine the crazy thoughts that have been going through my head!"

"Maybe you need to let them out. Share them with somebody. Tell me, Rue."

"It could be Marty Sutherland. He's been on the property. He's been in this house—I know, because he stole something, a clock that belonged to my grandparents."

"You know that for a fact?"

She nodded.

"You should have told me, Rue." He sounded almost angry, and his grip tightened on her arms.

"I know. But . . ."

"There's somebody else you suspect, isn't there?"

She shook her head. "I don't even want to think about it."

"Tell me, Rue."

She looked into his eyes. He stared back at her with an intensity that was almost frightening.

"My brother, Reg. Once, when we were kids, he locked me in that attic space. He was here in Amethyst the weekend Dawn disappeared. He goes off on his own, and his wife never seems to know where he is." Rue thought of the magazines under Gran's house, and the porno tapes she had discovered at Reg's house, with women in leather and bondage. She thought about the leather dog collar she had just glimpsed in the strong-box, and shuddered.

Juss's grip was painfully tight, but she almost didn't mind. The fingers digging into her flesh seemed to be the only things holding her up. "Who else, Rue? Who else knew about this house and might have used it? I have to know!"

She swallowed hard. "It sounds crazy, but . . . Dylan Jeffries, my friend from San Francisco. He was here in Amethyst when Dawn disappeared, and he never told me. I know he stayed at the motel. But so did . . ."

"Go on, Rue!" He gave her a shake. She felt like a rag doll in his grip.

"I don't want to say it, because it's so crazy! What kind of man could do such horrible things in the house where he grew up?"

Juss looked at her gravely. "You're talking about your father, aren't you?"

She nodded. "The man they convicted never confessed to the Corpus Christi murders, did he? My father lives in Corpus. He's always been a little strange." Saying the unthinkable out loud suddenly made it seem plausible. "He's a monster, Juss—whoever did this is a monster! When you see what's in there. . . ." Rue fought back a wave of nausea. "But he's left all kinds of evidence. Trophies—isn't that what they call them? Keepsakes. Things he can't bear to throw away. There must be plenty of stuff in there to prove who did it—fingerprints, DNA, items you can trace. Now that we've found his hiding place, it's just a matter of tracking him down." She shook her head. "But didn't you search the house yesterday, Juss? Why didn't *you* find that attic space? All you had to do was move that dresser."

His face was grim. "Here, show me what you found."

Rue shivered. "No, I can't go in there again."

"But I want you to show me." He turned her about, keeping a tight grip on her arms, and began to walk her across the room. Rue tried to resist, but he seemed determined to force her back toward the room.

They arrived at the wedge of open space between the dresser and the little door. "Step inside," Juss said. "Show me what—"

Juss abruptly stiffened. He heard the noise an instant before she did. Somebody else was in the house.

The sound of footsteps came from downstairs. Someone was walking from room to room, treading heavily, making no effort to keep quiet. The footsteps arrived at the foot of the stairway, then began to ascend.

"Get back, Rue," Juss whispered, releasing her arm and reaching into his jacket. "Go into the attic. Now! He may have a gun."

She shuddered and stepped backward through the little doorway, looking past Juss to keep her eyes on the top of the stairway.

A voice called out, "Rue! Are you up there?"

It was her father.

227

Rue felt a sinking sensation in the pit of her stomach.

"Goddamn it!" Juss muttered under his breath.

Emmett Dunwitty reached the landing and turned to ascend the last few steps. The grizzled top of his head came into sight.

Rue sucked in a breath and tried not to inhale the odors that surrounded her in the attic space—the fetid smell, and the other, sweeter smell that mingled with it. Suddenly she recognized that curiously pleasant smell—not a woman's perfume but a man's cologne, the same scent she always noticed whenever she was close to Juss. She could smell it on him now, its odor sharpened by his sweat. Under the brim of his Stetson she saw beads of perspiration on the back of his neck.

"Rue?" Her father called out again. He trod heavily up the last few steps. He came to a halt and stared at the two of them across the room—Juss standing in front of the attic door, Rue peering out from behind him. He looked puzzled. "What on earth's going on, hon? I said hello to your grandmother, then headed up toward the cistern. That's where she said you'd be. But I heard the door alarm and figured you must be here at the house. What's wrong, Rue? Who is this fellow?"

Rue felt unsteady and took a step back. A glimmer caught her eye. She turned her head and found herself staring at one of the pieces of jewelry hung on a nail—Dawn's silver signet ring, the one that matched her brother's. Rue's mind flashed back to the afternoon Juss climbed down to search the cistern while she and the sheriff watched. Rue had noticed something shiny near the spot where she had seen Dawn. Juss had picked it up but said it was nothing more than the pull ring from a cola can. Rue had been too far away to see for herself, but both she and the sheriff had taken his word for it. Juss had bagged it and slipped it into his pocket. Rue hadn't given the ring another thought.

"Juss!" she whispered hoarsely. He turned and looked at her over his shoulder. His jaw was stiff and his forehead was beaded with sweat. The eyes that stared back at her were those of a stranger. Rue felt sick and disoriented, as if the room had suddenly been turned upside down.

"Dad, run!" she shouted. "Get out of here, now!" She tried to step over the threshold, out of the attic, but Juss shoved her back and she banged her head painfully against the frame. She stumbled across the wobbly plywood. Juss blocked the doorway with his back.

"Now see here, young fellow!" her father said.

"Run, Dad!" she screamed. She shoved against Juss's back. He hardly budged.

Rue heard a shot. Her father cried out. She heard him stagger backward, stamping heavily, and then the sickening sound of his body tumbling down the steps.

For a moment time stopped, then started again when Juss turned to face her, bending to peer at her through the low doorway. As he stepped through, his Stetson caught on the frame, was pushed off his head, and tumbled onto the floor behind him. Rue had never seen him without it. She sucked in a breath, shocked to see that the top of his head was completely bald, as smooth and shiny as an egg. His expression was cold and hard, his eyes steady like flint. He looked like a completely different person, someone she had never seen before, no longer remotely handsome but ugly and repulsive.

He pointed the gun at her. "Sorry I had to kill your old man, Rue. But I don't imagine he felt much. Got him right through the heart. That's nothing, compared to what you're gonna feel. You think I need this?" He gestured with the gun. "Hell, no! More fun without it." He holstered his gun, then grabbed one of her wrists, moving so quickly Rue was unable to jerk away. He squeezed hard and bent her arm, making her yelp with pain as he pulled her toward the handcuffs hanging from the eye bolt. He forced her wrist inside one cuff and was about to snap it shut when Rue abruptly managed to snatch her hand free and stagger back.

He laughed—a high, unnerving giggle—and grabbed at her wrist again, but Rue pulled back, out of reach. She had the feeling he was toying with her. He was so much stronger, surely he could have handcuffed her already if he wanted to. Her head hit a rafter. She ducked and continued to back away, hunkering lower and lower, shrinking into the angular space formed by the sloping roof, like a frightened child trying to make herself as small as possible.

Steven Saylor

She desperately looked around for a weapon—something, anything, she could use to defend herself—but there was nothing.

"Why, Juss?" she said, her voice breaking.

He peered down at her and shook his head, looking disgusted. "That's what all you whiny Jezebels ask. 'Why, why, why?' Because you bring it on yourselves. You ask for it, just like Brother Zack says."

Rue felt a chill sweep over her. "I don't know what you're talking about."

"Brother Zack does. I write him letters. I think he gets a kick out of reading 'em on his show, giving a thrill to the old biddies who watch him. They all want the same thing—a man who's big enough to give 'em what they really want, rub their faces in it, make 'em squeal. You'll be squealing soon, Rue, just like the others did."

Something from Brother Zack's show flashed through Rue's mind. *Outcast from the Body of Christ*—that was how the writer signed his letters. *Corpus Christi* was Latin for "Body of Christ."

Juss took a step closer, looming over her. She could see he was sexually excited. "What did I tell you to do, Rue?"

She shook her head, not knowing how to answer.

He clenched his jaw and his voice trembled. "I told you to get the hell out of here, didn't I? I told you to stay away from this house and get out of Amethyst. But did you do what I told you? No!" The last word was a furious shout that made her cringe. "So here you are, you stupid bitch. Well, I hope you like it, because this is where you're gonna stay. This is home, Rue. You'll never leave this room again." He hunkered down and grabbed for her, but the confined space made moving awkward for both of them, and she managed to skitter just out of his reach.

"I like your short hair," he said in a low voice, no longer angry but crooning. "Makes you look pretty. Makes you look young."

"Not as young as the others," Rue whispered, her voice breaking.

A smirk crept across his lips. "Kandy and Brittany were bad girls. I caught 'em hitchhiking on the highway, running away from home, wearing nothing but skimpy shorts and tank tops. I ordered 'em to get in the car. Told 'em I had to handcuff 'em. And they let me. If they'd put

230

up a fuss I might have backed off, but they didn't. They liked being handcuffed."

"I don't believe that," said Rue.

"It's true. You know what they told me? They were headed for L.A. Gonna hitch rides with truckers. 'And how were you gonna pay your way?' I said. They giggled and said, 'Blow jobs!' Kandy stuck her tongue out at me. I decided to take care of her first."

"You brought them here?" Rue said. As long as they were talking, Juss seemed content to let her crouch in the cramped space next to the eaves.

"I pulled off the highway onto a dirt road. I made Brittany get in the trunk. She didn't want to. I had to hurt her a little, then she shut up and did what she was told. Drove here and brought Kandy upstairs. As long as I handled 'em one at a time, it was no problem. Once I showed 'em who was boss, they were meek as lambs."

"Where are they now?"

"Up on that hill, not far from the cistern. Kandy lasted a couple of weeks. Brittany lasted longer. They're buried next to Dawn."

"Buried? But they searched the hillside . . ."

He smiled. "Under my supervision."

Rue shook her head. "Why Dawn?"

"Why, why, why?" he said mockingly. "I just happened to pass her on the railroad tracks. There's a place where the road crosses the tracks and nobody can see, on account of the warehouses. I offered her a ride. She was in the car like a shot, making Jezebel eyes at me. I brought her here. She gave me a little trouble, but not much. It must get awful cold and lonely in this little attic when you're left alone for hours at a stretch. She was always glad to see me whenever I showed up. Eager to please. Everything was fine . . . until you showed up." His face darkened.

"Friday, when I got into town," Rue said, "Dawn was here—alive—in this room?"

He nodded. "Then I saw you at the football game. Somebody told me you were old lady Lee's granddaughter. Damn! I remembered what the old lady told me about you, back in the summer when I checked on this house for her and saw what a cozy love nest this attic would make. She told me she had a granddaughter who came home to visit every now and then and liked to go nosing around over here. And there you were, sitting up in the bleachers, giving me the Jezebel look." He shook his head. "I'd put out those traps to scare off trespassers, but I figured that wouldn't stop you. I couldn't let you find Dawn. It was your fault, Rue, that I had to get rid of her so soon. Real late that night, I came here and took care of her, just like I did with Kandy and Brittany. Gagged her and put a rope around her neck and marched her naked up the hillside, like a bitch on a leash."

"The flashlight I saw in the fields!" said Rue.

"Killed her with my bare hands. There's nothing . . . quite like that." His eyes glazed slightly and his tongue darted out to moisten his lips. "Brought a shovel so I could bury her right away, like I did the other two. But I didn't account for the cold. Damned earth was too hard to dig! Didn't want any animals messing with her, so I put her down in the cistern. Figured I'd come back the next day and bury her, but with one thing and another, Monday came around—and you found her. Then you called Bertha, and Bertha called me." He let out a low whistle. "Drove like a bat out of hell to get here ahead of Horace. Parked over here and ran up that hill. Got Dawn's body out of the cistern and hid her in the underbrush, then drove around to park at your grandma's house and came up behind you two, actin' like I was just showing up."

"Dawn was there all along—only a few feet away."

He nodded. "Remember when you and I searched the ground around the cistern and I yelled out that I couldn't find anything over in that thicket? I was standing right over her, playing with her. Had the tip of my boot shoved between her legs."

Rue shook her head. "You can't keep getting away with it. When Dwayne figures it out—"

"You think I'm afraid of that little fruit? People think he's some kind of football hero, but he's as queer as they come. Dawn told me so."

"I don't believe you. Why would she tell you that?"

"Dawn told me lots of things she didn't want to. I made her. I imagine you'll be telling me all sorts of things, too. Things you never dreamed you'd tell anybody." He giggled again, and the sound sickened her. "Once I get you locked up nice and tight—and have a little fun with you—I'll head up to the cistern and take care of Dwayne. Just like shooting fish in a barrel."

Her mouth was so dry she could hardly speak. "You can't get away with it, Juss. If Dwayne goes missing—"

"Everybody will say he went nuts and ran off to look for Dawn."

"And my father—" A sob caught in her throat.

"Nobody knows or cares where your old man is. Once I get rid of his car, nobody will even know he came here."

Rue felt ill. She looked past Juss, at the rusty box springs with handcuffs at each corner, and at the bloodstains on the plywood beneath. "Why, Juss?"

She expected him to mock her again, but his face was grim. "I'm sick. I know that. I've got a sickness. Charlie McCutcheon gave it to me. I'd never have done such things if I hadn't seen with my own eyes what he did to those girls down in Corpus. Once I'd seen what a man can do to a woman when he puts his mind to it, I couldn't sleep at night. I knew I had to do it, too. I'll tell you a secret: McCutcheon didn't do the last one. Trina Schaeffer was mine. Little Jezebel lived next door and used to leave her bedroom drapes wide open. Oh, she was asking for it! And I gave it to her. It was beautiful, the way she kept begging me to stop. I could have taken a lot longer with her, but I got nervous and rushed it, 'cause we were closing in on McCutcheon and I knew it was only a matter of time. I made it look like he did it. Since he never 'fessed up to any of the murders, nobody ever suspected Trina's was different. That's how I got my first taste. After that, I craved it. Thought about it night and day. But once McCutcheon was arrested I knew it was too dangerous to ever do it again in Corpus. Figured if I left Corpus and moved to some hole in the road, maybe I could control my impulses, keep myself out of trouble. But there's Jezebels everywhere. They just won't leave a man alone. They giggle and tease and flaunt themselves until a man just can't help himself."

He shook his head. "I told you to get out of town, Rue. I tried to scare you off—made that phone call in the middle of the night, called you a stupid bitch. And you are a stupid bitch, aren't you? You just wouldn't leave. Last night when I came by your grandma's house to see if you were still in town, I could hardly believe it when you came out on the porch to meet me. Were you naked under that coat, Rue? When you said everybody else was asleep, I suddenly realized I had my chance. I asked you to come with me. You almost said yes, didn't you? You liked it when I kissed you. Admit it." His face twisted with sudden rage. "Admit it, you stupid bitch!"

"Yes," she whispered, cringing as she remembered the kiss and the way he had turned away and walked off without a word when she declined to come with him. She had imagined a look of lovesick confusion on his face. Instead, his face must have looked as it did at that moment, hateful and smirking.

"You wanted to come with me, didn't you, Rue? Open your legs for a night of sin and then walk away like it never happened. Imagine how surprised you'd have been when I brought you here instead! You'd have been one of those women who just up and vanish overnight without a trace. Think how frantic your grandma and that wimpy boyfriend of yours from San Francisco would have been in the morning, waking up and finding you gone and knowing deep down they were never going to see you again. That would have made your boyfriend look mighty suspicious." He shook his head. "It could have happened that way, Rue. But instead it happened this way. Either way, I'm glad you decided to stay."

He flashed a sickening grin, then made a sudden lunge and grabbed her wrist. Rue struggled, but he was much stronger. Awkwardly, he scooted back and rose upright. He pulled her with him out of the narrow corner and toward the dangling handcuffs. A wave of sheer terror swept over her, drenching her with cold sweat. She had a sensation she had experienced only once before in her life, when she'd been in a rollover car accident. *This is it!* she had thought as the car hurtled through space and began to tip over. *This is happening—really happening. It's going to happen and nothing can stop it. This—is—it!*

Juss forced her wrist into the open handcuff. She gave a cry and gathered all her strength and tried to break free. They both lost balance and staggered to one side. The makeshift plywood wobbled under their feet.

Suddenly, Rue was off the plywood, pulling Juss with her. She stepped onto a rafter, then onto a patch of ceiling board.

The surface beneath her feet crumbled into thin air.

As they plummeted downward amid flying dust and debris, she heard her grandmother scolding her: *Don't you know it's dangerous up there? You could fall through the ceiling, you silly girl!*

31

Rue landed hard but remained upright, staggering and holding out her arms for balance. She coughed and wheezed, spitting cobwebs and dust from her mouth. A sharp pain shot through her ankle, taking her breath away.

She was in the living room, downstairs. She looked up and saw the ragged hole in the ceiling. A piece of broken chalkboard fell on her face. She staggered back and bumped into something. It was Juss, on his hands and knees. He shook his head, looking dazed.

Rue started running.

She pushed a chair out of her way. She skittered to one side and bumped hard against the wall. The pain in her ankle was excruciating. Behind her, she heard Juss getting to his feet.

To reach the front door she had to run through the little hallway at the foot of the stairs. She almost tripped over the large object that lay crumpled on the floor, and didn't realize what it was until she looked down and saw her father's face. His eyes were open and staring. Blood trickled from the corner of his mouth. Rue sucked in a shuddering breath and let out a long sob, then heard a noise behind her and rushed on.

Her father had left the front door open. Rue staggered across the porch and pushed open the screen door, sobbing with pain. She couldn't take high steps through the tall grass, but she shambled as fast as she could. The tangle of grass pulled at her ankles. Behind her, she heard the screen door slam back against the house. She wanted to scream but was too out of breath to manage.

He was going to catch her. He was going to grab her from behind, overpower her, and take her back to the attic. It was inevitable. Running was hopeless—if her lopsided, limping progress could be called running. But Rue kept moving anyway.

She reached the dirt drive and broke free from the sea of high grass. He was right behind her. She could hear his heavy breathing.

Then she heard an odd whoosh followed by a muffled crack and a stifled scream. She was so startled, she spun around. Juss was only a few feet away, but he had gone stiff, his body electrified with pain. He bent double and clutched his ankle. He had stepped on a metal trap in the grass, one of the traps he had put there himself.

Rue caught a breath and let out a bleat of triumph, then sucked it back as Juss opened the trap with his bare hands and extricated his foot. He was wearing thick leather cowboy boots. For a moment Rue thought he was unscathed. The she saw him wince and curse as he put some weight on his foot. He was hurt, after all. Rue felt a rush of hope—which crashed as soon as she turned around and tried to run again. It was a miracle she had made it this far. She had been running on pure adrenaline, but now that rush of energy was spent and the pain was unbearable. The least weight on her ankle felt like a knitting needle shoved into the joint. She felt something cold and wet on her face and realized that tears were streaming down her cheeks. Somehow, despite the agony, she kept hobbling forward.

Behind her, she heard him breathing heavily, cursing, growling her name. He stayed close, but he didn't seem to gain on her. Why didn't he draw his gun? She cringed, imagining a bullet in the back of her skull. Why didn't he shoot her? She knew the answer: he wanted her alive. He wanted her undamaged—at least to start with.

She made it past the old shed. A turn to the left, and it was a straight shot through a field of high grass back to Gran's house.

She glanced over her shoulder, but twisting her body shifted her weight and made her ankle hurt even worse. Juss was only a few steps behind her now. His face was pale, his body stiff with pain. He was limping as badly as she was. Oily spots swam before Rue's eyes and for a moment she thought she might faint. Then, out of nowhere, she felt a fresh surge of adrenaline.

Little by little, Gran's house grew nearer. She was going to make it! Then, suddenly, the fence loomed before her—the same fence Juss had helped her step over two days ago, returning from the cistern. The wire had been stepped over so many times that it sagged in the middle. Normally it was no obstacle, but to step over would require her to come to a full stop. Juss would catch up with her for sure, and then—

She had been a track star in high school. She had run high hurdles.

Rue gathered as much speed as she could. She made the leap and came down on her good ankle. When she stepped forward onto her bad ankle, she almost screamed from the pain—but she was still upright and moving. She had made it!

But now what?

She felt an impulse to run to her car—until she remembered she didn't have her keys on her, and the doors were locked. But what if she ran into the house and Juss managed to get inside before she could lock the door? It was unthinkable to put Gran in danger, but where else could she go? She staggered across the front yard and glanced over her shoulder. Juss had been slowed down by the fence, but he had just stepped over and was beginning to catch up with her.

Rue limped to the porch. She threw open the screen door and grabbed the doorknob, twisted it, and pushed open the door. She rushed headlong inside, almost falling, and spun about to slam the door shut. Juss was right behind her. The door struck his shoulder and he blocked it. Rue pushed again and the door caught his hand. Juss gave a cry and staggered back, just enough for her to slam the door shut. She pressed the little button in the doorknob. With a click, the door was locked.

Rue turned around, struggling to catch her breath, feeling light-headed and dizzy. Spots swam before her eyes, and after coming in from the daylight, the house seemed very dark. But she could see Gran over by the floor furnace, sitting bolt upright in her chair with a look of startled incomprehension on her face, looking frailer than Rue had ever seen her.

The room turned even darker. Rue's vision began to blur. Her ankle throbbed and her body felt clammy and cold. Her knees started to buckle and she could hardly stand upright. Suddenly she realized Gran wasn't alone. Dwayne Frady was sitting on the sofa across from Gran with a stunned expression on his face. He sat in an odd way, with the backs of his hands propped on his knees, his palms turned upright. His palms were solid red, raw and bloody as if they had been badly scraped. His face was filthy. The front of his jacket looked as if it had been dragged over sharp rocks.

He must have clawed his way out of the cistern. It seemed impossible that he could have climbed out without the ladder, yet there he was.

Rue heard a noise from the kitchen. With a look of alarm on his face, Dylan stepped into the living room. He was holding a dampened tea towel in one hand and a tube of first-aid ointment in the other.

"Dylan!" Rue managed to say, but that was all, before the door behind her gave way with a loud boom and a crash of splinters. The broken door struck her back, knocking her forward onto her hands and knees. A wave of cold air blew over her, raising gooseflesh on her neck.

"You stupid bitch!" Juss shouted. She looked over her shoulder to see his face apoplectic with rage. He was holding his gun. Rue tried to scramble to her feet, but she was too dizzy. The best she could do was to fumble forward on her hands and knees. She looked up at Gran, who seemed oddly still in her chair, her mouth agape and her eyes blank. Rue looked at Dylan, who stood frozen like a statue. Then a flash of movement drew her eyes to Dwayne. He had jumped up from the sofa and was making frantic movements with his damaged hands—unzipping his jacket, reaching inside, pulling out his gun.

But his hands were too badly hurt. He fumbled with the gun and dropped it. Juss laughed out loud.

In the next instant, moving faster than Rue would have thought possible, Dylan was down on his knees beside Dwayne, scooping up the gun.

Juss laughed even louder. Dylan clutched the gun as if it were a snake that might bite him, holding it away from him and staring at it with a look of panic on his face. Rue suddenly knew that he couldn't fire the gun—he was too afraid of it. She looked over her shoulder at Juss, who was raising his arm to fire. She looked back at Dylan and braced herself for the horror of seeing him shot. He was still clutching the gun, aiming it toward Juss but not firing.

Then, in the blink of an eye, the look of panic on Dylan's face changed into a look of sheer determination.

Rue covered her ears and closed her eyes. There was a gunshot. She opened her eyes again to see Gran give a start and nearly fall out of her chair.

Then Rue heard another gunshot.

And another.

32

The cars in the long procession slowly emptied the parking lot at the funeral home. They drove through downtown Amethyst, past the courthouse, through the park, and on toward the cemetery on the outskirts of town.

The dark green Oldsmobile that had belonged to Emmett Dunwitty was the first car behind the hearse. It seemed more dignified than Dylan's red Mitsubishi. Rue sat in the passenger seat. She cast a sidelong glance at Dylan behind the steering wheel. He was keeping his eyes straight ahead, driving slowly and carefully. He felt her eyes on him and turned to give her a reassuring smile, then reached over to place his hand on hers.

As had happened so often in the last several days, Rue found her thoughts following a long chain of "what if's." What if she hadn't confronted her father at the motel that day? But she did confront him, and as a result he had come to Gran's house later that afternoon. Even as addled as she was, Gran had managed to tell him that Rue had gone to the cistern, and Emmett Dunwitty had headed in that direction. A little later Juss had arrived at Gran's house, and was alarmed to see the unfamiliar Oldsmobile parked there. Both men heard the door alarm at the Dunwitty house when Rue briefly set it off; both immediately headed toward the house, but Juss was closer and Rue's father was a slow walker, and the two of them arrived several minutes apart. Because he showed up at exactly the wrong time, Emmett Dunwitty had been shot dead in the house where he grew up.

What if Dylan had done as Rue demanded when they spoke on the phone that afternoon, and had turned around and headed back to Austin? Instead, he continued on to Amethyst, and arrived at Gran's house to find Juss's patrol car and the unfamiliar Oldsmobile parked in the drive along with Dwayne's Toyota and Rue's rental car. He had found Gran alone in the house, but in a state of confusion, unable to tell him where everyone had gone. Even so, Dylan headed up to the cistern, where he found Dwayne exhausted from his frantic attempts to climb out, his hands badly scraped and bleeding. Dylan had lowered the ladder to Dwayne and then walked him quickly back to Gran's house. He was about to bandage Dwayne's hands when Rue burst into the house, followed by Juss.

In the critical moments that followed, when everything could have gone wrong, Dylan's instincts had been flawless. For an instant he choked, frozen by his fear of guns and policemen, but only for an instant. He had done what he had to do, and the single shot he fired struck Juss close enough to the heart to kill him almost instantly. Even so, as Juss fell backward he had managed to pull the trigger of his pistol twice in rapid succession. Both shots had gone into the ceiling.

In the days that followed, people who heard the story had been effusive in their praise of Dylan. Men stopped him on the street to shake his hand and women insisted on giving him a hug or a kiss on the cheek, much to his chagrin. "I didn't even have time to think, I just acted on instinct," he insisted. But wasn't that the very definition of a heroic act? Rue studied his profile behind the steering wheel and squeezed his hand.

And what if . . . ?

What if Rue had simply gone back to Austin, and that whole day had turned out differently? Dawn might still be missing. Juss Goodbody might still be alive and the killer would still be at large. But would Gran also still be alive? The shock of the door breaking in, followed by the gunshots, had been too much for Gran's heart—or so Rue had assumed. But Dr. Gilchrist, who performed the postmortem on Gran, thought otherwise. "It wasn't anyone's fault," he had assured her. From the symptoms Rue described, Dr. Gilchrist believed Gran had almost certainly had a stroke earlier in the day, perhaps a whole series of strokes. "They come in all sizes," he told her. "Some cause a little damage, some cause a lot. Do you know what I think? It was simply her time to go."

Dylan saw the brooding look on her face and gravely shook his head. He knew what she was thinking. Like the doctor, he kept telling her that Gran's death wasn't her fault. "Today isn't about you or me, anyway," he had told her with surprising bluntness as they dressed for the funeral that morning. "It's about your grandmother. Don't think about how she died. Think about how she lived, and all that she meant to you."

As they drove through the cemetery gates, Rue was struck by how bleak the place looked at this time of year, with its cold marble monuments and naked trees that cast long shadows. They had been here only yesterday for her father's funeral, to bury him alongside his parents. Her mother's grave was only a short distance away, not far from the flagpoles at the center of the cemetery, where a U.S. flag and a Texas flag fretfully stirred and snapped, blown by a bitter wind from the north. Years ago, not long after her divorce, Rue's mother had purchased two plots on an installment plan, one for herself and another for Gran.

An attendant from the funeral home guided them into a parking spot. Dylan got out first and circled around the Oldsmobile to open Rue's door. The firm touch of his hand on her arm made her feel strong enough to go through with the funeral. Standing, she winced a bit and leaned more heavily against him. Her ankle was still not fully healed.

Cars kept arriving. More and more people gathered around the canopy beside the grave site. Amid so many people dressed in black, the hothouse flowers around the coffin dazzled Rue's eyes: purple irises and red tulips, pink roses and yellow daffodils—all Gran's favorite flowers were there.

Rue scanned the crowd. Everyone in town seemed to have turned out for the funeral. Ginger Sutherland gave her a tentative, sheepish nod.

Marty looked at the ground. Milton and Maybelline Schneider were there, and Horace Boatwright and his wife. Dub and Patty Ireland, and DeeDee Botner and her husband.

And there was Dwayne Frady in an ill-fitting suit, standing next to his mother. Liz Frady looked older and frailer than a woman her age should, but not from ill health. Her medical tests had given her a clean bill of health. Rue had been thankful for that news, at least.

Reg was suddenly next to her. Rue looked past him and saw that Cathy was back at their station wagon fussing over the kids, who looked unhappy in their dress clothes. Attending two funerals in two days was too much for them. While Rue watched, Tyson pulled the head off the doll Shawna was carrying, and Shawna began to cry.

Rue took Reg's hand. Grandmother and Grandfather Dunwitty were dead. Both of their parents were now gone, and today they were saying good-bye to Gran. They were truly orphans now, the last of the Amethyst Dunwittys. Rue and Reg had spent a lot of time together over the last few days, making arrangements for the funerals, going over their father's will, and trying to make sense of his recent trips to Amethyst. It turned out there was a developer in Mayhew who had a scheme to build houses on the hillside above the ruined cistern, and Emmett Dunwitty, in his usual secretive way, had been trying to wrangle a deal to trade that strip of land for some ranch property in Amethyst County with good deer hunting. That was why he had been coming to Amethyst—to look at properties and to go hunting with the developer. It was a deer rifle Rue had seen him putting into the trunk of his car at the motel. Afterward he had driven to Mayhew for a brief meeting with the developer before he came to see Rue at Gran's house.

His will left everything to Rue and Reg in equal shares. What would they do with the old Dunwitty house? Considering the awful things that had happened there, Rue's first impulse was to tear it down. But that decision could wait. First they had to pay their respects to the dead.

Asking Reg about his affair could also wait—because Rue was almost certain he was having one. Why else had he been deceiving both his employer and Cathy about his whereabouts? But when Rue considered the far more terrible suspicions she had entertained about her brother, an affair seemed almost trivial.

The last of the funeral procession arrived. The family took seats under the canopy. The ceremony began. Dylan sat beside her, holding her hand the whole time. Rue cried, but not as uncontrollably as she feared she might. She heard almost nothing of the preacher's words, except the familiar phrases that seemed to echo from her father's funeral the previous day, and from her mother's funeral two years ago—"Ashes to ashes, dust to dust."

After the ceremony and the words of comfort from the long line of mourners, the crowd gradually dispersed.

Rue took a last look at the newly turned earth that covered Gran's coffin, then headed back to the Oldsmobile. Dylan opened the door for her. She was about to get in when she noticed a figure standing alone, off toward the edge of the cemetery.

"Wait here," she told Dylan.

She walked past row after row of headstones, feeling the cold north wind on her face. Dwayne Frady was standing over a bare site in one of the newer sections at the very edge of the cemetery. Rue laid her hand on his shoulder.

"This is where they're going to bury her," he said. "Tomorrow. They're going to dig a hole right here. They're going to put Dawn in that hole, and then cover her up forever."

"I'm so sorry, Dwayne."

"I know. But I'm glad that you—I mean, if it hadn't been for you . . ."

She nodded. At least they knew the truth. Dawn's body had been found and reclaimed by those who loved her.

"I didn't stand in the line and say so, but I'm sorry about your kinfolk," he said. "I never met your father, but your grandma was a nice lady."

Rue nodded. For all her grief, how could she compare what she felt to Dwayne's suffering? Rue had been estranged from her father for years, and Gran had lived a long life and had died of natural causes, whatever the circumstances. Dawn had been so young, and she and her brother had been so close.

Dwayne sighed and shut his eyes. "Someday . . . someday I'm leaving all this behind me. As soon as I graduate, I'm out of here. I'm leaving Amethyst for good. Leaving Texas."

"Where will you go?"

He opened his eyes. "Where do you think? San Francisco."

Rue smiled. Everyone needed a destination. "It's not easy to make a go of it there."

"I never thought it would be. But nothing could be harder than this."

He was right. She reached into her handbag. "Dwayne, take this card. It's got my address and phone numbers. Stay in touch. Call me the day you graduate. We'll get you to San Francisco. We'll find you a job or get you into school. We'll make things work out for you, Dwayne. I swear we will."

"Who's 'we'?"

She smiled. "I guess I mean Dylan and me."

"Are you two going to get married?"

She thought for a long moment. "I'm not sure. But . . . after my mother died, I promised myself that I'd never marry any man unless Gran met him first and approved of him. I'm guess I'm glad Gran had the chance to meet Dylan. I'm glad she liked him."

Dwayne flashed a faint smile of understanding, then frowned. "Are you coming to Dawn's funeral tomorrow?" he asked.

Rue sighed. "I can't, Dwayne. I've got to get back to San Francisco, and so does Dylan. And with Gran gone . . ." She shook her head. "Without Gran in the house, I can't spend another night in Amethyst. Not yet. Maybe I'll come back in the spring."

He nodded, then took her hand and held it for a long moment while the two of them stared at the plot of earth where Dawn would be laid to rest.

Rue counted the landmarks as she and Dylan drove out of town. They passed the courthouse and the big Texaco sign. They passed the little historical marker by the ruined windmill, the ugly little power substation, and the dirt road that turned off the highway toward the American Legion Hall. An open vista of hills and trees spread out on either side of the highway.

Amethyst was behind them. Rue was heading home.